Madness Maketh the Man

by

Rebecca Xibalba and Tim Greaves

(from an original idea by Rebecca Xibalba)

Productions

Madness Maketh the Man

PART I

CHAPTER 1

Since starting secondary education, hiding in the toilets had become something of a regular occurrence for Terence Montague Hallam. It didn't always work, but if he pulled up his legs to prevent the school's personal education teacher, Mr Keane, from spying him under the stalls, he would sometimes get away with it.

But not today.

Keane always made a quick sweep of the cubicles to locate errant students.

'Hallam!'

The man's voice boomed out, echoing around the tiled walls of the toilet block.

Terence held his breath and fiddled nervously with the collar of his canary-yellow sports shirt.

Keane let out an exasperated sigh and banged the flat of his hand against the door of the second cubicle in the row of five. 'Come on, I know you're in there, you lazy little scrote.' The tone was impatient but not angry. 'Get your lardy backside out here now.'

It was always hard for Terence to muster much enthusiasm for anything, but sport was the ultimate chore. He disliked it immensely and whenever possible, would find a way to avoid participating. Even though the very idea of running about on a muddy field filled him with slothlike complacency, he could at least understand the competitive spirit generated by football or a cricket match. But the passion for running eluded him. As far as he was concerned, it was a pointless waste of one's energy; trotting aimlessly around the country lanes that surrounded the Bagshott Boarding School for Boys in Milton Abbas in the most frightfully cold and wet conditions was something he would go out of his way to shirk. The knowledge he would probably get caught by attempting to duck out – and subsequently be subjected to chastisement or, worse yet, ridicule – never once dissuaded him from trying.

It was a bonus that Mr Keane wasn't the sharpest tool. Like many school sports masters, he was a legalised bully with a sadistic streak a mile wide, not to mention academically inept, with most of his brains having taken up residence in his biceps. Playing sport and keeping fit were his sole purposes in life and he had precious little time for anyone who didn't subscribe to the same way of thinking.

Keane ran a hand through his head of thick black curls. 'Well?' The patience had diminished. He banged his balled fist on the cubicle door. 'Are you coming out, or am I busting the lock?' The question hung in the air for a moment, then he added, 'Which, incidentally, your parents will be billed for.'

Terence knew it was an empty threat, at least the sending a bill to his parents part; he wasn't so sure about the door being broken down. Nevertheless, there was no point exacerbating the situation now. Lowering his legs, he stood up, slid back the bolt and opened the door.

'Sorry, sir, I wasn't feeling very well.'

'*Again*? Becoming a bit of a habit, isn't it lad?'

Shuffling his feet, Terence stared down at his trainers. They weren't the Adidas ones he'd begged his parents for; on the contrary, they probably couldn't have found a cheaper brand than Speedee if they'd tried.

Keane glared at the boy. 'You must think I was born yesterday.'

Terence continued to stare at his shoes.

'I hope you weren't playing with yourself in there, lad!'

'I wasn't, sir.'

There was hatred in the man's eyes now. 'You need to sort out your attitude, Hallam. I don't think I've ever encountered such a lazy little scrote in all my days.' The sports master put his hands on his hips and his expression softened a little. 'You understand the benefits of keeping fit, don't you?' He slapped his hands against his outer thighs, which bulged out of the

the leg holes in his obscenely tight pair of shorts. 'Build up a bit of muscle?'

Terence didn't reply.

'Look at me when I'm talking to you, lad!' The ire had returned.

Terence raised his head. 'Sorry, sir,' he mumbled quietly.

'What? Speak up!'

'Sorry, sir,' Terence repeated.

Keane shook his head resignedly. 'You really are a useless specimen. I'm telling you, if you don't buck up your ideas you'll end up looking like Billy Bunter.' He eyed the boy standing in front of him and made a little snorting noise that might almost have been a snigger. 'You're well on the way as it is.' Bending both arms, he flexed his muscles and they swelled, stretching the fabric of his T-shirt sleeves to almost splitting point. 'You don't think I got to look this good by hiding in the bogs, do you?'

Not just sadistic and a bully, but arrogant too.

Terence shook his head. 'No, sir.'

'Alright then. Get out there and join the others and work some of that blubber off.' Keane reached out and slapped the boy on his stomach with the back of his hand. 'It's hanging over the top of your shorts, lad. It's disgusting.'

6

He waited until Terence had gone, then walked to the end of the row of cubicles and banged on the closed door. 'Come on, you too, Gillam.'

*

Despite the fact that Terence despised boarding school – its teachers, his fellow pupils, the very building itself and everything it represented – he didn't enjoy weekends at home either. There was his beloved poodle, Harvey, given to him by his aunt on his birthday last year against his father's wishes. But that was about it.

Arthur and Emily Hallam were not what anyone would describe as doting parents. Of the two of them, Arthur was particularly remote. In emotional terms, he kept his son well at arm's length in order to, in his own words, 'knock some of the softness out of him, toughen him up, make a man out of him'. That had been his own father's method of parenting and, in Arthur's opinion, it had been a successful one. It had certainly been the making of him. Yet sending Terence to boarding school hadn't been an entirely altruistic move; he had little patience with the boy and the less time he had to spend interacting with him, the better. He was far from being a pillar of fatherhood.

Emily, marginally less harsh than her husband, had no maternal instinct about her whatsoever. Indeed, she was unashamedly vocal about never having wanted to be a mother in the first place; Terence had been a mistake – conceived after birthday celebrations that left her somewhat tiddly – and it was something about which he was reminded with cruel frequency.

Arthur was the owner of Hallam Toys, established by his father, Montague, in 1932. The company specialised in the manufacture of tinplate toys, and although in Montague's lifetime it never brought him the success he so badly craved, its annual turnover enabled it to pootle unremarkably along for 25 years.

It was in 1957 that everything changed. Montague suffered a fatal heart attack, leaving his 27-year-old son, Arthur, holding the reins. Having been inducted into the company in 1952, the same year that his mother was taken by pneumonia, young Arthur had watched silently from the sidelines as his father toiled to keep Hallam Toys afloat. Having become a shrewd businessman, no sooner was Montague in the ground than he shut down the production plant and shifted his focus to overseas, where costs were a fraction of what they were in the UK. Arthur struck a lucrative deal with a Japanese manufacturer – it didn't matter to him one jot that Montague would have been turning in his grave at the very idea – and designs were drawn up for a range of clockwork robots with see-through breastplates that sparked, a simple but satisfying effect generated by friction as the legs moved.

Within a year the Martian Robo-Fleet put Hallam Toys firmly on the map, turning them into a household name. "Collect all Six!" the advertising exclaimed, and they were so phenomenally popular, that it became difficult to keep up with the demand; there wasn't a boy in Britain who didn't pray he would find one in his stocking on Christmas morning.

When the company hit a road-bump, after much soul-searching and deliberation, Arthur sold forty-nine percent of the business to an entrepreneurial acquaintance, Paul Crawford. He was an ambitious young man and, before long, his no-nonsense go-getter approach had reinstated Hallam Toys' footing in the healthy profit zone.

It was the icing on the cake when, in 1959, the company received a Queen's Award for Enterprise.

Arthur had more than any young man of his age could ask for. He had status, he had wealth and he had an enviable four-bedroom thatched cottage in Seatown in Dorset, which he'd inherited from his father.

Then, in 1958, he married his childhood sweetheart, Emily Griffiths, and his life was complete. They couldn't have been happier. But then Emily fell pregnant, and nine months later their first and only child came kicking and screaming into the world.

*

Following his humiliating extraction from the school changing rooms, the rest of Terence's day didn't get any better.

Out in the lanes he ran into problems with Clive Willingham. He was one of the school prefects, a consummate bully who went out of his way to make the other pupils' lives a misery, and Terence had fallen foul of him on his first day at Bagshott.

Having been instructed by Mr Keane to bring up the rear, Clive had been trotting along behind Terence for a mile or so, making derogatory comments about his lack of speed and his attire.

Most of the boys at the school had Fred Perry sports kits. Terence did not. As with his trainers, all his clothing had been bought on the cheap. It had never been a case of Arthur and Emily being unable to afford something better, indeed they were as well-heeled – if not more so – than any of the boys' parents. It was merely that they refused to spend the money.

As the distance between Terence and Paul Vear, the boy in front of him, continued to widen, so Clive's jibes became more caustic. As Paul disappeared around

10

a bend up ahead, putting Terence and Clive out of sight of the rest of the class, the older boy rushed up and gave Terence a hard shove.

He let out a cry as his ankle twisted and he lurched forward, lost his footing and pitched headlong into the hedgerow.

Clive stood with his hands on his hips and howled with laugher. 'Oops!'

Rolling over and sitting up, Terence gingerly attempted to free himself from the brambles.

'Come here, you moose.' Clive stopped laughing and reached down to assist the floundering boy.

Gratefully grasping hold of the outstretched hand, Terence wasn't quite on his feet when the older boy purposely let go of him and he fell backwards into the hedgerow again, tearing a gaping hole in his shirt in the process.

Clive was bent double with laughter. 'I can't believe you fell for that!'

Terence wasn't so much worried about the gash in his midriff as he was the prospect of having to explain to his parents about the ruined garment. It would have been bad enough if it simply meant having to buy a new one, but the yellow shirt had actually been Arthur's hand-me-down from his own school days and he wasn't going to be happy with what he would undoubtedly claim to be Terence's lack of respect for property.

With his ankle throbbing, when he hobbled back into the changing rooms an hour later, Mr Keane demanded an explanation. Terence saw Clive Willingham staring at him, the slits of his eyes just daring him to tell the truth. It was obvious that grassing the boy up would lead to problems later on, so he lied and claimed that he'd caught his foot in a pothole and tripped.

Keane's sympathetic response? 'Oaf! You'll learn to pick your feet up next time, won't you? Go on, get yourself along to matron and get that wound cleaned up. And make it snappy, I don't want blood all over my changing room floor!'

Matron cleaned the cut with TCP – Terence squealed as she dabbed it on – but once the blood was gone, it wasn't anywhere near as bad as it had looked. She rubbed some Germoline on and smiled at him. 'Good as new.'

Getting ready for bed in front of the other boys was something Terence avoided like the plague, so that night, as he always did, he buried himself under the bedclothes to change. But as he was struggling to get his feet into his pyjama bottoms, Martin Bream spotted what was going on, scuttled over and whipped off the blanket. With a whooping noise, he wrenched the pyjamas from Hallam's hands. His eyes widened and he burst out laughing.

'Here, Hallam's got no pubes!'

His face crimson with embarrassment, Terence wrestled the trousers away from the cackling boy and used them to cover his crotch.

'Leave me alone!'

To compound his humiliation, several other boys came over and gathered round the bed.

'He's got girl titties too!' Graham Lavis sniggered.

Bream grinned. 'And a tiny todger.'

'You *what*?' Lavis said, a glint of mischief in his eye. 'How would *you* know?'

The others all turned and looked at Bream questioningly.

'I just saw it, didn't I!' Bream added hastily. 'No pubes and a tiny todger.' He held up his thumb and forefinger with a tiny gap between them. 'Just like a tadpole it was.'

'Bender!' Lavis snorted.

At that moment, Mr Fielding, the housemaster, appeared in the doorway. 'Come on, lads, into bed and lights out.'

With tears of restrained rage brimming his eyes, Terence rolled over to face the wall. Then the light went out and the room was cloaked in darkness, bringing another unbearable day at Bagshott Boarding School for Boys to a close.

Trying to ignore the giggling sounds on the other side of the dormitory, Terence felt under his pillow and withdrew a small polaroid photograph. He turned it into the shard of light peeping through the curtains from the yard outside and gazed at the image of himself sat on a park bench with Harvey cuddled up on his lap. He smiled as his thoughts reminded him that in just a few days' time he would be back home with his best friend.

CHAPTER 2

For Terence, the prospect of another miserable couple of days spent at home was improved solely by the comforting thought that he'd get to spend time with Harvey.

It was Friday afternoon and all the other boys heading off for the weekend had been collected just after four o'clock. Terence had been left sitting alone on the steps outside the school waiting for his father to pick him up.

It had just started to rain when, at precisely four-thirty, Arthur Hallam's sky-blue Ford Anglia appeared through the gates of Bagshott. Spotting his son, he half-heartedly raised a hand and Terence cautiously returned the gesture, wondering what sort of mood his father would be in today.

The car drew up at the steps and Arthur leaned over and opened the rear door behind the passenger seat.

'Come on, stop loitering and get in!'

Throwing his duffel bag and two plastic carriers loaded with dirty washing across the back seat first, Terence clambered in and the door banged shut. He winced, realising he'd pulled it harder than he'd meant to. Maybe it hadn't been as loud as he thought. Maybe…

'For Christ's sake,' Arthur snapped. 'Why the hell do you insist on slamming it every single time?'

Well, that answered the question regarding his father's mood at least.

There would be no apology for the fact he had arrived half an hour late. It was unlikely it would even be mentioned. Terence couldn't remember ever having heard his father apologise for anything. Not even the time the family had been out for a picnic, his parents had been arguing and Arthur lashed out at Emily, leaving her with a cut on her cheek.

There was a faint scent of petrol inside the car; Arthur must have filled up on the drive over. Terence hated that smell; it always made him feel queasy. As they set off, he sat back and, as best as he could, tried to put it out of his mind.

The journey from Milton Abbas to the cottage in Seatown took just over an hour.

'Good week, boy?'

Regardless of the fact Terence's week had been another typically wretched one, he sat in the back of the car trying to sound as enthusiastic about it as he could. Not that his father was actually interested. He never was. Terence wondered why he even bothered to ask.

'It was okay, I suppose,' he said without much gusto.

'Stop mumbling, boy!'

Terence thought for a moment and started talking about a chemistry class he'd actually enjoyed, but only a minute had passed before Arthur cut him off by reaching down and switching on the radio. 'Let's have some music.'

The upbeat sound of Christie singing *Yellow River* filled the car.

Terence's face lit up. 'I love this one. Can we have it a bit louder please, Dad?'

Arthur had started tapping his hand on the wheel along with the beat, but for no other reason than to be contrary, he promptly turned it off. 'Call that music? Bloody racket. I'd rather listen to your incessant prattle.'

'It's really good,' Terence protested weakly.

'*Good*?! Don't make me laugh. Garbage is what it is. Bunch of long haired layabouts! I tell you, there's something seriously wrong with you if you think that's good.'

After a moment's pause, Terence tried to lighten the mood. 'So how was *your* week, Dad?'

'I don't want to talk about it.'

'What *shall* we talk about then?'

'Nothing! Just zip it, for Christ's sake. I'm driving.'

The remainder of the journey was spent in silence. Terence rested his head back and idly stared up at the window beside him. He picked out two streaks of rainwater and, as the wind blew them chaotically across the glass, he followed them with his eyes, willing his favourite to make it to the finish line first. He did that several times, then when he grew tired of it, he gazed sullenly out at the countryside as it whizzed by. How he wished he could be out there running free instead of being held prisoner in a life he never asked for.

When they arrived home and stepped through the front door, Harvey came bounding down the stairs and along the hall to greet them.

Terence dropped his bags, squatted down and Harvey ran straight into his outstretched arms. 'Hello, Harv!' Terence lifted him up off the floor and hugged him close. 'Did you miss me?' As if in response to the question, Harvey eagerly set about giving the boy's face a lick-wash. Terence giggled.

'Stop buggering around with the dog,' Arthur said curtly, removing his jacket and hanging it on the coat stand. 'Go and say hello to your mother.'

Knowing better than to argue, Terence set Harvey down. With Arthur bringing up the rear, the little dog followed Terence through to the kitchen. Emily was standing at the stove overseeing something bubbling away in a saucepan.

'Hi Mum!' Terence flung his arms around her.

Emily stopped what she was doing and held him to her apron for a few seconds. It was more a rote gesture than a show of affection. Then she released him and pushed a displaced strand of hair back over her ear. 'Hands!'

Terence dutifully held out his hands for inspection.

'Hmm. Well, I've seen cleaner.' Emily afforded him a smile. 'Go on with you, get upstairs and clean up, there's a good boy. Dinner will be on the table shortly.'

Terence crossed to the kitchen door. Harvey was still scampering around his feet.

'Not you,' Arthur said firmly. He opened the back door and glared at Harvey. 'Out you go.'

'But Dad, it's raining!' Terence said glumly.

'You know the rules. No dog in the house while we're eating.'

'But he'll get soaked and...' Terence trailed off as he saw the blood beginning to rise in his father's face. He bent down to Harvey and ruffled the curls on his head. 'Go on then, boy. I'll see you later.'

Dinner, as was always the case, was eaten in silence. Only when they had finished dessert, Terence had helped Emily clear the plates, and Arthur had retired to the living room to enjoy his evening cigar in solitude, did the subject of the school week arise.

'So how was school, dear?' Emily asked, running hot water into the washing up bowl.

'Not too bad.'

'Not too *good*?'

Terence attempted to dodge the question. 'Can I let Harvey back in now?'

'When you've helped me with the washing up. So? How *was* school?'

Terence hesitated. 'I'm still getting picked on by the other boys.'

Emily shook her head and sighed. 'Not *that* again, Terence.' She turned off the tap and began washing the dishes. 'I thought you'd had all this out with your father.'

'I did. It's easy for him to say stand up to them, but he doesn't understand. He's not *there*. They're all bigger than me.'

'Then just learn to ignore them. All bullies thrive on getting a response. I've told you that before. If you don't give them one they'll soon get bored and leave you alone.' Emily pointed to the drying-up cloth on the hanger beside the sink. 'Towel.'

Terence reached it down and Emily handed him a plate.

'Ignoring them doesn't work either.' Chewing his bottom lip, Terence wiped the suds off the plate. 'There's something I've got to tell you.'

Emily handed him another plate. 'What's that, dear?'

'We had to do cross country running this week and my shirt got ripped.'

Emily stopped what she was doing and looked at her son. 'Your yellow sports shirt? Your *father's* shirt?'

Terence nodded.

'Oh, Terence. How could you?'

'It wasn't my fault! Clive Willingham pushed me into a hedge!'

'Your father will be *very* angry about this.'

'I know. Can we maybe not tell him?'

Terence could see the disappointment in his mother's eyes. Disappointment in *him*. She handed him a dish. 'How badly torn is it?'

'Quite badly,' he replied dejectedly. 'And there's a bit of blood on it too.'

'I suppose I can take a look and see if I can sew it up. But if it means a new one, you'll just have to speak to your father and own up.' As if to suggest it was something Terence wasn't already painfully aware of, she added, 'He'll be very upset, you know. That was his shirt when he was captain of the school football team.' And then a final twist of the knife: 'It's *very* precious to him. He trusted you with it and you've let him down.'

Terence wished he could explode and scream at her that he never wanted the damned shirt anyway; it was ugly and smelt funny, and he wanted a Fred Perry kit like all the other boys so they would have one less piece of ammunition to use against him. But he knew

21

that a display of contrition was his only option, so instead he just said, 'Sorry, Mum.' It didn't escape him that Emily didn't even query the mention of blood on the shirt, or ask him if he'd been injured.

He returned the drying-up cloth to the hanger. 'Can I let Harvey in now please?'

'Yes, go on.'

Terence opened the back door and the sodden dog shot past him into the kitchen, leaving a trail of muddy pawprints across the linoleum. Skidding to a halt beside the fridge, he shook himself vigorously and a mist of water droplets peppered the wall.

Tutting, Emily handed Terence a tea towel. 'Wipe that off before your father sees it. Then take Harvey upstairs and dry him off properly.'

The evening was spent in the usual manner, without much conversation. For Terence and his mother that meant the company of the television while she darned Arthur's socks. Friday evening's fare was a western series, *The Virginian*, followed by popular gameshow *It's a Knock-Out!*, then *Look - Mike Yarwood*, the nation's favourite impressionist. For Arthur it meant *The Times* crossword. He only occasionally looked up to mutter his disapproval at something or other on the screen, and didn't set the paper aside until the *Nine O'Clock News* came on. This also signified Terence's bedtime.

Harvey had been curled up snoozing quietly on his lap. Sitting beside the fireplace was an elegant vase that had belonged to Arthur's grandmother and, as Terence rose to go upstairs and change for bed, Harvey jumped down and knocked it over. It toppled and hit the marble hearth, shattering some of the porcelain filigree petals.

'Jesus Christ!' Arthur leapt up from his armchair and lashed out at the dog, catching him a glancing blow.

'Dad, don't! He didn't do it on purpose!'

Harvey whimpered and fled across the carpet, disappearing through the door into the hall.

'That bloody dog!' Arthur exclaimed, kneeling down to inspect the remains of his precious vase.

Emily mouthed at Terence to go after Harvey and he went out into the hall. He gathered up the dog in his arms and stood quietly outside the living room door listening.

Emily went over and knelt down beside her husband. 'Is it badly damaged, dear?'

Arthur turned his head towards her incredulously. 'What the hell do *you* think, woman? You've got eyes in your head, haven't you? Of course it's damaged! It's completely ruined!' He carefully collected up the broken fragments of porcelain. 'Gran was given this as a wedding present.' There were tears in his eyes. 'It's more than 70 years old,' he added bitterly. 'It survived two world wars just to get smashed up by that's boy's mangy, flea-bitten mutt!'

'It wasn't intentional, dear. It was an accident.'

Arthur stood up. 'Yes, well, it's the last one,' he said angrily. 'He's a damned menace. First he destroyed my tomato plants and broke a pane of glass in the greenhouse, two weeks ago he chewed through the telephone cable...' – he held up the broken vase – '...and now *this*. I tell you, Emily, his days aren't numbered. They're over. When we get back from dropping Terence off at school on Sunday, Harvey goes to the pound.'

Emily put a hand to her mouth. 'Oh, Arthur, you can't mean it. It'll break his heart.'

'Too bad. If my pisshead sister had actually paid attention and listened to *my* wishes, we wouldn't have had the damned thing in the first place. She knows how much I hate dogs. And who gets saddled with looking after it while he's away at school? Us!'

'But Terence loves Harvey *so* much. If you do this he'll never forgive you.'

'I don't give a shit! Don't you defy me on this, Emily. That boy spends far too much time fawning over that bundle of brainless fuzz as it is. Life isn't all sunshine and roses and the sooner he grows up and realises it, the better.'

24

Outside the room, Terence was still listening. He hugged Harvey close to him. 'Don't worry, boy,' he whispered. 'I won't let them take you, I promise.' He planted a soft kiss on the dog's head. 'I'll think of something.'

CHAPTER 3

Terence managed to keep out of his father's way for most of the weekend. When he got up on Saturday morning, the sun was bright. Packing a rucksack with a cheese and pickle sandwich wrapped in clingfilm, a couple of bags of ready salted Golden Wonder crisps, a flask of lemon squash and a bottle of water for Harvey, he set out on a long hike along the coast. He found a quiet spot and settled down on the sand, where he poured some water into a bowl for Harvey. The sun was warm on his face and he sat munching on his sandwich, gazing out at the expanse of green water and trying to work out what he was going to do the next day. There was no way on earth he was going to let his father take Harvey to the pound. It wasn't going to be easy, but he'd somehow have to smuggle him back to Bagshott.

On Sunday morning, Terence watched from his bedroom window as Martin and Vanessa Turner – his parents' best friends – picked them up for their usual weekend doubles tennis match.

While they were out, Terence collected a spare sports bag from his bedroom closet and put Harvey inside. Zipping it up and leaving just an inch open at the end, he carried the bag downstairs and sat in the lounge with Radio One playing quietly. To his delight, Harvey didn't make a sound and when he carefully unzipped the bag a little over an hour later, the dog was curled up inside sound asleep. So that was the way he would do it. He would smuggle him back to Bagshott that afternoon. It was risky; he had to pray that Harvey would keep quiet. If he got caught out there would be hell to pay. But if he actually managed to pull it off… well, he would figure out what he was going to do next once he got there.

Aware that Arthur and Emily would be back at noon, Terence went outside to the garden shed and rummaged around in his father's toolkit. Then he went back through the house to the garage. Bending down, he raised the hammer and, with all his might, drove a three-inch nail deep into the tread of the rear tyre. Then he went round to the other side of the car and did the same thing with two more nails. Stepping back, hands on his hips, he surveyed his work. A satisfied smile crossed his face. Part two of his plan had been successfully implemented.

Feeling pleased with himself, he returned the hammer to his father's toolbox, then went back into the house and glanced at the clock. It was almost noon. Before his parents had left, his mother had asked him to prepare the chicken salad lunch for their return, so he washed his hands and busied himself with that. He had only just finished laying out the plates when he heard the rattle of keys in the front door.

'Oh, bloody hell!'

The cry came from outside the house.

It had just turned four o'clock and Terence was upstairs packing his clean clothes for the week into a carrier bag. Arthur had gone out to the garage to reverse the car onto the driveway.

Terence went to the window and peered down from behind the curtain at the scene below. His father was on his hands and knees at the back of the car. His mother appeared beside him.

'What's happened, dear?'

'Flat tyres. Bloody nails in both of them at the back! I don't believe it! How the *hell* did that happen?'

'Oh no!' Emily bent down to see. 'We must have driven over them coming back from the carpet centre yesterday afternoon. Can you do anything about it?'

'Like *what*?' Arthur got up off his knees. 'I've only got the one spare.'

'Is there anywhere we can get another?'

'You really do ask some stupid questions, woman. Of course there isn't. Not round here on a Sunday. Anyway, that's not the immediate problem. We have to get Terence back to Milton Abbas.'

'I could ring Vanessa and ask if they'd mind. I'm sure they'll help if they can.' Emily rested a hand on Arthur's shoulder, but he brushed it away.

He was still staring at the tyres. 'I just don't understand it. *Both* of them!'

'Don't be angry. These things happen. We'll sort it first thing in the morning. I'll go and give Vanessa a call.'

Terence smiled to himself. Things were going exactly as he'd planned.

He was a little worried about how Harvey's absence would be explained when he said goodbye; the little dog was always there to see him off. As it turned out, he'd worried unnecessarily. When the Turners arrived to collect him, Arthur had been in the back garden letting off steam by chopping wood. And Emily, possibly distracted by the worry over the car, didn't even seem to notice that Harvey wasn't there.

The drive back to school was far more enjoyable than the one home on Friday afternoon had been. The radio was on and Terence sat in the back of the Turner's car with the window open a couple of inches, enjoying the feeling of the cool breeze blowing through his mop of blonde hair. At the wheel, Mr Turner puffed quietly on his pipe, filling the car with the pleasant aroma of Condor tobacco. Mrs Turner – looking particularly attractive in a summer dress, Terence thought – was chattering away, occasionally feeding him a barley sugar.

He kept checking the sports bag on the seat beside him, but there really was no need. Harvey was as good as gold and there wasn't a peep out of him all the way back to Bagshott.

The Turners deposited Terence at the steps of the school. He thanked them for their kindness and, before leaving, Mrs Turner leaned in close. Terence caught the sweet scent of her perfume as she planted a goodbye kiss on his cheek; it gave him a funny sensation in the pit of his stomach and made him blush. Then she handed him the rest of the bag of sweeties to keep.

As the car pulled away, Terence heaved a sigh of relief. The easy part was over. Now the real challenge was underway: Keeping Harvey hidden. Not only from the schoolmasters, but from his dorm mates too.

Walking round the side of the building to the back entrance, he stopped out of sight of the windows beside some rhododendron bushes. There was a sudden rustling sound and a squirrel shot out and disappeared up among the branches of a nearby oak tree.

Terence opened the bag to see Harvey's inquisitive little face gazing up at him. 'Good boy,' he said, putting Harvey's leash on. 'Time for a tinkle.'

After the dog had relieved itself, Terence put him carefully back into the bag. This time, Harvey put up a bit of a struggle; he'd clearly had enough.

Terence managed to calm him down. 'Just another couple of minutes, pal.' He zipped up the bag and made his way cautiously into the school through the rear doors.

When he got to the dormitory, he was relieved to discover that none of the other boys had returned yet. He quickly let Harvey out of the bag and sat him on the bed, then he withdrew a small porcelain bowl from a sidepocket on his holdall. He patted Harvey on the head – 'Wait there a minute, there's a good boy.' – and went along to the toilets where he filled the bowl with cold water. He had barely put it down before the poodle pounced on it.

Prior to leaving home, Terence had pilfered some sliced ham from the fridge. He broke it into small pieces and Harvey wolfed it down, then returned to the water bowl.

Terence took the little dog's head in his hands, stroking him behind the ears with his thumbs. 'Now listen. You're going to have to be *really* quiet. You'll have to stay here while I attend classes tomorrow, but I'll make you a nest under the bed and you'll be safe as long as nobody knows you're here. I'll leave you fresh

31

water and I'll bring some food at lunchtime. Do you understand?'

Harvey just stared at him and tried to lick his hand.

Terence sighed. 'No, of course you don't. But it's *so* important, Harv. If we're caught, we'll both be in big trouble.'

Harvey's tongue flicked out and he licked Terence's wrist enthusiastically.

'Okay, let's make your bed for you before the others get here.'

It was fortunate that Terence had the corner bunk. Collecting a couple of fresh blankets from the linen closet at the end of the dormitory, he bundled them up and pushed them up against the wall beneath the bed. No sooner had he coaxed Harvey underneath with the last piece of ham – 'Now stay, there's a good boy.' – and tied his leash to the leg of the bedstead than the double doors clattered open and Bream and Lavis appeared.

Lavis eyed Terence with amusement. 'You're back early, Hallam' he said as he crossed the room to his bunk. 'Little goody-goody.' Dropping his bags beside the bed, he jumped on, stretched out and put his hands behind his head. 'Good weekend, Bream?'

The other boy had already started to unpack. 'It was okay I suppose. Mum took me to the pictures on

Saturday night and this morning I went to the rugby with Dad. You?'

'Spent the whole weekend out on my grandfather's yacht. Did some sunbathing. Got a bit of swimming in too.'

'Excellent!'

Lavis yawned. 'It was a bit tedious to be honest with you. But you know how it is, the whole family was there, so…' He saw Terence looking at him. 'What are you gawping at Hallam?'

Terence could only dream of spending his weekends doing the things these boys were describing. He shook his head and averted his eyes. 'Nothing.'

Lavis sat upright and pulled up his legs, wrapping his arms around them. 'What did *you* get up to at the weekend then? Scare a few crows?' He picked idly at a scab on his knee.

Bream guffawed. 'He's got the right face for it!'

'That's an insult to scarecrows!' Lavis shot back.

Before Terence could summon up a suitable response, the doors swung open and three more boys – David Parrish, Barney Talbot and Greg Hockley – appeared. Lavis turned his attention to them and Terence busied himself unpacking his fresh clothes. He urgently wanted to take a look under the bed to ensure Harvey was settled, but he resisted the temptation; he hadn't made a sound when the boys came in, plus he didn't want to risk drawing attention to himself.

Just before six-thirty, when the others went off to the canteen for dinner, Terence hung back for a moment and took a quick peek. He smiled. Harvey was curled up in a little ball, sound asleep.

His peace of mind was short-lived.

At dinner, Lavis – who was seated next to Terence – flicked custard from his dessert spoon onto a boy seated at the next table, who jumped up with a cry.

The attending master, Mr Pearson, strode over.

'What's going on?'

The boy was scooping custard off his neck. 'One of them two chucked custard at me, sir.' He pointed at Terence and Lavis.

Pearson turned to them angrily. 'Which one of you did this?'

Before Terence could answer, Lavis gave him a shove in the ribs. 'It was Hallam, sir.'

Pearson glared at Terence. 'Well? Was it, boy?'

Terence wanted to deny it, but the words wouldn't come. He just sat there, tongue tied, tears in his eyes and rapidly turning red.

'Right,' Pearson said. 'My office.'

'But…'

'Now!'

Terence wasn't actually that worried about being in trouble again. Although he was completely innocent, he was well accustomed to taking the blame for things he hand't done. What *did* bother him, was his delay in getting back to the dormitory.

Ten minutes and two swipes of a wooden ruler across the back of his hands later, he ran back as fast as his legs would carry him. When he got to the doors, he paused outside to catch his breath before going in. That was when he heard the raucous laughter. He pushed open the door and immediately saw Bream, Lavis and his other three dorm mates gathered around his bed.

Terence's heart leapt into his throat.

Amidst the jeers of his cohorts, Lavis had Harvey's lead in his hand and was dragging him out from under the bed.

In that moment, Terence realised he'd made a terrible mistake. He hadn't thought his plan through to its inevitable conclusion. What had he been thinking? How could he have possibly hoped to keep Harvey hidden from the other boys? Of course he had meant well, but he'd been so focused on saving Harvey from a terrible fate at the hands of his intolerant father that he had potentially brought him into a much more dangerous one.

He stood rooted to the spot as, almost as if it were playing out in slow motion, he watched Lavis yank on

35

the lead and raise it high above his head. With a yelp, Harvey was lifted off his feet, whimpering and spinning on the end of the lead. Suspended in mid-air, his back legs dangled beneath him, with his paws a good inch or more off the floor.

'Leave him alone!' Terence demanded, marching towards the gathering.

His face alive with mischief, Lavis lowered the lead. As his feet touched the ground, Harvey tried to scamper away but Lavis held the leash taut. He grinned at Terence. 'You been dognapping, Hallam?'

Harvey spotted Terence and started to bark, straining fruitlessly against the leash.

'He's mine!' Terence exclaimed angrily. 'Give him to me!'

Parrish and Hockley stepped forward, positioning themselves between Terence and Lavis.

'Back off, Hallam,' Hockley said threateningly.

'Just give me my dog!'

'What dog? Oh, *this* dog!' Lavis bent down and lifted the squirming poodle into his arms. Harvey snapped at him but Lavis wasn't the least bit concerned. He held Harvey out at arm's length. 'This thing's got more spunk in it than you have. It can't be yours.'

'But he *is*!'

'Nah. If you really owned a dog, it would be a poofter. Just like you!'

The other boys chortled. Terence could feel the tears coming.

'Besides,' Lavis continued, 'dogs aren't allowed in school.' He grabbed hold of Harvey's left ear and twisted it hard. 'Especially not ugly ones like this.' The little dog yelped and tried to break free, but Lavis held him tight.

'*Please* don't hurt him!' Terence cried, as Parrish grabbed hold of him, restraining him in his strong arms.

'Hurt him?' There was a glint of pure malice in Lavis's eyes. 'Why would I hurt him?' He laughed. 'Oh, wait, you meant like this.' He twisted Harvey's ear again, eliciting another yelp. 'No, I would never do that.'

Talbot had stood away to one side as if he didn't want to get involved. Parrish released his hold on Terence, perhaps because he also felt things were getting out of hand. Lavis, however, had already registered the signs of impending mutiny on Parrish's face. He thrust Harvey into Bream's arms, darted round to the far side of the neighbouring bed and held out his arms. 'To me, Bream!'

One moment Harvey was in Bream's hands, the next he was somersaulting through the air. Lavis caught him awkwardly and his back leg twisted under him. He let out a yelp.

Terence rushed round the bed, but as he reached Lavis, the boy shouted, 'Hockley!' and hurled the poodle towards the startled boy.

Harvey flew through the air again, but Hockley was taken off guard and missed the catch. The bundle of flailing legs spiralled past him, went down hard, skidded across the floor and collided with the wall.

Harvey twitched once and lay still.

With a howl of anguish, Terence ran over and dropped to his knees. Weeping, he carefully lifted the limp little body into his arms. Almost immediately Harvey stirred and looked up at his master.

Terence glanced back over his shoulder. Everyone was standing looking at him. 'You bastards!' he said bitterly.

'Is he okay?' Hockley asked. There was genuine concern on his face. 'We didn't mean nothing.'

The others all nodded.

Except for Lavis. He was remorseless. He stepped forward, pushing Hockley aside. 'Who cares if it's hurt or not? It's only a stupid dog. It shouldn't be here anyway. I wonder what the headmaster would have to say about Hallam trying to keep a dog in the dorm? What do you reckon, Parrish?'

'He'd be quite cross,' the boy replied nervously. Things had clearly gone much further than he was comfortable with, yet he was still too afraid of riling Lavis by standing up to him.

'Just what I was thinking,' Lavis said with a sadistic grin. 'Let's go and ask Fielding.'

'Ask *Mr* Fielding *what*?'

The boys all turned to see their housemaster standing in the doorway.

'Nothing, sir,' Lavis muttered. He suddenly seemed to have lost his puff.

'It must be *something*, lad. I clearly heard you say let's ask Mr Fielding.' He caught sight of Terence, who was still on his knees. 'What are you up to, Hallam?' He raised his eyebrows as he saw what Terence was trying – but failing – to keep out of sight. 'Just a minute. Is that a dog you've got there, lad?'

'No, sir.' Even as the words left Terence's mouth, he realised what a facile response it was.

'It damned well looks like one to me!' Fielding frowned. 'Bring it here.'

Terence got to his feet and came over.

'Is it yours?'

Terence nodded miserably. 'They were being horrible to him, sir.'

'Be that as it may, what do you think you were doing bringing a dog into school? Surely you didn't think you'd get away with it.'

Terence shrugged.

'You could be expelled for this, lad.' Fielding looked at the bundle in Terence's arms and his expression softened. 'What's his name?'

'Harvey.'

'Harvey, eh?' Fielding smiled.

Terence shuffled his feet. 'What's going to happen to him, sir?'

'I don't know. But I suggest you get yourself along to my office and wait for me there.' As Terence trotted resignedly to the doors, Fielding glared at the other boys. 'As for you lot, get over here right now!'

When he reached the end of the corridor, Terence paused and glanced back to ensure there was no sign of his housemaster. Then, instead of going right and along to the office as he'd been instructed, he turned left, ran down a flight of steps and hurried out of the door.

CHAPTER 4

If there was one thing Arthur Hallam disliked intensely – and in truth there were many – it was the telephone ringing after six o'clock on a Sunday evening. As far as he was concerned, the dying embers of the weekend were sacrosanct; it was his last opportunity to relax before another frantic working week got underway, and any intrusion upon that was intolerable.

Occasionally he would just let the phone ring, but this evening, as he happened to be walking past, he reached out and irritably snatched up the receiver. 'Seatown double-four-seven-five.'

He listened for a few moments and his face darkened. 'He did *what*?!'

Two hours earlier, puffing and panting as he'd made his way down the narrow lane heading away from Bagshott – with Harvey on his lead scampering along behind him – Terence had no idea what he was doing or where he was going. His sole intent at that moment was to put as much distance as possible between himself and the school. No matter how much he might have pled Harvey's case with Fielding, he knew there was no way he would be allowed to keep the dog with him. And the outcome, were he to be returned home, was unthinkable. As it turned out, he had covered less than a mile before a Morris Mini Minor appeared round the bend in the lane behind him. Its horn sounded twice.

Tugging at Harvey's lead to get him out of the road, Terence stepped up onto the verge to let the car pass, but as it drew up alongside him the engine shut off.

The driver wound down the window and Terence's stomach tightened when he saw the man's face. It was Mr Fielding.

'Get in.'

Tired and defeated, Terence walked around the car and Fielding leant over and opened the passenger side door. Terence lifted Harvey up into his arms and climbed in.

'Shut the door.'

Terence did as he was told.

Instead of starting the car again, Fielding twisted in his seat and looked at the boy. Rather than being angry, he spoke patiently. 'So come on, lad. Are you going to tell me what's going on?'

Terence didn't reply.

'You can tell me here, or you can tell me back in the headmaster's office. It's no skin off *my* nose.'

There was nothing to be done now but tell the truth. After a moment's thought, Terence said sullenly, 'My

Aunt gave him to me for my birthday, but my Dad wants to get rid of him.'

'Why would he want to do that?'

Terence shrugged. 'Because.'

'Because what?'

'Because he hates him and he's always being mean to him.'

'Why? There must be a reason.'

'He just doesn't like dogs and every little thing Harvey does makes him mad. The other day he broke a vase. He didn't mean to, it was an accident. But afterwards I heard Dad telling Mum that when I came back to school he was going to take Harvey to the pound.'

Fielding nodded. 'I see. Well, he was probably just angry about the vase. I'm sure it was just an idle threat.'

'You don't know him. It wasn't a threat, he meant it. The only way to stop it happening was to bring him back here with me.'

Fielding thought for a moment. 'Well, listen Hallam, I'm sure you know you could be expelled for your hamfisted indiscretion.'

Terence didn't respond.

'You do realise you can't keep him at school?'

Terence nodded sadly.

'Alright then, here's what's going to happen. Against my better judgement, I'm not going to report this to the headmaster. I totally understand that you love your dog, and what you did... well, it was done with the best of intentions. But it was also extremely foolhardy. I'm going to have to call your father and have him come and collect the dog.'

'Please don't.' There were tears welling in Terence's eyes.

'I don't have any choice, I'm afraid.'

'He'll be absolutely furious.'

'That can't be helped. I can overlook what you did and we'll say no more about it, but the dog has got to go.'

Terence looked down sorrowfully at Harvey in his lap, and stroked the tight curls on his head. 'He'll send him to the pound.'

Fielding turned the key in the ignition and started the car. 'Let's just see, shall we?'

His face like thunder, Arthur slammed down the telephone receiver and walked through to the lounge where Emily was doing her sewing and half-watching *Songs of Praise*. With no regard for the fact she might be enjoying the show, he strode over to the television set and switched it off.

'That damned boy!'

Emily's brow furrowed. 'Who? Not Terence?'

'Of course Terence. Who do you think, Prince Charles?!'

'What's happened?'

'That was one of his teachers on the phone. He only took the bloody dog back to school with him! Christ knows how.'

After Terence had left with the Turners that afternoon, it had been over an hour before Emily had finally noticed Harvey's absence. From outside in the garden, Arthur heard her calling the dog's name and came in to see what the fuss was about. As unlikely as it seemed, after a thorough search of the house failed to locate him, they concluded he must have somehow escaped from the garden. Despite Emily's assertion that they ought to go out and look for him, Arthur was adamant that they do no such thing. Harvey would probably return of his own volition, he'd said. And if he didn't? All well and good then, as far as he was concerned; it would save him a trip to the pound the next day.

'I thought it was odd he'd run away,' Emily said, returning her attention to her sewing.

Her apparent insouciance merely fanned the flames. 'This is no bloody laughing matter! Never mind the fact he shouldn't have had the dog there in the first place, he made matters worse by taking off when he got caught.'

'What do you mean, taking off?'

'Taking off. Scarpering. Running away! Unsurprisingly, they take a very dim view of truancy. The teacher said if the headmaster had found out about any of it, Terence would probably be in line for expulsion.'

'You can't really blame him, Arthur. You know he loves that dog to bits. If he overheard you talking the other night...'

'It's gross defiance and I'll not stand for it! This is my house and he'll live by my rules. If I say the dog has to go, the dog has to go and that's the end of it! Just wait until I get my hands on him. He won't sit down for a week!'

'So what's going to happen? Are they bringing Harvey back?'

'Of course they aren't. This guy – Fielding I think he said his name is – expected me to drive over there and collect him right now. I told him in no uncertain terms the earliest that was going to happen is tomorrow after I've got the new tyres fitted. And even then, not until I've finished work. But he was insistent it's to be taken care of tonight.'

Emily put down her sewing. Her face now showed a trace of concern. 'What are we going to do?'

'I'm calling Clara. She can go and get it.'

'Make sure you ask her nicely, Arthur.'

'I'm not *asking* her. I'm *telling* her. It's her fault we ended up saddled with the damned thing in the first place.'

'What if she says no?'

'She'd better not.'

'But what if she does?'

Arthur glared at his wife. 'She'd better not,' he repeated though gritted teeth.

Clara answered the phone within two rings. Immediately she spoke, Arthur could tell she was inebriated.

'Arthur, darling, how lovely to hear from you!'

'It's not a social call. I need you to drive over to Bagshott School and collect Harvey.'

Clara sniggered. 'Don't be so ridiculous, darling. Collect the dog from school?' She made a small hiccupping noise. 'Whatever next!'

'Don't be stupid.'

'Surely you mean Terence!'

'No,' Arthur said tersely. 'Harvey…'

Clara wasn't listening. 'Just a minute, it's Sunday night isn't it? Why does Terence need collecting from school? Surely he's only just gone back for the week. Oh dear me, he's not fallen ill has he?'

'No, he hasn't. It's the dog that needs collecting, not Terence.'

'Why's Harvey at the school, darling?' Clara made a noise somewhere between a snigger and another hiccup. 'Do they actually allow dogs there?'

Arthur was beginning to lose his patience. 'For Christ's sake, have you been drinking?' He knew the question was redundant.

'I might have had a little drinky-poo.' Clara sniggered again. 'Or maybe it was two.'

Or five, Arthur thought. 'Never mind. Just listen to me. Somehow – and I'm not exactly sure how yet – Terence smuggled that stupid mutt back to the school with him this afternoon. Unsurprisingly, he got found out and someone has to go and pick it up.'

'Ohhhhhh.' Clara chortled. 'Silly me. I was starting to think you'd lost your marbles, Arthur. Dogs at school and all that. Whatever next?' She hiccupped again.

'So will you do it?'

'Do what?'

'Go and get the damned dog!'

'Of course, darling. I'll go first thing in the morning.'

'No, not tomorrow, *tonight*!'

'Tonight? Oh, I don't know about that. I was planning an early night. Can't you go?'

'Why the hell would I be calling you if I could go myself? I've got a couple of flats on the car and I can't get it sorted until tomorrow. The dog needs to be collected tonight or Terence will be expelled.'

'Expelled? Oh deary me. Bloody tyrants. Well, we can't have that, darling?' She hiccupped again. 'Of course I'll go.'

'Thank you. It's going to the pound tomorrow anyway.'

Clara snorted. 'Oh, Arthur, you're such a card!'

'I'm not joking. It's a bloody nuisance. It blotted its copybook for the last time the other night when it broke grandma's vase.'

Clara didn't even remark upon the lost heirloom. 'Don't be so awful, darling. If he goes to the pound they might put him to sleep.'

'Hallelujah to that!'

'You're serious, aren't you?'

'Never more so.'

Clara seemed to sober up a little. 'Oh, Arthur, how could you suggest such a thing?! Poor little Harvey. I'll take him. He can live here.' She thought for a moment. 'Alfie will be alright, he won't stand for any nonsense, but I don't suppose Rhubarb will be too happy.'

Arthur frowned. 'I thought she died.'

'That was Rhubarb One, darling. I'm talking about Rhubarb Two. She's extremely territorial, bless her.'

Arthur had even less time for cats than dogs, and as for Alfie, Clara's spoilt macaw parrot, he'd hated the bird since the day it took a chunk out of his thumb. 'More fool you if you take it on. But I'm telling you straight, if you bring it back here, it's off to the pound tomorrow.'

'You always were a cold-hearted bastard, darling.' Clara hiccupped. 'I'll take him.'

Clara arrived at Bagshott a little before ten. Arthur had telephoned Fielding to let him know it was his sister who would be coming, and he was duly waiting with Harvey in his arms on the steps at the front of the building. Terence was standing forlornly beside him.

'Terence, my darling,' Clara cried as she clambered out of her battered Volkswagen Beetle, cursing under her breath as she caught her blue, feather-ruffed chemise on the door handle. With a good hour's drive ahead from her home in Christchurch to the school, she had decided not to dress, pausing only to throw a knee-length blue-and-green tartan coat over her nightgown.

'How lovely to see you.' She chortled, stepped over to Terence and gave him a wet kiss, depositing a smear of crimson lipstick on his cheek. 'A shame it's in such awful circumstances.' She took a step away and gave Fielding a disparaging glance. 'You must be Fielder.'

He didn't correct her. 'Thank you for coming. It was essential for Terence's sake that the dog be returned home this evening.'

Clara was staring at him dispassionately. 'I suppose you expect me to be grateful.'

'Well...'

'I'll have you know I don't take kindly to being dragged out at this time of night.'

Fielding's demeanour changed slightly. 'Be that as it may, Mrs Hallam...'

'It's Ms. *Mrs* Hallam is my brother's wife.'

'Of course. Humble apologies. As I was about to say, Terence bringing his dog into school was beyond foolhardy and – let me be perfectly clear on this – had it been somebody other than myself who found out, things could have ended very differently for him. This way we get the minimal amount of fuss and nobody else ever need know it happened.' He smiled and winked at her.

Clara hiccupped. 'Is there something wrong with your eye?' She suddenly became aware that her overcoat was hanging open, exposing a generous swell of unfettered bosom over the top of her gown. She hastily wrapped the coat around herself and pulled the belt tight. 'Pervert. Just give me the dog.'

51

Looking slightly affronted, as Fielding handed Harvey over to her, he recoiled at the pungent smell of alcohol on her breath.

Terence, who hadn't said a word up until now – not even to greet his aunt – suddenly spoke up. 'Dad's going to take him to the pound, Aunt Clara.'

She shook her head. 'Don't you worry about that, darling. He's coming to live with me. You can visit whenever you like.'

Terence's face lit up. 'That's amazing! Thank you so much!' He ran forward and flung his arms around Clara, almost squashing Harvey between them.

Fielding coughed. 'Alright, Hallam, I think you need to get yourself to bed now.' Standing upright with his hands behind his back in a very officious stance, he waited until Terence had said goodbye and gone back inside before speaking again. 'I don't think you realise the gravity of the situation. Terence could have been expelled for this, or at the very least suspended. I've been incredibly lenient on this occasion, but I shan't be again. One more strike and he's out. I'm sorry if that seems harsh, but that's the way it is.'

'Horseshit is what it is!' Clara mumbled, putting Harvey on the passenger seat of the car and closing the door. She turned and pointed a finger at Fielding. 'You haven't heard the last of this.'

'Ms Hallam. If I might offer you a couple of pieces of advice? For the sake of Terence's future here at Bagshott, I sincerely hope it's the last we'll *both* hear about it.'

Clara knew he was right and she had no intention of taking the matter further, but neither was she going to be seen to back down.

However, before she had a chance to answer, with an undisguised note of sarcasm Fielding added, 'Delightful to have met you.' He turned away. 'I bid you goodnight.'

Clara felt her blood begin to rise. 'Don't you turn your back on me, you rude man! You said a *couple* of pieces of advice.'

Fielding paused at the door. 'Driving under the influence of alcohol is against the law in this country. If it were to be reported, it's a punishable offence – most likely imprisonment.' He gave her a thin smile. 'But I'm sure you know that. Nevertheless, I really can't recommend strongly enough that you give it the consideration it deserves. And then hopefully, very much like this reckless matter with the dog…' – he waved a hand in the air – '…neither of us will hear any more about it.'

Clara glared at him. 'Are you threatening me?'

'Goodnight, Ms Hallam.' Fielding turned away and strode inside' letting the door swing shut behind him.

CHAPTER 5

Terence spent the next two weekends at home missing Harvey desperately. However, Bagshott's Sports Day was coming up and his father said that, as a reward for performing well, his mother might – emphasis on *might* – take him to visit Aunt Clara and the dog. While it gave Terence hope and a touch of incentive to excel, it did little in the short term to allay the overwhelmingly dismal feelings of emptiness.

When Sports Day arrived, despite the fact Terence loathed any form of sport, he was fully prepared to give his all; mentally, at least, if not exactly physically.

Having been informed by Mr Keane that he would be competing in three events, he was mildly optimistic about his chances in the shot put and tug-of-war. He felt much less confident about the hundred-metres dash. Entering him into that particular event had surely been an act of demented vindictiveness on the sports master's part, Terence thought. Nevertheless, he consoled himself with the thought his father hadn't actually said he needed to *win* anything to claim a visit to Harvey, only that he had to perform well.

It was a blazing hot afternoon and things got off to a bad start before he'd even left the changing room. Terence knew full well that he'd packed his shorts and yellow shirt – which his mother had thankfully managed to repair – when he'd left home on Sunday. Yet, in the changing rooms, he unzipped his bag to discover they weren't inside. His heart sank. Then he caught sight of Lavis and Bream, conspiratorially huddled together, watching him from the opposite bench.

Lavis had that all too familiar mischievous smirk on his face. 'What's up, Hallam?' he said. 'You look bothered.'

'Someone's taken my kit.'

'Oh, that's bad luck. Don't you reckon, Bream?'

Bream sniggered.

Terence stood up. 'Did you take it?'

Lavis looked at him innocently. 'Moi?' He touched a hand to his chest. 'What would I want with *your* stinky old kit?'

'*Please* tell me where it is. I've got to be on the field in ten minutes.'

Lavis stood up. The humour disappeared from his face. 'You don't hear so good, do you Hallam?' He stabbed a finger into Terence's left breast, making him wince. 'I told you, I haven't got it.'

'Then who has?'

Lavis shrugged. 'Not my problem. You'd better tell Mr Keane.'

Feeling angry and humiliated, Terence walked over to the annexe that the sports master used as his office. The door was slightly ajar. He could see Keane dressed in his black tracksuit, filling in names on a chart of the day's events with a felt pen.

Terence tapped nervously on the door. 'Excuse me, sir.'

Keane didn't look up. 'Not now. I'm busy.'

Terence pushed open the door and took a step inside. 'Someone's stolen my kit.'

Sighing, Keane put down the pen and spun his swivel chair to face Terence. '*What*?'

'Someone's stolen my sports kit, sir.'

'Is that the best excuse you can come up with, Hallam? A stolen kit?'

'It's not an excuse, sir. It was in my bag and now it's not.'

Keane shook his head. 'You must think I was born yesterday, lad. Stop wasting my time and go and get changed.'

'But...'

'Stop arguing with me, lad. Get changed!'

'Isn't there a spare I could use?'

'No, there isn't. If you haven't got your own kit you'll just have to strip down to your pants and vest, won't you?' He stood up. 'Come on, chop-chop, first race in ten minutes.'

Terence was struggling to hold back the tears. 'I *can't*, sir.'

Keane's response was completely out of proportion to the situation. 'You *can* and you *will*!' he screamed, giving Terence a shove. 'Now get out of my office! If you're not changed and on that field in five minutes I'll have you in detention every night for a month!' He slammed the door shut.

Terence knew that if anyone else's kit had been stolen, Keane would have given every boy in the changing room a grilling. He was also aware that there were always spare kits kept in one of the lockers and, had Keane been anything other than the cruel bastard that he was, he would have let Terence use one. This was just another opportunity for the sports master to degrade him. Regardless, he did as he had been told and tried to focus on the fact today was simply a means to an end; getting to see Harvey again was all that mattered.

A few minutes later, clad in his string vest and mustard yellow Y-fronts, with a piece of card emblazoned with the number 13 dangling around his neck, he made his way outside, anxiously trying to ignore the laughter of the other boys.

The hundred-metres dash was even more of a disaster than he expected it to be. As soon the geography master, Mr Randall, pulled the trigger on the starting pistol, David Parrish stuck out his foot and sent Terence sprawling onto the grass. By the time he managed to scramble to his feet, the cluster of other runners was already half way across the field and well on the way to the finish line.

To the sound of jeers from the crowd, Terence came in last. As he made his way back across the field, he caught sight of his father and mother among the hundreds of parents lining the perimeter. He put up a hand and waved. Emily waved back and gave him a smile of encouragement. Arthur did not; he rolled his eyes and slowly shook his head.

The shot put tournament went as well as Terence could have hoped. The sun was beating down and he could feel it burning the back of his neck as he picked up the stainless steel sphere and, with a cry of exertion, hurled it a remarkable 47 feet. The shot earned him third place. The enthusiastic applause from the crowd, the impressed nod from Mr Keane and – more than anything – the sight of his father clapping vigorously, filled him with encouragement and he approached his third and final event with optimism. This time he wouldn't be on his own. The tug-of-war was a team effort and even if the blues were defeated by the reds, the shame of losing wouldn't be his alone to bear.

With two teams of seven boys each readying themselves alongside the rope, Terence took up his position with the blue team, one from the end, immediately in front of the anchor; it was Clive Willingham, the boy who had pushed him into the hedge on the cross country run a few weeks beforehand.

Willingham smirked at him. 'Nice pants, Hallam.'

Terence ignored him.

'Ready, lads? Pick up the rope!' Mr Keane shouted.

Terence lifted the length of twisted cotton rope from the ground and thought about Harvey. He smiled to himself. He'd be seeing the little dog soon.

The two teams shuffled backwards until the rope was taught. Then Keane bent over and pressed a small flag into the earth below the central marker on the rope. 'Take the strain!' he commanded, his brow now glistening with sweat.

The boys all leaned backwards and dug their heels into the grass.

Invigorated by his triumph on the shot put, Terence was feeling as confident as he ever had before. Even Willingham whispering to him from behind – 'You'd better have brought your muscles with you, blubber boy!' – wasn't going to distract him.

'And pull!' Keane yelled.

One moment the boys in the blue team were preparing to pull for all they were worth, the next they were dragged forward off their feet and piled in on top of one another.

The crowd cheered.

'Reds win!' Keane exclaimed as the boys in the red team jumped around, jubilantly slapping each other on the back.

As Terence got up off the grass, nursing his palms from the rope burns, a pair of hands descended on either side of his hips and before he realised what was happening, his underpants were down around his ankles.

Willingham stood back in hysterics. 'Look at that fat arse!'

Hearing the shout, the other boys all turned to look and promptly burst out laughing.

Mortified, Terence bent to pull up his pants, but they got caught on the heel of his SpeeDee plimsole and he toppled over sideways.

It took the spectators a moment to cotton on to what had happened, but then one of the fathers pointed and cried out, 'Hey, look at the chunky kid! He's lost his pants!'

The laughter in the crowd built from a few isolated chuckles to a deafening uproar. To compound the ultimate humiliation, from his prone position on the grass, Terence could see his mother and father had joined in.

Keane came running over and dragged him to his feet. 'Stop making a fool of yourself,' he fumed as Terence managed to pull up his Y-fronts. 'You were determined to show me up, weren't you?!' Keane waved to the crowd and grinned broadly. 'Show's over, no harm done.' Then he leant in close to Terence and snarled, 'Get your lardy backside indoors and get dressed. I'll speak to you later.'

CHAPTER 6

Although, for Terence, the Sports Day had been catastrophically awful, his father actually deigned to praise him for his sterling efforts in the shot put. The harrowing incident at the end of the tug-of-war match was never once mentioned, and Arthur – being as good as his word – authorised a visit to Clara's to see Harvey. The initial plan to drive over was scuppered when an opportunity to go trout fishing with Martin Turner presented itself, and Arthur didn't hesitate to change his plans.

So the following Saturday morning, Emily and Terence boarded the eight-twenty eastbound train on their own. Destination: Christchurch.

The journey took almost three hours, with changes at Salisbury and Southampton and onward to Christchurch. Emily passed the time snoozing, or gazing out of the window at the countryside as it sped past. Terence meanwhile lost himself in the swashbuckling adventures of the novel *Treasure Island*.

To save them having to complete the final leg by bus, Clara was waiting for them at Christchurch. She was standing beside her Beetle at the far end of the car park and, as Emily and Terence came out of the station, she put up a hand to catch their attention.

'Where's Harvey?' Terence asked, as he squeezed into the back of the car and Emily took the front passenger seat.

Clara waved a hand breezily in the air. 'Oh, he'll be pootling around in the back garden somewhere I expect.'

'You don't know?' Emily said with a note of concern.

'I run a loose ship. He pretty much does as he pleases.'

'Is he okay though?' Terence asked.

'Of course! I told him you were coming and he'll be absolutely cock-a-hoop to see you.'

Terence felt slighty deflated. He had rather expected Harvey would be here to greet him.

Emily screwed up her nose. 'What on earth is that…'

'Oh, the smell? Yes, I'm sorry about that, darlings,' Clara said. 'Had to take Rhubarb to the vet in the week – tummy problems, I'll spare you the grim details.' She chortled and theatrically wafted a hand in front of her nose. 'She had an accident all over the back seat coming home. A bugger to clean up, I don't mind telling you.'

Terence looked at the dark stain on the seat beside him and shifted uncomfortably.

Emily had noticed something else. 'I think there's some poo on the floor as well,' she said, moving her feet to avoid getting any on her patent leather shoes.

'There is. That was your Harvey when I brought him home. The little tinker.'

Emily frowned. 'That was weeks ago! Would it not have been an idea to pick it up?'

Clara appeared to consider the question for a moment. 'I intended to, but to be honest I clean forgot. It's not doing any harm.'

'It's not very hygienic to just leave it here though.'

Clara caught sight of the revulsion on Emily's face. 'It's just a bit of poo, darling. It's not going to bite you.' She sniggered. 'Imagine that, eh Terence? A turd with teeth! Grrrrr!'

Terence laughed, but Emily put a hand to her mouth as if she was about to be sick.

'If it's really bothering you, darling, just open the window and bung it out. Honestly, there's nothing to worry about, it'll be dry by now.'

Emily gagged. 'I need some air!' She wound down the window and inhaled deeply. The nausea quickly subsided as the cool morning breeze enveloped her.

Clara was a demon behind the wheel, frequently blasting the horn at other drivers. But aside from a near miss when they took a sharp bend in Somerley and several empty bottles rolled out from beneath the passenger seat – which distracted her and almost resulted in the murder of a pheasant – the drive to Christchurch was uneventful. Terence sat in the back reading while Emily stared out the window embracing the fresh air.

Clara chattered away incessantly about everything and nothing, while Emily – who was only half listening – occasionally threw in an appropriate "uh-huh", or "oh, really?", or "I see", or made little grunting noises to give the impression that she was paying attention.

Clara opened the front door and Rhubarb immediately appeared, weaving in and out of her legs. She chivvied the cat away. 'Move yourself, Rhu, we've got guests.'

The cat scampered away across the lounge and took up a watchful spot beneath the television set.

Terence and Emily stepped in behind Clara and were immediately assailed by the overwhelming stench of ammonia.

'Can I go and find Harvey?' Terence said.

Before Clara could reply, Emily made a little noise – 'Ugh!' – and put a hand over her face.

Clara chuckled. 'I know. It's shocking, isn't it, darling?'

'*Bloody awful! Bloody awful!*' With a loud squawk, the macaw – wedged into a cage that was far too small for it – hopped from one perch to another, flapping its wings and whipping up a cloud of plucked feathers.

'Hush, Archie!' Clara said.

'What in God's name is it?! Emily exclaimed from behind her hand.

'The smell?'

Emily nodded.

'It was Rhubarb.' Clara saw Emily glance down at the cat with disgust. 'Oh, not this little princess.' She squatted on her haunches and ruffled the cat's head. 'You wouldn't do that, would you, Rhu?' Clearly perturbed by Clara's heavy-handedness, the cat hissed at her.

She stood up. 'No, it was her predecessor, Rhubarb One. She would so insist on widdling on the carpets. Dreadful habit. I tried to get her to take her business outside, of course, but she wasn't having it. I gave up in the end. When she passed, I thought about replacing the carpets, but I thought why waste the money? I'd kind of got used to the smell by then.'

Emily eyed one particularly large, unsightly stain on the worn russet pile.

'Anyway,' Clara said. 'Tea? Or something a tad stronger?'

Emily glanced at the clock, hanging slightly askew on the wall behind the television. 'It's only just turned eleven.'

Clara winked. 'It's always five o'clock somewhere, darling.'

Emily didn't attempt to hide her disapproval. 'Tea will be fine.'

Clara nodded. 'Orange juice for you, Terence? It's the only soft drink I keep in, I'm afraid.' She winked at Emily again. 'Nothing quite like a gin mimosa to start the day off with a buzz.'

'Yes please,' Terence said. 'May I see Harvey first?'

'But of course, darling!' Clara escorted them through to the kitchen and unlocked the back door, which led out to a small conservatory piled high on both sides with a ramshackle assortment of cardboard boxes. 'Just go on through.'

She picked up a couple of mugs from the sideboard and blew the dust out of them. 'I hope a mug is alright, I don't think I have any clean cups at the moment.'

Arthur and Clara didn't see much of each other and, on those occasions when they did, it was usually in Seatown or, once in a blue moon, at a location for a day out somewhere halfway between there and Christchurch. As such, Terence had only visited his Aunt Clara's house twice in his life, and only one of those times was he old enough to remember.

There had been a lovely little garden at the back of the house, with a well-kept lawn bordered by flowerbeds abrim with dazzling colour. At the end in front of a high fence was a patch devoted to bushes hanging heavy with some of the most delicious soft fruits that Terence had ever tasted. And beside that, a small pond, where he had sat drinking lemonade and marvelling at the mass of frogspawn.

What faced him as he stepped out of the conservatory door bore no resemblance whatsoever to the memories of his last visit several years earlier. The whole garden had fallen into the most shocking state of neglect. The grass – where it hadn't been scorched away by the sun – was knee high and strewn with thistles. The flowerbeds were full of weeds and the pond was obscured by a bank of stinging nettles. Worse yet, the fruit bushes – from which once dangled oodles of raspberries and gooseberries and blueberries – were barely visible beneath a wall of ugly brambles and twisting ivy. Even birdsong was conspicuous in its absence.

In an instant Terence's excitement evaporated. He surveyed the sad piece of ground. There was no sign of Harvey.

He called out. 'Harvey!'

The silence was almost deafening.

He tried again. 'Harvey! Where are you, pal?' Trying to avoid the prickly thistles, he made his way gingerly through the long grass towards the end of the garden. Then he heard a scuffling sound. It appeared to be coming from a large, upturned wooden crate near what used to be the pond.

When he reached it, he could see the slats were broken at one end. He bent down. 'Harvey?' he said warily. Getting onto his knees, he peered inside. What he saw broke his heart.

Harvey – for a fleeting moment Terence wasn't even sure it *was* him – was hunched up in the corner. He had always been a skinny dog, but even without close inspection it was clear he'd lost weight. The dark fur looked damp and there were patches of loss where pink skin was showing though. His whole body was trembling as he peered out nervously at Terence.

Terence was lost for words. He could hardly conceive that Aunt Clara would have treated his faithful friend with such neglect. Yet here in front of his eyes was evidence of just that.

All of a sudden the animal seemed to recognise his master. The shaking ceased abruptly and with an excited yipping noise he darted out into Terence's arms.

'Oh, Harvey! What's happened to you, pal?' Terence held the little dog close and let him lick his face. He made his way back up the garden and through the conservatory to the kitchen, where Clara was just handing Emily a mug of tea.

'Auntie, I don't think Harvey's very well.'

Emily saw the dog cradled in Terence's arms and almost dropped her mug. 'He looks awful!'

'Nonsense, darling.' Clara walked over and studied Harvey for a moment. 'He's alright.' She ruffled his curls. 'Aren't you, boy?'

Harvey licked her hand.

'You see?' Clara went back to the sideboard and picked up her mug of tea. 'I suppose it was remiss of me not to mention that he hasn't been eating much. And he likes to sleep out in the garden. He prefers it out there to indoors. I can't think why. But I fashioned an old packing crate into a shelter for him.' She took a sip of her tea. 'He seems to like it.'

Terence saw that his mother was looking sorrowfully at Harvey. 'Could we not bring him home with us, Mum? I swear I'll make sure he doesn't do anything else to upset Dad.'

Emily shook her head. 'I'm sorry. Your father's word was final. He won't have a dog in the house any more. He'll just take him to the pound.'

'But he obviously isn't happy here. Look at him! He's all thin and he's losing his fur.' Terence suddenly scratched his forearm and cried out. 'Ugh, what's that?'

Emily leaned over. 'Is that a flea?' She looked aghast.

Terence screeched! 'Get it off, get it off!'

'Don't be such a namby-pamby.' Clara reached out and brushed it away. 'It's only a little flea.'

Terence looked at his mother imploringly. 'I've never seen Harvey this skinny. I can feel his ribs.'

'I can see he's in a bad way. It's very sad, but I'm sure Clara's doing the best she can for him.' Emily didn't believe her own words, but she couldn't entertain the suggestion of taking Harvey home with them either.

Clara nodded. 'I do my best. But I can't force him to eat if he doesn't want to.'

'It's true,' Emily said. 'It's much better for everyone if he stays here.'

'It's not better for Harvey,' Terence said, fighting back the tears. There was no way to win this argument and yet he couldn't just leave Harvey here to die. Then an idea popped into his head. He set the dog down on the floor. 'May I take him for a walk?'

71

Clara beamed. 'Of course you can, darling.' She reached over and lifted Harvey's lead off the hook on the back of the kitchen door. She handed it to Terence. 'He doesn't get many walks.' She patted the side of her leg. 'The old gammy hip stops me walking too far these days. Stay out with him as long as you like.'

'I'll take him to the beach.'

'Good idea!' Clara fumbled in her purse. 'Here's ten shillings. You can buy yourself an ice cream if you like.' She counted out ten shillings into Terence's open hand.

The boy's eyes lit up and he tucked it in his pocket. 'Thanks Auntie Clara!' He attached the lead to Harvey's collar but as he walked across the kitchen, Emily gasped and pointed at the floor.

'Terence!'

Looking to where his mother was pointing, he saw that he'd managed to traipse dog mess into the house. He looked up at Clara apologetically. 'I'm sorry, Auntie.'

She chuckled. 'Think nothing of it. Happens to me all the time. Come and sit in the lounge Emily.'

As Clara flounced off back into the living room, Emily pulled Terence to one side. 'Don't be gone too long. We're not staying in this house any longer than we have to!'

'Auntie's always drunk, Mum. She can't look after Harvey properly.'

'We'll talk about it later. Go on, go and have your ice cream.'

When Terence left, she walked through to the lounge. Clara was splayed out on the settee. She patted the cushion beside her. 'We've so much to talk about, we haven't seen each other for ages.'

'Shouldn't we clean up the kitchen floor first?'

Clara noticed the look of repugnance on Emily's face. 'Honestly, darling, you really have got a hang-up about poo, haven't you?'

She nonchalantly reached a small hipflask out of her handbag and unscrewed the cap. 'Bottoms up!'

Terence spent the next couple of hours down at the beach. He bought a 99 cornet from a vendor on the seafront and sat down on a nearby bench to eat it. Harvey crawled underneath and lay down in the shade.

Breaking the end off the cone, Terence scooped some of the soft, white ice cream into it and bent down and fed it to Harvey, who grabbed it from his fingers and gulped it down.

When he'd finished his treat, Terence lifted the little poodle up onto the bench next to him and unhooked the lead from his collar.

'Listen to me, pal. I'm afraid it's time for us to say goodbye. I really wish I could take you home with me, but if I do, Dad will be furious and he'll take you to the pound. But I can't leave you with Aunt Clara either. She's just not looking after you properly. I'm afraid if you stay with her you'll get sick and die.'

Terence picked up the dog and hugged him close. 'I've come to a decision that's best for you. I'm going to leave you here now. You may have to fend for yourself for a bit, but hopefully someone will find you and take you home and love you just as much as I do.'

Harvey licked Terence's nose. 'I know. I'm going to miss you too. Badly. But you have to understand it's for the best.' Kissing the top of Harvey's head, he lifted him down from the bench and stood up. 'Love you, pal. Go on now.' He flapped his hands at the slightly bewildered-looking dog. 'Shoo!'

Harvey just sat on the pavement looking at him. Tears streaming down his cheeks, Terence turned away, but as he started to walk, Harvey got up and trotted after him.

'No!' Terence shouted, trying to wipe away the tears with the back of his hand. 'Bad dog! Go away. I don't want you any more!'

Harvey paused, uncertain what was happening.

'Go on! Away with you!'

Terence started to walk again and this time Harvey didn't follow. When he reached a break in the promenade wall, he paused and couldn't resist looking back. The little dog was still sitting in the middle of the path watching him curiously.

Every fibre in Terence's being was screaming at him to run back and pick up his beloved pet and return him to Clara's. But he didn't. With his heart breaking, he turned away. As he did so he heard a child squeal with delight.

'Mummy, look at the little doggie! Do you think he's lost? Can we keep him, Mummy? Can we, can we?'

With the words echoing in his ears, Terence set off back to Clara's house. Through his tears, he managed to smile.

Harvey was going to be fine. Just fine.

PART II

CHAPTER 7

Terence tapped his fountain pen on the paper in front of him, applying the final full stop to his thesis on the introduction of the Welfare State to Great Britain in 1946.

With a satisfied sigh, he picked up the antique silver ink blotter that his mother had bought him upon his enrolment at the Univeristy of Warwick and rocked it back and forth over the last few lines on the page.

He would be the first to admit that he had been dubious about the Business and Economics Course that Arthur had pushed him in to. Yet, much to his surprise, he'd discovered he had a natural aptitude for the subject. Determined to succeed – not only to impress his father, but to prove to himself he could do anything he set his mind to – he had been diligent throughout the first three months of the course and his thirst for knowledge had rapidly burgeoned.

In the evenings – when most of his fellow students would be out drinking or engaging in what Terence deemed to be dubious and ill-advised carnal liaisons – he would remain alone in his room in the halls of residence where, if he wasn't busily writing, he could be found with his head buried in a book.

Now, as he carefully tucked his essay into the top drawer of his writing desk, there was no doubt in his mind that depriving himself of unnecessary distractions had paid off.

Terence glanced at his watch. It was only a cheap Timex, but, having been a gift from his mother when he started college, it was precious to him and he loved it for that reason alone. It was only just after nine. He smiled. Perhaps he might push the boat out tonight and allow himself a small celebratory drink.

He briefly considered going to one of the nearby pubs that were popular with the other uni students, but the last time he'd done so, everyone else was in their own little groups of friends, nobody spoke to him and he ended up spending the evening drinking alone.

For everybody else, university life seemed to double as an excuse to have fun; there was one big party going on inside, and Terence felt like he was always left outside the window looking in on it. It didn't really bother him, in fact it was an analogy that rather amused him. He preferred his own company anyway.

He decided instead on the Rose & Crown, ten minutes walk from the campus.

Slightly befuddled by the friendly smile afforded him by the barmaid as she handed over his change, he made his way over to the quietest corner of the room where he took a seat to enjoy his half-pint of draught Taunton Cider and a bag of Big D peanuts.

Things hadn't been easy for Terence since he walked out of the doors at Bagshott for the last time three years earlier. Elatedly shaking the dust off his shoes as he went, he had naïvely expected that life would improve away from its cruel corridors. It wasn't to be the case. It turned out that Weymouth College was equally as soul-destroying as boarding school, if not more so; different kids perhaps – at college he was mixing with both boys and girls for the first time in his life – but the same roster of bullying and humiliation ensued.

One particular incident left him badly scarred. He had been eating lunch in the dining room when he noticed a fellow pupil at the adjacent table. The boy had what could best be described as a pretty face, framed by long blonde hair that hung loosely around his shoulders. He was enviably slender, but muscular with it, and when he smiled he lit up the room.
Terence had been idly watching him, wishing he looked as handsome. But the boy caught sight of him staring and gave him a mouthful, accusing him of being queer. After that, the name Homo Hallam stuck, muttered by sniggering students – just loudly enough for him to hear – with cruel frequency.

One good thing did come out of the incident, however. His weight had made him a cheap target for the bullies at Bagshott, and it had been joined by snidey implications of homosexuality. So he pledged that he would lose some of his childhood fat. His second year at college had been spent eating healthily and the pounds dropped away. He had arrived for his first day at Warwick University weighing in at a lean ten and a half stone, not only almost four stone lighter, but having matured into a very handsome young man with strong features and a great head of hair.

Another significant change had come about during his second year at Weymouth. Arthur claimed that, should Terence be prepared to put his back into his academic studies, a bright future with Hallam Toys awaited him. Thereafter, he had taken a far greater interest in his son's education.

Terence thrived on the paternal attention and milked it for all it was worth, although not for the reasons Arthur thought; he would never have said so, but he had no intention whatsoever of following in his father's footsteps. The very notion of sitting behind a desk negotiating the sales of toy robots filled him with dread. Of course, that didn't mean that he didn't intend to work hard. On the contrary, he was smart enough to know that doing well at college would pave the way to university, which in turn would facilitate an escape route from the dreary prospect of working for his father.

Tragedy had struck the family when Clara Hallam was killed in a road collision a year earlier. After the mysterious disappearance of Rhubarb, who Arthur asserted had probably fled to live somewhere less like a pigsty, Clara found solace in the bottle and her state of mind had progressively worsened. Indeed, it had reached the point where she was more often inebriated than sober. She would regularly get behind the wheel completely plastered and, as such, a collision was something just waiting to happen and wouldn't have surprised anybody, but for one thing:

She had been summoned for jury service and was driving to court to attend her second sitting on a drink driving trial – the irony escaped no-one – and she had actually been stone cold sober. Pulling out of a junction without looking, she was clipped by an articulated lorry. The Beetle went into a spin and hit a lamp post driver-side on. The the man behind the wheel of the artic had slammed on his brakes, but Clara was dead before it had even come to a halt.

Arthur was grief stricken and riddled with guilt over not having done more to help his only sister. He had always worried Clara would go the same way as their mother, who'd had serious mental health issues and often suffered crazy episodes; on more than one occasion, he had remarked, 'She's lucky they never locked her away!'

Unlike his father, Terence was secretly pleased that Clara was dead. He had never forgiven her for her ill treatment of Harvey and as far as he was concerned the world was a better place without the old drunk in it.

Two days after his trip out to the pub, Terence was sitting in the dining room on campus trying to find a measure of enjoyment in the unappetising ham salad sandwich he'd chosen for his lunch. He had just finished the last mouthful and washed it down with a swig of apple juice, when a girl carrying a lunch tray walked passed his table and came to a stop alongside him.

'Hello again!'

Terence looked up, blinking against the early afternoon sun. It was glaring through the window directly behind the girl's head, forming a halo of light around her auburn feather cut.

'Oh, hello,' he replied uncertainly.

'You're looking very smart today.'

'Am I?'

In Terence's opinion, how he presented himself in public was of paramount importance. Many of the students at the university were so casual in their choice of attire that some of them appeared as if they could barely be bothered to get dressed at all.

'You are.'

Terence wasn't sure who the young lady was, but it was rarely, if ever, that he received a compliment, and certainly not from a member of the opposite sex. He adjusted his tie. 'Well, thank you.'

Rather than walking away as he expected her to, the girl laughed. 'You don't remember me, do you?'

'Er... yes.' He immediately regretted the lie.

'No you don't. I can see it in your eyes.'

Terence felt himself beginning to blush. 'Er... no, I'm sorry, I'm afraid I don't.' Suddenly feeling rather foolish, he picked up his glass of juice and took another mouthful.

The girl laughed again. 'I could tell from your face you didn't. The Rose & Crown? A couple of nights ago?'

Terence frowned, trying to remember. 'You'll have to forgive me, I can't...'

'I was working behind the bar. If I recall rightly, you had half a cider and a bag of nuts.'

Of course. Terence remembered her now; she had smiled at him. 'That's correct, I did.'

'It's a nice pub. A bit quiet, but kind of homely.'

'I don't really drink as a rule. I was treating myself for completing an essay. A small celebration if you will.'

The girl laughed again. '*Very* small. You only stayed about twenty minutes.'

Terence endeavoured to conjure up a smile. 'Well, perhaps calling it a celebration was gilding the lily somewhat.'

Terence hated small talk. He always had. Mostly because he wasn't very good at it. He was permanently at a loss for something interesting to say and more often than not he would become tongue-tied. As such, rather than endure aimless conviviality, he would nip it in the bud at the earliest opportunity. He drained the last of his juice. 'Well, nice to see you again,' he said, hoping the words would sound final enough that she might take the hint and go away. He reached for his dessert – a small pot of chocolate mousse.

'I'm Joanne, by the way. Joanne Cormack.' The girl perched her tray on one hand and extended the other towards him.

Terence half-heartedly shook it. 'Hallam. Terence Hallam.' Why wouldn't she just leave him alone?

'Thank you, Hallam Terence Hallam, I'd love to!'

'I'm sorry?'

Joanne pulled out the chair opposite him and sat down. 'Join you for lunch.'

Terence frowned. This was becoming annoying. 'As you can see, I've almost finished,' he said, peeling the damp cardboard lid off his mousse.

'Don't worry, I'm a fast eater. I'll catch up.'

Terence eyed up the food on her tray: a small, rather flaccid-looking beefburger in a bun alongside a meagre portion of overcooked chips, a strawberry milkshake – the sight of which made his stomach turn – and a dessert similar to his own, only a different flavour.

Joanne tapped the lid of the mousse. 'Snap. Well, almost. I find the chocolate a bit sickly. Strawberry's the best. It's my favourite flavour in the whole world.'

'I have to say I'm not keen.'

'No?' She picked up the burger and took a large bite out of it. 'It's so refreshing.'

Now she had moved out of the sunlight, Terence was able to observe her properly. She was wearing flared jeans and a plain white T-shirt. The smallest swelling on her chest suggested it probably wasn't necessary for her to wear a bra, yet the outline of straps over her shoulders attested that she did anyway.

Terence looked at her face. The standout feature was her dazzling green eyes, which looked as if they might be incapable of ever conveying anything other than excitement. She wasn't wearing make-up and her pale skin was unblemished but for a small mole on her left cheek. Her lips were a delicate shade of pink. She was certainly pretty, Terence concluded, but not exactly what he personally would have called beautiful.

Trying to think of something to say, he spooned some chocolate mousse into his mouth and sucked the spoon clean. 'So what are you doing here?'

'Excuse me?' There was a tiny dribble of tomato sauce on her chin. Terence cringed inside.

'Here at the university.'

Joanne swallowed the bite of burger and popped a couple of chips into her mouth. 'What do you think I'm doing?' She smiled. 'Same as you. Studying for a degree.'

'I see.' He finished his mousse. 'What are you studying?'

'Architecture.' She screwed up her face and spat the chips out on to the side of her plate. 'Pardon my manners. They're horrible. Look…' – she pointed at the mush of chewed potato – 'That one's burnt.'

Terence made a point of not looking. 'Don't you find studying somewhat difficult between tending the bar?'

'Silly sod! I'm a full time student. I only work alternates at the Rose – Monday, Wednesday and Friday evenings. Oh, and every other Saturday lunchtime.' She shoved the last piece of her burger into her mouth and pushed the plate aside. 'It puts a few pennies in the purse, you know?'

'I would imagine it does.'

Joanne swallowed her food and, much to Terence's relief, dabbed her mouth with a serviette, wiping away the blob of ketchup from her chin in the process. 'You *imagine* it does, do you?' She laughed. 'You do talk funny.'

Terence frowned. Now she was mocking him. 'And how precisely would you have me speak?'

Joanne saw the expression on his face. 'Oh, no offence intended.' She put a hand over his and kept it there for a second or two longer than necessary.

Terence felt a tingling sensation at the back of his neck. 'None taken, I can assure you.'

'See? There it is again. So polite.' She smiled. 'It's rather sweet. There aren't many people round here as eloquent as you.' Pushing the carton of mousse aside – 'I don't think I fancy that now.' – she changed the subject. 'I've seen you in here before, but you never seem to be at any of the socials.'

'I prefer to study.'

'Every night?'

'I find it invaluable to extend my knowledge. It's a far better way of spending one's time than going out partying.'

'Surely it wouldn't hurt to let your hair down once in a while?'

'It's really not my thing.'

Joanne closed her lips around the end of the twin straws and sucked on her milkshake. 'Tell me then, Terence Hallam...' Her eyes widened playfully. 'What exactly *is* your thing?'

Was she flirting with him now? Terence hadn't the faintest idea. He'd never had a girl show any interest in him before. He shifted uncomfortably in his seat.

Joanne could see she had embarrassed him. She grinned. 'Sorry, I'm teasing. Honestly though, you ought to get yourself out a bit. You could take me to the disco next Saturday night if you like. It'd be fun.'

'I don't think so. I'm not really too fond of crowds.'

'I can see why you chose the Rose and Crown then!' Joanne chuckled. 'Come on with you. It would be fun.'

'The problem with discos is they're usually full of dreadful drunks.'

'Well you're not adverse to a drink yourself.'

'There's a difference between unwinding with a small alcoholic beverage and drinking until you can barely stand up!'

'Fair point. But not everyone is like that.'

'Too many in my experience.'

'Forget the disco then. How about you and me go out somewhere where there isn't a crowd. Just the two of us.'

Terence's collar suddenly felt tight. He ran a finger around the neckline. 'I'm not sure. I'm quite busy at the moment.'

'Let me guess. Studying?'

'Precisely.'

Joanne sucked on the end of the straws and swallowed. 'Tell you what. There's a new Wimpy bar in town. The burgers have got to be better than the ones here. Why don't we go try it out?' She saw the look of hesitation on Terence's face. 'It'll be my treat.'

Terence sighed. Perhaps if he agreed, she would go away and he could think up a reason not to go later. 'I suppose it couldn't do any harm. Just the once, mind you.'

'Fab!' Joanne stood up and picked up her lunch tray. 'Meet you beside the front gates at six tonight.'

Terence felt his stomach tighten. 'Tonight? Aren't you working?'

'I told you. Mondays, Wednesdays and Fridays. It's Thursday today.'

'Ah, yes.' Terence sighed again. 'So it is. I stand corrected.'

Joanne grinned. 'See you tonight then.' Without giving him an opportunity to think up an excuse, she walked over to the serving area and deposited her tray on the end of the counter. Then she turned, blew him a small kiss and disappeared through the doors.

CHAPTER 8

The moment he set foot inside the restaurant, Terence wanted to turn around and walk straight back out again. The place was heaving and the noise of chatter and laughter was almost deafening. He cursed himself for agreeing to come.

'It looks full.' He was hoping that Joanne wouldn't notice the one empty table that he'd spotted beside the far wall. 'Shall we go somewhere else?'

She laughed. 'You're not wriggling out of it that easily, Hallam Terence Hallam!' She pointed to the empty table. 'There's a free one over there.'

Terence made a concerted effort to sound pleased. 'Ah, yes, so there is.'

They made their way over, squeezing between the other tables and Terence politely pulled out a chair.

Joanne slipped her hands into the pockets of her jeans and bobbed a small curtsy. 'Why thank you, kind sir.'

Pulling out a handkerchief, Terence brushed some crumbs and a stray chip off the table, evidently left there by the uncouth previous occupant. Then he walked round to the other side and took a seat opposite Joanne.

There was a menu on the table. She opened it and studied it hungrily. 'What do you fancy?'

'I'm not sure. I don't usually eat this sort of food. I'm not too partial to burgers.'

'They have other stuff.' She spun the menu so that Terence could see it and pointed. 'I can recommend the Egg Bender.'

A memory flashed through Terence's head. He was laying on his bunk at Bagshott, fighting to conceal his modesty, and Lavis was there with that dimwit grin on his face, calling Bream a bender.

'I think not,' he said.

'Okay. What sort of things do you like?'

'Do they offer some variety of salad perhaps?'

'They do.' She pointed at a photo on the menu. 'The Delta Salad. Looks quite tasty, doesn't it?'

It didn't, but Terence nodded. 'I'll have that.'

'I think I'm going to spare no expense and have the International grill.'

Terence peered at the menu. 'That's fifty-four pence!'

'I know. I've only had it once before when my Mum and Dad took me out for my birthday, but it's worth it for the steak alone.' She pushed the menu to one side. 'And a knickerbocker glory for afters.'

'A what?'

93

'You've *got* to be joking.' Joanne looked at him with amusement. 'Are you honestly telling me you don't know what a knickerbocker glory is?'

Terence shook his head.

'You'll have to wait and see then. You're in for a real treat.' She sat back in her chair and cast a glance around the restaurant. 'Quite nice here, isn't it?'

'Is it?'

Joanne laughed. 'Lighten up, for God's sake! Try to have some fun.'

Terence forced a smile. 'I am.'

'Well, you've got an odd way of showing it, Hallam Terence Hallam.'

'Why do you keep calling me that?'

'Because it's funny. That's how you introduced yourself to me at lunchtime.'

'Did I?'

'You certainly did.' She pulled a stern face and adopted a posh accent. 'Very formal.'

'Oh.'

She smiled. 'What do you like to be called then?'

'Just Terence.'

'Not Terry?'

'No.'

'What about Tel?' She put her hands on her hips and swaggered left and right. 'Awright over there are ya, Tel-boy?'

She giggled and Terence caught the glint of mischief in her eyes. He had to admit that she had quite the winning smile. 'I suppose Terry would be acceptable.'

Joanne slapped the flat of her hand on the table. 'Terry it is then. And you can call me Jo.'

Terence suddenly felt the familiar sensation of awkwardness grip hold of him. He'd run out of things to say. Joanne was looking at him expectantly; she was sure to be waiting for him to say something interesting, he thought. He panicked and in desperation said, 'Did you know that the Wimpy brand originated in the United States of America?'

'Did it?'

'Indeed it did. In Bloomington, Indiana in 1932, no less.'

'Really?'

Joanne looked decidedly underwhelmed by the tidbit of information, but if Terence noticed he didn't let it deter him. He'd found something worthwhile to talk about and he ran with it.

'Yes, it's absolutely true. Forty-six years ago.' Terence was getting into his stride. He looked at Joanne excitedly. 'And when do you think they first opened a restaurant in this country?'

'I don't know.'

'Go on, have a guess.'

'Er... 1933.'

'No, that's only a year after they'd established themselves in America. Have another go.'

'1934?'

Terence smiled. 'You're not trying, are you?'

Joanne sighed. 'Honestly, I've really no idea. 1940? 1950? 1960?'

Terence raised a hand to stop her. 'Pretty much in the middle. 1954 in London. Isn't that interesting?'

The expression on Joanne's face made it clear that it was anything but. 'Incredibly.'

'And by 1970, Wimpy had over a thousand outlets in twenty-three countries around the world. That's quite remarkable, isn't it?'

'Amazing,' Joanne said flatly. She couldn't have looked less interested if she tried. 'How come you know all this useless information?'

Terence let her slightly ignorant "useless" remark pass and smiled proudly. 'I went along to the library and researched it on the microfiche this afternoon. I thought as we were coming here a little bit of prior information would be beneficial.'

Joanne rolled her eyes. 'And yet you don't know what a knickerbocker glory is.'

'Er, no. It's the business side of things that interests me. How they expanded and flourished and made their fortune.'

'You do make me laugh, do you know that?'

'Do I?'

'Yeah. I'd have been more interested in looking up the menu.' Exactly as she had done at lunchtime, Joanne reached out and rested her hand upon his. 'I rather like you, Terry.'

Terence hastily withdrew his hand from beneath hers. 'That's nice.'

'Aren't you going to say you like me too?'

'I don't really know you.' He realised how blunt that sounded and added, 'Clearly I must, or else I wouldn't have agreed to come out to eat with you.'

Joanne laughed. 'That figures.'

Terence fiddled awkwardly with his tie.

'Stop fiddling with it,' she said, reaching over and lightly smacking the back of his hand. 'It's all sideways now.' She straightened it for him. 'That's better.'

Another moment of awkward silence was broken by the appearance of a spotty-faced lad beside the table. He was wearing a small square cap and an apron emblazoned with the Wimpy emblem, and he had a notebook and pencil clutched in his hand.

'Sorry for the wait, folks, we're very busy this evening. What can I get for you?'

They ordered their food and the lad jotted it down on his pad. 'Is that everything?'

Terence and Joanne both nodded.

As the lad started to turn away, Joanne caught sight of the name badge pinned to his shirt: **MARK TIBBS**. She grinned. 'Do they call you Mister Tibbs?'

The boy paused and looked at her blankly. 'What?'

'Do they call you *Mister* Tibbs?' she repeated. 'You know, Sidney Poitier in…'

Terence cut her off. '*In the Heat of the Night*. Absolutely first class film!'

Joanne's face lit up. 'Isn't it though! It's one of my favourites.'

'Mine too,' Terence enthused.

Evidently either unfamiliar with, or completely disinterested in the celluloid oeuvre of Sidney Poitier, the lad walked away to pass their order to the chef.

'My Mother allowed me to sit up late and watch it with her a few years ago,' Terence said. 'A splendid piece of film-making, and much superior to the sequel in my opinion. In fact, I would posit that it's Norman Jewison's finest work.'

Joanne nodded. 'I really like *Fiddler on the Roof*. *The Thomas Crown Affair* too. But I agree, *In the Heat of the Night* is his best.

Terence sat up enthusiastically.

'I confess I'm a bit biased,' Joanne continued. 'I've got a bit of a thing for Sidney Poitier. *To Sir, with Love*….' She placed a hand over her heart and patted it. 'He made my legs go to jelly in that. I should be so lucky to ever have a teacher like *him*! Lulu was *so* lucky – the bitch!' She laughed. Her eyes were alive with excitement. 'It's the tiny, tight corkscrews of hair. It's such a turn on. I think black men are so…' Perhaps realising she had gone too far, she trailed off. 'I have a thing for blonde hair too,' she added quickly. Then: 'Sorry, that u-turn made me sound a bit of a phoney. I really do though. Yours reminds me a bit of Jan-Michael Vincent's in *Damnation Alley*.'

Terence wasn't interested in her preferences in men's hair. He was delighted that they had finally found some common ground. 'You know your films, I see.'

'Yeah, I *love* films.'

'Have you seen Vincent in *The World's Greatest Athlete*?'

'Is that the Disney one that Robert Scheerer directed?'

Terence couldn't have been more impressed. 'Now you're just showing off!' He chuckled. 'You really *do* know your films.'

'A walking encyclopedia of all things cinema, that's me.' Joanne smiled at him warmly. 'You know, this is the most animated I've seen you since we got here.'

'I'm glad I came,' Terence said. Five minutes earlier he would have been lying, but now he meant it.

'I'm glad too.'

'Listen. Perhaps we might go and see a film together one evening?'

Joanne's smile faded and she frowned. 'Oh, I don't really know about *that*.'

'Only if you feel like it, of course,' he muttered, wishing he hadn't made the suggestion. 'You could choose, naturally, but it's absolutely fine if you'd rather not. I didn't mean to…'

Joanne broke into a grin. 'I'm teasing, you silly sod. I'd love to!'

Their meals arrived and they both tucked in. Terence discovered that he was suddenly feeling hungry and the Delta Salad he'd ordered looked far more appetising and turned out to be much tastier than the picture on the menu had suggested.

The conversation flowed and not once did Terence struggle for something to say.

He declined to order dessert, but watched with mild amusement at the speed with which Joanne managed to demolish her knickerbocker glory.

It had been a delightful meal and when they'd finished, Terence offered to pay before walking her home. Joanne put up a half-hearted argument – after all, she explained, she had invited him out, not the other way round – but he insisted.

She looked slightly awkward. 'I wouldn't have had the International if I'd known you were going to pay.'

Terence chuckled. 'I know. Fifty-four pence! Scandalous!'

Joanne stood up. 'Thank you, Terry. I just need to go and spend a penny before we leave.' She gave him a peck on the cheek. 'I shan't be a minute.'

Terence sat back in his chair and sighed. It had been a wonderful evening. And to think, he'd been contemplating coming up with an excuse to pull out.

His eyes wandered over to the door just as it opened. A young man who looked to be about the same age as him came in. There was something vaguely familiar about the face, but Terence couldn't quite put his finger on it.

The young man stopped just inside the doorway and surveyed the restaurant. He couldn't be looking for a table, Terence thought; unlike when he and Joanne had arrived, the place was half empty now. No, he appeared to be looking for someone.

As Terence watched, trying to ascertain from where and how he might know the man, a hand went up among a group of people seated near the window and someone shouted.

The words made Terence's blood run cold.

'Lavis, you old bugger. I thought you'd stood us up!'

101

CHAPTER 9

The stroll back to the halls of residence wasn't as pleasant as it might have been. At least not for Terence. Joanne hooked her arm through his – which he had to admit he found quite pleasurable – and chattered away about her favourite films, a few of which Terence hadn't even heard of, let alone seen. He threw in the odd response, but he wasn't really listening to her. His mind was elsewhere.

The day he walked out of Bagshott Boarding School for Boys, he'd hoped to never again see the likes of Graham Lavis, or Martin Bream, or Clive Willingham, or any of the others who ruthlessly tormented him. He had hardly been able to believe his eyes and ears when Lavis walked into the Wimpy bar fifteen minutes earlier. What on earth was he doing in Warwick? Lavis hadn't been the brightest student at Bagshott, so Terence couldn't quite believe he was a student at the university. The very thought that he might be, made him feel sick. If he was, he would almost certainly have started ten months ago when Terence did, and surely they would have come across each other before now. Of all the places in the country he could have ended up, perhaps by some cruel quirk of fate he actually lived in Warwick. That would be just Terence's luck.

As they approached the building that housed the girls' rooms, Joanne was saying, 'I know the world and his wife rave about it, but it bored my tits off.' She laughed. 'Now I suppose you're going to say that you loved it, aren't you?'

There was a silence and Terence became aware she was looking at him, waiting for an answer. 'Sorry, loved what?'

Joanne stopped by the entrance door and unhooked her arm from his. She spun to face him. 'I'm not boring you by any chance am I?'

'Not at all!'

'You haven't been listening to a word I've said, have you?' she said slightly reproachfully.

'You're mistaken. I believe that you said that *The Time Machine* set the bar to which all time travel films should aspire.'

Joanne frowned. 'Yes, I *did* say that.'

'You see, I told you I was...'

'*Two* minutes ago! We've moved on since then.'

Terence shuffled his feet. 'Ah. I see. Then I must apologise.'

'I got the impression you enjoyed the Wimpy.'

'I did. Very much.' As an afterthought he considered she might appreciate, he added, 'The company too.'

'And yet you've hardly spoken two words since we left. What's wrong?'

'It has nothing to do with our evening together, I assure you.' Terence sighed and tucked his hair back over his right ear. 'I just have a few things on my mind, that's all.'

Joanne stepped up close to him and rested her hands up on his shoulders. 'Like what?'

'This and that.'

'What about the other?'

'The other?'

'Never mind.' She dropped her hands and smiled. 'Are you going to kiss me goodnight, or not?'

Terence scratched his chin. 'I hadn't really thought about it.'

Joanne laughed. 'If just about anyone else said that to me I'd call them a liar. But I actually believe you mean it!'

'I do.'

'Well are you going to kiss me or aren't you?'

Terence just stared at her awkwardly.

'Oh, for God's sake, come here.' She threw her arms around his neck and their lips met.

Terence had never been kissed that way before. There had been the cursory greeting and farewell pecks on the cheek from his mother when he set off for, or arrived home from school. Plus, of course, the slighty slobbery ones from Aunt Clara. And he'd not forget that little moment when Mrs Turner had kissed him on the cheek and made him tingle. But he'd certainly not been kissed with passion and the moment of intimacy was thrilling. With no clue as to what he was doing, Terence pressed back against Joanne's lips. He kept his mouth shut, but hers was moving sensually as if she were trying to devour him. When he felt her tongue trying to prise his mouth open, he pulled quickly away.

'Well, that was… nice.'

'There's more where that came from!' She giggled and turned away. 'See you in the dining hall tomorrow lunchtime. We can decide what film we're going to see on Saturday.'

Terence smiled. 'Just a moment…'

Joanne looked back, tossing her hair as she did so. For a fleeting moment, in the dim glow of the light above the door, Terence thought she actually looked beautiful.

'Yes?'

'What was it you were referring to just now that you thought I would claim I loved?'

'*2001*.'

'You mean Kubrick's *2001: A Space Odyssey*?'

'Yeah.'

'Remarkable special effects, but ultimately a lot of old tosh.'

Joanne smiled and blew him a kiss. 'Goodnight, Terry.'

*

Terence tried to banish Graham Lavis from his mind. As was his unwavering routine, he had expected to be travelling back to Seatown the following evening. But the thought of accompanying Joanne to the cinema on Saturday night excited him and, after they'd said goodnight, he had come to the decision he would call his mother the following morning and let her know he wouldn't be coming home for the weekend.

Despite his best efforts to distract himself with pleasant thoughts, when he climbed into bed, he struggled to get off to sleep, with memories of his childhood nemesis haunting him.

When he finally managed to drift off, he slept badly.

Periods of semi-consciousness were punctuated by a succession of fractured bad dreams. The last and most disturbing one found him seated in a packed cinema watching *2001: A Space Odyssey*. Joanne was beside him and in the light reflected from the screen he had disconcertingly become aware that they were both naked. He nudged her and asked if they could go and buy some new clothes, but she shushed him and told him not to worry; nobody would notice. His crawling feeling of panic intensified and then suddenly the house lights came on. Struggling to get up, he realised he was rooted to the seat. He turned to Joanne for help, but she had vanished. As he looked around desperately to see where she had gone, the people in the row in front turned in their seats and Terence saw the gloating faces of Mr Keane, Willingham, Hockley, Talbot, Parrish, Bream and… there in the seat right in front of his, was Lavis. As Terence dropped his hand to cover his nakedness, he felt hot breath on his ear and a woman's voice whispered, 'Hallam's got no pubes!'. He turned to see Joanne, now fully clothed, grinning at him demonically. 'And no *cock*!' He looked down and saw to his horror that where his penis used to be there was nothing.

It was at that point Terence woke up. His heart was pounding and his pyjamas were soaked in sweat. Instinctively, he thrust his hand under the blankets; the feeling of relief as he realised his genitals were intact was immediately dulled by the shameful realisation that he'd wet himself.

He propped himself up on his elbows and looked at the bedside clock. It was a little after six-thirty.

Sleepy-eyed and with the gnawing disquiet provoked by the horrible dream still hanging over him – particularly the expression of cruel mockery on Joanne's face – he got up. Cursing, he stripped off his soiled nightclothes and crammed them into a carrier bag to take home with him that evening.

He now had no intention whatsoever of staying in Warwick for the weekend. He would come up with an excuse and tell Joanne something unexpected had happened at home that required him to return. He felt no guilt about the prospect of lying to her. She seemed a nice enough girl and he wouldn't deny he'd enjoyed their evening out together. But he had forgotten that dating attractive girls wasn't for the likes of him, and he had dropped his guard and allowed himself to be tempted by a pretty smile and a kiss. It was probably best he nipped things in the bud now; he had studies to concentrate on and distractions – especially those of the female variety – were something he could well do without and would inevitably end badly.

Then, of course, there was Lavis to worry about. Terence knew that time had moved on and that fretting about childish pranks which happened five years ago achieved nothing. But he could still scarcely believe the boy had come witlessly strolling back into his life after all this time, bringing his destructive self-doubt and anxiety to the surface again. It wasn't beyond the realms of possibility that Lavis had changed. Maybe he was a nicer person now. Terence seriously doubted it, however, and he had no intention of allowing an encounter to take place that would enable him to find out.

Half an hour later he had showered away the remnants of his nightmare and was feeling a little more like his old self. Deciding on the first best course of action with regard to Lavis, he quickly got dressed and headed off to the dining room for a bite of breakfast before his morning class.

*

'So we can get a bite to eat first, then it's either Eastwood and the monkey, *The Deer Hunter*, or the Alan Alda one.' Joanne smiled. 'I know which one I'd prefer, but I'll be gracious and let you choose, Terry.'

They were sitting in the Uni dining room having some lunch and Joanne had been talking almost non-stop since they'd got there.

'What was the choice again?'

She gave Terence a slightly withering look. 'That's the second time you've zoned out on me. *Every What Way...* something or other – I can't remember what it's called – *The Deer Hunter* or *Same Time Next Year*. Or, if you really want to slum it, *The Wiz*.'

'What's that?'

'I told you just now, that musical with Diana Ross and Michael Jackson.'

'Ah, yes, so you did.'

'But the trailer wasn't very exciting and it's not getting very good reviews, so unless you're *really* keen I'd sooner give it a miss.'

'I see.'

'So?' Joanne looked at him expectantly. 'Which one?

Terence had been putting off the evil moment, but now she was pinning him down he was left with no choice but to spit it out.

'I'm very sorry, but I'm not going to be able to come.'

Joanne's face dropped. 'Oh, why not?'

'Personal reasons. I think it's best you find someone else to go with.'

'I don't understand.' She looked disappointed. 'What's changed since last night? I mean, I know you seemed a bit distracted on the walk back, but …'

'I'm really sorry. Something unexpected came up.'

'Yeah? Like what?'

Was there was a hint of unfriendliness in her voice, or was Terence imagining it? He sighed. He'd rather hoped she would just accept it was for some reason or other he didn't wish to discuss and not question him any further. But clearly she wanted something more.

'My Mother needs me home for the weekend,' he said. 'She's at her wits' end. It's my father, you see, he's not well.'

The last part of the statement wasn't so far from the truth. Arthur had been having breathing difficulties for some time. A trip to the doctor five weeks earlier had resulted in the recommendation he cease smoking or risk his chances of lung cancer. Further tests were pending. Indulging in a Montecristo Especial cigar was one of Arthur's greatest pleasures and going cold turkey hit him hard. Nevertheless, he followed his physician's instructions to the letter; initially at least. While his breathing didn't improve one iota, his temperament worsened. Within two weeks he'd decided he could live with the congestion and had resumed his four-a-day regime.

'His doctor believes he may have lung cancer,' Terence continued. 'They need to carry out further tests.'

Joanne hadn't finished her food, but she crossed her knife and fork and slid the plate to one side. 'I'm so sorry.' She looked at him sadly. 'Your father is ill and here I am wittering away about going to the pictures. You go home and help your mother, we can go out another time. Maybe one evening next week.'

111

Terence shook his head. 'Actually, about that... I've given the matter some consideration and I really don't think it's a very good idea.'

'Oh.' Joanne looked a little taken aback. 'You were okay with it yesterday.'

'I know, but what with my father being unwell, I'm probably going to be tied up at weekends for a while and it's imperative that I don't neglect my studies.'

Joanne eyed him suspiciously. 'This sounds like a brush-off to me. A pretty weak one at that.'

Terence didn't reply. He looked at her awkwardly, steeling himself for the inevitable vitriol and hoping it would be brief. Then she would get up and storm off and that would put an end to the matter.

But the anger didn't come. Much to Terence's surprise, Joanne smiled at him.

'Listen here, you. I'm not giving up that easily.' She leant forward in her seat and Terence caught the heady scent of her perfume. 'It sounds to me like you might have got cold feet because I came on a bit heavy last night.'

'No, it's not that at all, it's...'

She reached up and pressed her finger to his lips. 'I totally understand and I'm sorry. I have a tendency to take the things I want without thinking about it too hard. Life's way too short not to. I could have picked anyone in this room to go out with last night, but I didn't want just anyone. I wanted you. So if you're prepared to give me another chance, I'll try to control my…' – she grinned – '…animal urges. I can't promise, mind you. I don't mind admitting, I fancy the pants off you. But I *will* try.' She sat back and looked at Terence hopefully.

He had been watching her intently as she spoke and chastising himself for daring to think she wasn't beautiful. She was absolutely enchanting. And refreshingly honest too. What she had said might have smacked of conceit, but it was also true: she could indeed have had her pick of anyone in the room. Yet here she was talking to *him*, interested in *him* – plain-as-they-come Terence Montague Hallam. He decided that he may have been too rash in dismissing the chance of getting to know her better.

'That was quite a speech.'

Joanne nodded her appreciation. 'Thank you.'

'Very eloquently put.'

'Well?' She smiled at him. 'What do you reckon?'

'What was it you said?' Terence raised his eyebrows. 'You fancy the *pants* off me?'

Joanne looked a little embarrassed. 'I believe I might have said that, yes.'

'I see.'

'After all, it's true.'

Terence now regretted making an excuse not to see her at the weekend. But having done so, he wasn't about to backtrack either. He would go home to Seatown as planned. And there was, as Joanne had suggested, always next week.

'What are you doing on Tuesday?'

'I don't know.' She put her elbows on the table and rested her chin on the back of her hands. 'Going to the pictures with you, maybe?'

'Maybe.'

She smiled. 'Is that a *definite* maybe?'

For the first time since they had sat down, Terence smiled back at her. 'It's a *maybe* maybe.'

'Terence Hallam, you're an awful tease.'

CHAPTER 10

When he boarded the train bound for home that evening, Terence was still of a mind that he'd made the wrong decision in acquiescing to Joanne. Although the very notion of getting into a relationship with a women – a bit of head-turner at that – filled him with anxiety, there was something about her that intrigued him. She was forthright, confident and fully engaged with the enjoyment of life; everything he wasn't. Perhaps, he concluded, a spell in her company would pay dividends and some of those enviable qualities might rub off on him.

'It's not *what* you said, you silly bitch. It's the way you said it!'

The seats opposite Terence had been empty when he got on. He turned his head and saw that they were now occupied by a man and a woman. He had been so lost in his thoughts, that he hadn't noticed them board.

The woman was quite petite, with cropped, slightly unkempt mousey brown hair. She was wearing jeans and a shabby, low cut vest shirt with a CND logo spray-painted on it. The man's attire was similarly scruffy, except his shirt had **SeX PisTOls** scrawled across it. The sides of his head were shaved, and the spiky strip running from the top of his forehead to the nape of his neck was dyed bright green. His pasty skin was lightly sweaty, and he looked slightly unwell. The can of Special Brew clutched in his hand was probably contributory to that, Terence thought.

The man took a swig. 'Well?!' he demanded. 'Don't just sit there lookin' at me like some kind of fuckin' spastic!'

'I'm sorry,' the woman said. 'I didn't mean it, it's just the way it come out.'

'You wanna watch yourself, girl.' The man leaned over and banged his can on her forehead. 'Or else.'

'I said I'm sorry.' She rubbed her head. 'Don't get all angry like, Len. It'll ruin our night out.'

The man looked at her sourly. 'Then stop flappin' your lips and let me enjoy my can. Or I'll ruin *your* day good'n'proper.'

'I only meant…'

Before she could finish her sentence, the man's empty hand flashed out and struck her hard across her temple. 'I said belt up!' As he sat back in his seat, he caught sight of Terence looking at him. 'Problem, mate?'

Terence looked quickly away. But sensing a bit of fun, the man got unsteadily to his feet, came over and perched himself on the seat opposite. 'Don't fuckin' pretend you didn't hear me, mate. You know I was talkin' to you.' He smacked Terence's knee with the

116

back of his hand. 'Oi! You! I asked you what your problem is.'

'Nothing.'

The man had a small, silver crucifix hanging on a thin chain around his neck and he lifted it up and kissed it. On one hand it was an innocuous enough thing to do, but on the other the gesture was alive with tacit threat, and – already aware of a burgeoning air of peril – Terence felt himself starting to perspire.

The man let the crucifix slip through his fingers. He pointed at Terence. 'But you was gawpin' at me.'

'I wasn't.'

'I saw you and you was gawpin'. So come on, why was you gawpin'?'

'Leave 'im alone, Len,' the woman said. She was watching nervously from her seat. 'He ain't worth it.'

The man shot her an angry look. 'Button it, you!' He turned his attention back to Terence. 'Well?'

'I can honestly assure you I wasn't.'

'Was it *'er* then?' He jerked a thumb towards the woman. 'Was you gawpin' at my bird's tits?'

Of all the things that might have been running through Terence's mind at that moment, bizarrely he found himself wishing the man would stop saying "gawpin".

'He wasn't, Len!' the woman exclaimed. She could sense trouble coming.

117

'Absolutely not,' Terence blustered.

'Huh?'

'I said absolutely n…'

'I 'eard you!' The man took another swig from his can. 'Say you're sorry.'

'What?'

'Say sorry to my bird.'

'For *what*?'

'Are you gonna say sorry, or…'

This was getting ridiculous. But determining that an apology might be the only way to diffuse the situation, Terence looked at the woman and said, 'I'm sorry.'

She smiled at him, but she looked embarrassed.

The man lifted the crucifix to his lips and kissed it again, and the fire in his eyes appeared to burn out. 'Alright then. But wind your neck in.' He got up and returned to his seat, cuffing the woman around the side of her head again. 'And I told you to shut the fuck up!'

Terence turned away and stared out of the window. He wasn't stupid; he knew such things went on. But it was the first time in his life that he'd witnessed such an uncalled for display of brutality first hand. As he stared out across the countryside, he found himself wishing ill fortune upon the man named Len.

Although Terence returned to Seatown every weekend, it was more out of habitual duty than a desire to see his parents. He certainly didn't enjoy the visits. On the contrary, he hated them. His relationship with Arthur and Emily had never risen above that of parents-to-be-respected and child-who-should-know-his-place. And whenever he was in their presence, he always became the awkward, introverted creature that most young people cease to be long before they reach eighteen years of age. He now preferred being away to being home. He had adapted to university life reasonably well and, unlike his days at boarding school and college, there was nobody picking on him. Nor, until Joanne came along, was there anyone paying him much attention at all. But he was content with that.

When he arrived home, his mother greeted him with her customary indifference. 'Your father's working late, so it'll be just you and I for dinner this evening.'

Terence was secretly pleased, but he offered a nominal, 'Oh, that's a shame.'

Over their meal, as was always the way, Emily told Terence about her week. It was seldom that anything interesting had occurred, but Arthur wasn't interested and it seemed to give her pleasure to have someone to talk to. Tonight was a little different however. She appeared troubled.

'Your father isn't a well man, Terence. His breathing is getting worse. He knows he shouldn't be smoking those damned cigars, but he does it anyway.'

119

Terence sat in silence, allowing his mother to offload. Her face was ashen as she finished, '…but there's nothing I can say or do to make him see sense. If he insists on killing himself, so be it.'

Terence didn't really know how to respond, but before he could summon a few suitable words of consolation, Emily suddenly smiled and changed the subject.

'Oh, I almost forgot. I finally joined the Seatown Ladies' Pottery Society this week. I threw my first pot. I'll show you after dinner. I thought it was a slightly mediocre effort myself, but Mrs Anning – lovely lady, she runs the Wednesday class – said it was one of the best first efforts she'd seen.'

'That's good, Mum,' Terence said. 'Well done.'

Only when Emily had relayed all her own news and they had moved on to dessert was the subject of Terence's week addressed.

'So tell me about you. How was school? What have you been up to?'

On the journey home Terence had wondered whether to mention Joanne, but now the opening had presented itself, he thought better of it. 'Pretty much the same old thing. I did complete one of my essays though.'

'That's nice.'

Terence hesitated and set down his spoon in his dish of berry crumble. 'I'm on the horns of a dilemma, Mum.'

'Oh?'

'I saw someone this week that I used to know at boarding school.'

Terence had never revealed the full extent of the triade of bullying he'd endured at Bagshott. But now, provoked by his encounter with Lavis playing on his mind, he felt compelled to raise the subject.

Emily smiled. 'Well, isn't that nice!'

'It isn't actually. We didn't get on that well. It was a bit of a shock to see him to tell the truth. Fortunately it wasn't at uni, it was off campus.'

'What did he say?'

'Nothing. He didn't see me.'

'Silly boy. You should have spoken.'

'Why? He hated me!'

'But that was years ago, Terence. Water under the bridge. People do change as they grow up, you know.'

'Maybe. But I doubt it where *he's* concerned.'

'So what's your dilemma?'

'If it turned out he was at uni, I'm not sure I could continue there.'

'That's a preposterous thing to say, Terence!'

'You don't know how bad it was at Bagshott, Mum. He was horrible to me.'

'Don't let your father hear you talking like that.'

'Hear him talking like *what*?'

Neither Terence or Emily had heard Arthur come in. He was standing in the doorway of the dining room.

'Hello, Arthur. Your dinner's in the dog.' It was a silly expression his mother had used for as long as Terence could remember, but in the wake of Harvey's unceremonious eviction from the family fold, it always made him bristle.

Arthur grunted. Without even acknowledging the presence of his son, he disappeared into the kitchen, collected his plate of steak and kidney pudding from the oven and returned to the dining room carrying it on a tray. He took his usual seat at the head of the table and looked at Emily. 'So what was it I'm not supposed to hear?'

'Terence was telling me he bumped into an old friend from Bagshott.'

'He *wasn't* a friend,' Terence said. 'I just saw someone I used to go to school with. He wasn't very nice to me back then. He was a bully.'

'So I was suggesting that Terence let bygones be bygones. Maybe speak to the boy next time he sees him.'

'And I'm hoping I never see him again!' Terence exclaimed.

122

Arthur appeared to be preoccupied with his food. The room fell silent as he chewed thoughtfully on a piece of meat. No-one could have been more surprised than Terence when he swallowed and said, 'I'm on Terence's side. If this kid used to bully you, just ignore the blighter. Worst case scenario...' – he punched a fist in the air – '...be sure you get the first punch in. If *he* gets the first punch in and you get a chance to throw the second, make sure it's hard and fast enough that he doesn't get up for the third.'

Terence laughed. He'd never heard his father talk quite like this before. Yes, he used to tell Terence to stand up to his persecutors, but resort to violence? That really was a first.

Emily was less amused. 'You shouldn't be encouraging the boy to fight, Arthur!'

Arthur waved a dismissive hand at her. 'Oh, shoosh, woman. Terence can defend himself. Can't you boy?' He punched his son playfully on the shoulder.

Terence was delighted by his father's display of faith in him. If only he had it in himself. 'I'm a bit tired,' he said, bringing the subject to a close. 'I've got a book I want to finish, so I think I'll have an early night.'

When Terence had gone upstairs and Arthur heard the click of the bedroom door, he looked at Emily.

'Bloody poofter, that boy. Couldn't throw a half decent punch if his life depended on it.'

After the dishes had been cleared, they retired to the living room where, despite his wife's tutting, Arthur lit up a cigar and eased himself into his armchair.

Emily switched on the television. 'Oh, I'd forgotten the new series of *Dawson's Watch* starts tonight. I *do* like Les Dawson.' She chuckled. 'He's so funny.'

Arthur rolled his eyes and turned his attention to his *Times* crossword.

As the clock on the mantle struck ten-thirty, Emily yawned. 'I'm off up the wooden hill.' She stood up and stretched.

Arthur looked up from his paper and tapped it with his biro. 'Tough one today. I'm nearly finished.'

Emily kissed him lightly on his forehead. 'Don't be too long. You look tired.'

'Ten minutes.'

When she'd gone, Arthur went over to the antique oak drinks cabinet that, as family legend would have it, his great grandfather had collected as part of a gambling debt from a peripheral member of the Royal Family. Pouring himself a measure of Johnnie Walker Old Scotch Whisky, he returned to his chair, where he lit up a fresh cigar and stared at the two remaining clues on the page.

124

Four across: *Greed is a sin overwhelming all rogues initially.* Fourteen down: *Obsession of woman entertaining native Muscat, possibly.*

Tossing the paper aside, he swallowed his drink in one gulp and put the empty glass in his lap. He rested his head back. It had been another tough week and he was so tired. The Japanese manufacturers with whom Hallam Toys had enjoyed a profitable working relationship for several decades were playing hardball over their new line, demanding more cash up front than Arthur could afford. If he could negotiate with them to bring their demands down by just ten percent, he could stretch to it, otherwise there were only two options left open to him: meet with the bank to see if he could arrange an extention on his loan, or start sourcing new product from elsewhere. Neither appealed to him.

He closed his eyes and took a long draw on the Montecristo, hissing the smoke out between his clenched teeth…

'For God's sake, Arthur! Wake up!'

His eyes snapped open. How long had he been asleep? Disoriented, it took him a moment to register where he was. For some reason he couldn't quite grasp, Emily was standing beside him beating the side of his armchair with what appeared to be a wet towel.

'Wake up!' she screeched again.

Then the horror of what was happening hit him like a brick in the face. He leapt up, sending his empty glass flying. As he did so, Terence came running into the room and hurled a bucket of water over the flames that were licking up the side of the armchair. With a hiss of protest, they immediately died back and went out.

'You stupid, *stupid* man!' Emily cried as she flung open the living room window.

Still slightly bewildered, Arthur stared like a lost child at the smouldering side of the chair beneath the right armrest. On the patch of carpet there was a pool of charred, molten mess where the vinyl synthetic leather had melted away from the frame. 'What happened?' he exclaimed.

Emily was almost apoplectic. 'What do you *think* happened?!' She bent down and picked up the limp remnant of the Montecristo cigar. 'Not content with killing yourself with these foul things, now you're trying to burn us *all* to death!'

'I'm sorry,' Arthur said shakily. 'I must have dozed off.'

Although there was still a lingering haze in the room, the night air had quickly dispersed the worst of the acrid smoke.

'Are you okay, Dad?' Terence asked, setting down the empty pail.

At the sound of his son's voice, Arthur appeared to regain his composure. 'Of course I am, boy. Panic over. You get yourself off to bed and leave me to clean up this mess.'

Her anger gone, Emily took her husband in her arms. 'Thank God I came down for a glass of water. I smelt the smoke from the top of the stairs.' She buried her face in his neck. 'I couldn't bear to lose you.'

Arthur hugged her tightly. 'Never.'

At the doorway, Terence paused and looked back. He had never seen his mother so angry. But more than that, he'd never seen his father appear so vulnerable. For once, he had actually shown that he was human. As he watched his parents embracing, a curious wave of emotion washed over him. He'd never seen them so openly show their feelings for one another.

Climbing the stairs to bed, he couldn't help wishing that his father had burned there and then in his chair. Their father-son relationship had never been based upon affection, but the years of lovelessness and negligence had manifested themselves into burning hatred; Terence would have been the last person to shed a tear if Arthur had perished.

CHAPTER 11

On the Tuesday following Terence's return to Warwick, he and Joanne visited the small independent cinema near the campus where they watched *Same Time Next Year*. It wasn't Terence's cup of tea at all. Joanne had wanted him to choose – and, truth be told, he rather fancied *The Deerhunter* – but since she'd already hinted at having a preference, he had played the gentleman and let her decide. So the Alan Alda and Ellen Burstyn headliner it had been.

The film, which jumps forward five-years at a time, chronicles an affair between two married people who only manage to see each other once a year and the whole story spans several decades. It provided a few chuckles and, unsurprisingly for a romantic comedy, a few tears too. During one particularly poignant scene, Terence heard a sniffling sound and realised that Joanne had started to cry. At first he didn't know what to do, but then, almost instinctively, he slipped his arm around her. Sobbing quietly, she leaned appreciatively against him and nuzzled her face into his shoulder. They remained that way until the end credits rolled.

'Sorry about the snot and tears,' Joanne said as they left the cinema. 'I hope I haven't ruined your shirt.'

'Think nothing of it.'

'It's really not like me at all. But that bit when he told her his wife had died just touched a nerve. I lost my Mum when I was twelve.'

'I'm so sorry.'

'Don't be. I've made my peace with it. I mean, obviously it was awful when it happened and I hated the whole world for taking her away from me. I was really horrible to my Dad too, at a time we were supposed to be supporting each other. I've not regretted much in my life, but I do regret that.' She smiled. 'Still, it was a long time ago. We're best mates now.'

'It must be hard losing a parent so young.'

'It was. You've never mentioned your parents.'

'There isn't much to tell. It's all rather boring to be honest with you.'

Joanne smiled. 'I don't mind. Bore me.'

As they walked back to the university, Terence imparted just enough information about his mother and father to sate her interest. When they walked in through the gates, the faint sound of music drifted over from the open windows of the social club.

'Do you fancy a nightcap?' Joanne asked.

Terence didn't, and even if he had, the last place he would choose would be the commotion of the campus social club. But he was enjoying Joanne's company and felt reluctant to end their evening just yet. He nodded. 'A small one might be nice.'

129

It was a warm evening and the room was particularly busy. The combination of the jukebox pumping out *Oliver's Army* at full volume and the hubbub of chatter was deafening and Terence wished that he'd declined Joanne's suggestion.

'You find a table,' she said, 'I'll get the drinks.'

'No, I'll pay,' Terence said, reaching into his pocket for his wallet.

Joanne smiled and put a hand over his. 'Uh-uh. You paid for the film tickets. And the popcorn! These are on me.'

'Very well. Thank you.'

'Strongbow for you?'

'Please. Just a half.'

Joanne laughed. 'I could have guessed that.'

As she pushed her way between the tables to get to the bar, Terence spotted a group of four people vacating some seats behind him. They were right beside the jukebox, so hardly ideal, but as he couldn't see another table free, he quickly nabbed it.

The Elvis Costello song that had been playing came to an end and a man standing nearby stepped over to the jukebox, inserted a coin and touched a button. He returned to the friend he was drinking with, and Terence watched the fascinating mechanism through the glass front of the jukebox, as the vinyl disc on the turntable was lifted away, dropped into a slot and

130

replaced on the rubber mat by another. Then the Squeeze number *Up the Junction* started playing. Terence hadn't heard the song before. It told the depressing tale of a hard-working man who becomes worthless when he forfeits his wife and daughter to the lure of gambling and alcohol. In his considered opinion, wastrels like that – those too ignorant to appreciate what they have until they no longer have it – had no place in this world.

He looked over towards the bar, but there was no sign of Joanne amongst the sea of people. The Squeeze song came to an end and he fumbled in his trouser pocket for some change. Standing up, he surveyed the selections on the songlist. Making his choice, he inserted a coin and sat back down to watch the machine's mechanism cycle through its magical rotation. Then *This Town Ain't Big Enough for Both of Us* burst into life. Terence started to tap his foot. He had never been particularly passionate about music, but Sparks was an idiosyncratic American band he'd followed keenly since their meteoric rise to fame in Great Britain.

He smiled as he pictured the discord on his father's face. Arthur had hated the lead singer's falsetto voice and was always telling Terence to turn it off.

The song hadn't even reached the first chorus when a young man carrying a half-full pint glass forced his

131

way through the crowd and stopped beside the jukebox. 'Who put this shit on?' he said loudly.

The voice was slurred; evidently the worse for wear, Terence thought. He looked up and his heart shot into his mouth.

Standing not three feet away from him was Graham Lavis.

Lavis pounded the side of the jukebox. 'How do you make it stop?' He looked enquiringly at Terence as if it had been more than a rhetorical question. 'Utter, *utter* shit, isn't it?'

Terence didn't reply. He was waiting for the inevitable look of recognition to appear on Lavis's face. But it didn't come.

At that moment, Joanne appeared carrying two glasses. She caught sight of Lavis and smiled broadly. 'Gray!' she exclaimed, apparently delighted to see him.

Lavis turned to see who had called him. 'Jo-Jo!' To Terence's consternation, he threw an arm around Joanne and gave her a big hug, almost causing her to spill the drinks in the process.

Momentarily, the whole room became a blur of movement and colour, and the music faded to a muffled background buzz. Terence snapped sharply back into focus as he heard Joanne saying the crushing words, 'Come and join us, Gray.'

She set down the drinks on the table and took a seat opposite Terence. As the music stopped, Lavis slumped down into the chair between them.

'Terry, this is Graham. Graham this is Terry, my... well, boyfriend, I suppose.' She looked at Terence expecting a reaction, but he didn't respond. In fact, he suddenly looked a bit sick.

Lavis slapped him on the shoulder. 'Pleased to meet you, Terry.'

Terence hadn't been mistaken in his initial assessment; Lavis was definitely drunk. Almost choking on the word, he managed to respond, 'Likewise.' In truth he was willing the ground to open up and swallow him whole.

'Gray started in my class two weeks ago,' Joanne said. 'He transferred down from... Leicester was it?'

'Yeah.'

'James Harrington asked me if I'd mind helping him settle in. You know, James? Our student liaison officer?'

'Not really,' Terence said.

'Ah, okay. Well, he's a really nice guy, isn't he, Gray?'

Lavis didn't reply. He was squinting at Terence. 'Do I know you from somewhere?'

'I don't believe so.'

'I'm pretty sure I've not seen you in here before.'

'No.'

Lavis shook his head and wagged a finger at Terence. 'There's something *really* familiar about you. I'll be buggered if I can place you though.'

The jukebox fell silent and Terence picked up his glass and took a sip. He looked across the table at Joanne and managed to conjure up a half-smile. 'We'd better drink up and get moving.'

'We only just arrived! Loosen up a bit and enjoy your drink.'

'Help me out here, mate,' Lavis said. He was still staring at Terence. 'I know you from *somewhere*.'

'I'm sure you don't. I just have one of those nondescript sort of faces.'

'What's your surname?'

Terence's stomach turned. This was the moment he'd spent the last few days dreading. But before he could answer, Joanne spoke for him: 'Hallam.'

Lavis reeled back in his chair as if he'd been slapped. '*Hallam*?! Not *Terence* Hallam?'

'That's him!' Joanne laughed. 'You know each other?! That's amazing. Where from?'

Terence squirmed. 'I really have no idea.' He was desperately trying to think of the quickest way out of the situation. What was it his father had said? Get the first punch in? He adopted a puzzled expression. 'What did you say your name was again?'

'Don't be a prick, Hallam! It's me. Graham Lavis! From Bagshit.'

Feigning uncertainty, Terence peered at his old nemesis. 'Oh, yes. Graham Lavis. Of course.'

Joanne gave Lavis a quirky smile. 'What's Bagshit?'

'He means Bagshott. We were pupils there together. Bagshott Boarding School for Boys.'

Lavis cackled. 'We called it Bagshit.'

'You may have done, but I most certainly didn't.'

Catching Terence off guard, Lavis flung an arm around his shoulders and gave him a friendly shake. 'I knew I recognised you. But, Christ, you haven't half lost some weight!' He looked at Joanne and laughed. 'He used to be a right blob did Hallam.'

Terence looked at Joanne awkwardly. 'It was just puppy fat.'

Lavis guffawed. He withdrew his arm and patted Terence hard on his stomach. 'Too many doughnuts is what it was!' He sat back in his chair. 'Well, bugger me. Who'd have thought it, eh? It's good to see you Hallam.' He laughed again. 'Here, did your pubes ever grow?' He looked at Joanne again. 'Thirteen years old and he didn't have a single hair on him! Tiniest winkie you ever saw too.' He held up his little finger.

Terence felt himself blush. He took another nervous sip of his cider.

135

'We had some right old laughs at Bagshit though, didn't we?'

'You and your friends did, yes,' Terence said sullenly.

'Do you remember that sports day when we hid your kit and Keane made you do it in your Y-fronts? Fuckin' hilarious!'

Joanne could see Terence was uncomfortable. She had felt sorry for Lavis when he first arrived in Warwick; to her he'd seemed somewhat lost and alone. She had gone above and beyond James Harrington's request to help him "settle in", going so far as to befriend him and subsequently finding him to be pleasant company. But it was becoming abundantly clear his past relationship with Terence hadn't been mutually benevolent and she didn't like what she was hearing.

'So you bullied him?' she said bluntly.

Lavis looked slightly taken aback. 'Bullied him? Nah, of course not. It was just a bit of fun, wasn't it, Hallam?' He laughed and looked to Terence as if he genuinely expected he would agree.

Terence didn't reply. He was staring sadly into his glass.

Joanne attempted to change the subject. 'You never said why you moved down from Leicester, Gray.'

Lavis sat back in his chair and waved an idle hand in the air. 'It was a lot of old bollocks really. I got accused of something I didn't do.'

'What was it you did? Or rather what was it you were *accused* of doing?'

'Something stupid. Doesn't matter now.' Lavis's expression had changed. The boisterousness seemed to have left him.

'I was always being accused of stuff I didn't do when I was at school,' Joanne ventured. It was a lie, but her curiosity was piqued and she sensed that, if she pressed gently, Lavis might spill the beans.

Before she could say anything more, a voice called out – 'Graham!' – and a young man in his mid-twenties, with long, wavy, blonde hair and a neatly trimmed beard approached the table. 'How are you getting on?'

'Fine thanks.'

'Good, good.' The man rested a hand on Joanne's shoulder. 'And Jo's looking after you properly?'

'Yeah.' The man's arrival appeared to have made Lavis uneasy.

Joanne noticed that Terence was looking at the man apprehensively. 'Oh, Terry, this is James Harrington, our liaison guy. Jim, this is Terry.'

The man held out his hand. 'Nice to see you again, Terry.' He thought he detected uncertainty on

137

Terence's face, so he added, 'We met at orientation week last year.'

Terence gave the hand a cursory shake. 'I don't recall,' he replied. In actual fact, he did, but he also remembered having taken an immediate dislike to the man; he had been far too gregarious for Terence's liking, and his unwavering smile had come across as insincere.

'I do.' There was that smile again now. 'I never forget a face.' Harrington turned back to Lavis. 'So you're settling in okay then, Graham?'

Lavis nodded.

'Good, good. Any problems or anything you need to discuss, you know my door's always open.'

Lavis nodded again. 'Sure.'

'Alrighty then. I'll leave you guys to enjoy your evening.'

Lavis waited until Harrington had walked away, then he picked up his glass and drained it. 'Another?'

Both Terence and Joanne declined.

'You sure?' He waggled the empty glass. 'I'm buying. Listen, I need to take a piss – my back teeth are floating – then I'll get us in a round.' He punched Terence playfully on his shoulder. 'What do you say, Hallam? One for old time's sake?' Without waiting for a reply, he got up and pushed his way through the tables towards the toilets.

'Can this please be our cue to go?' Terence said.

Joanne nodded. 'Absolutely!'

They stood up to leave, but Terence paused. 'Wait just a moment.' He pulled a coin from his pocket, put it into the jukebox and pressed the selection button.

They left the bar to the sound of *This Town Ain't Big Enough for Both of Us*.

CHAPTER 12

Walking back to the halls of residence in silence, they were almost at the steps when Joanne finally spoke. 'I wonder what Lavis did that got him booted out of Leicester?'

The very same thought had been circling round in Terence's mind. It was the tiniest thing, but he also noticed that Joanne had stopped referring to his nemesis as "Gray"; it made him feel a little better about the nightmare he'd just endured.

He sighed. 'It could be just about anything, I suppose. A leopard doesn't change its spots. He wasn't a very nice boy, ergo it's not unreasonable to assume he's not a very nice man either.'

They walked up the steps and stopped at the door. Joanne turned to look at him. 'I'm sorry you were bullied at school.'

'It's fine. I've put it behind me.' That couldn't be further from the truth, but it felt like the right thing to say.

'It's *not* fine, Terry. Bullies are the lowest of the low. Sad, insecure, cowardly little bastards. It breaks my heart that it happened to you.'

Joanne leant forward and kissed him softly on the lips. Her arms snaked around his neck and the embrace

140

became more passionate. She pressed her body to him and, this time, when the tip of her tongue eagerly worked its way into his mouth and engaged with his own, he didn't shy away.

The kiss ended and they stepped apart. Joanne smiled. 'Thanks for the movie. I'm really sorry I let Lavis take the shine off the evening.'

'Forget it.' Terence desperately wanted to hold her again. The feel of her body pressed against him – wanting *him* – had melted away the horrors of the last hour. 'Can I see you tomorrow?'

'For lunch if you like.'

'That would be nice. But I meant tomorrow evening.'

Joanne shook her head. 'It's Wednesday, remember? I'll be working.'

'Of course, sorry. Thursday perhaps?'

'It's a date.'

They kissed again – briefly this time. Then, with a playful giggle and a goodnight, she was gone.

The following morning before class, Joanne paid a visit to James Harrington's office. She knocked on the door, which was slightly ajar, and it swung open.

Harrington was sitting at his desk, his fingers rapidly tapping away on a typewriter. At the sound of the knock, he looked up and smiled broadly when he saw who it was. 'Jo!' He stood up 'To what do I owe this pleasure?'

'Sorry to bother you, Jim. I wondered if you might be free for a quick word?'

'For you? Anytime. Come on in.' He beckoned for her to sit. 'You look a little bothered. Everything okay?'

'Yes, I'm fine.' As Harrington sat back down, Joanne closed the door and took the seat opposite him. 'I wanted to ask you something about Graham Lavis.'

Harrington's brow furrowed and his relaxed posture changed perceptibly. 'He's not causing you problems, is he?'

'No, it's nothing like that.'

Harrington appeared to relax again. 'Okay, that's good to hear. You guys seemed to be getting along okay yesterday evening. So what is it you wanted to ask?'

'When we were talking last night he mentioned that he left Leicester under a bit of a cloud.'

'Did he now?'

'Yes.' Joanne tried to read Harrington's face, but his expression remained impassive. 'He was saying he'd been accused of something he hadn't done.'

'I see.' Harrington's eyes narrowed a fraction. 'What exactly did he say?'

'Not much more than that really, I was wondering if you might be able to tell me what went on up there?'

Harrington gave her a knowing look. 'Come on, Jo. You know full well I can't do that. All student's records are confidential.'

'Yes, but I was hoping you might make an exception as it's me. I mean, you did task me with keeping an eye on him. If he's a wrong'un, surely it's only fair I should be aware of it. I mean, he might be dangerous. I've a right to know.'

Harrington grinned. 'You offer a reasonable case, I'll give you that. But he's not dangerous and it's still a no.'

'Can't you at least give me a hint as to why he was booted out of Leicester?'

'There's no mileage in pursuing this, I assure you.' Harrington stood up and crossed to the door. He opened it and waited for her to get up. 'Was that all?'

Joanne looked at him imploringly. 'He was saying some horrible stuff last night and he was completely oblivious to the fact it was upsetting Terry. They knew each other when they were kids. He was making a joke of the fact he used to bully him. Then it turns out he got thrown out of Leicester under circumstances he doesn't want to talk about. It strikes me he's not a very nice person.'

Harrington was poker-faced. 'You might be right, but I can't help you I'm afraid.'

'*Please*, Jim. I swear I won't say anything to Graham. I just want to know. Whatever you tell me will be strictly between us.' The top two buttons of her blouse were open. She was toying with the third and it came loose. 'I'll make it worth your while.'

Harrington hesitated for a moment, then he closed the door. He walked over and stood beside her. 'How so?'

Joanne popped the fourth button. Her top was now open to the midriff and from where he was standing looking down on her, Harrington could see the lace stitching of her pink bra and the twin mounds of soft, pale flesh. Suddenly he bent and kissed her and she responded enthusiastically. As she raised a hand and ran it through his blonde locks, he broke away.

'Wow, that was amazing,' he said. 'I've wanted to do that for a long time.'

He crossed to a filing cabinet beside the window, opened the top drawer and rifled through the collection of suspended document wallets inside. Pulling one out, he returned to his desk and sat down.

Joanne refastened her blouse. 'Thanks, Jim.'

Harrington flipped open the folder. 'If you breathe a word about this, we'll both be in deep shit.'

'I won't.' Joanne pressed her lips tightly together and mimicked a zipping motion.

Looking at her doubtfully, Harrington extracted some stapled pages from the folder and laid them on the desk in front of him. 'Okay, let's keep this brief. Graham was – still *is* as far as I'm aware – heavily into his sport. When he signed up at Leicester last year it was to study for a degree in Sport and Exercise Science.'

'Not Architecture?'

'No. He switched subjects when he came here. That's nothing to do with me. But he's mad about cricket and he got friendly with the groundskeeper. This was…' – Harrington studied the paperwork – '…about two months ago. The guy asked him if he'd give his son some extracurricular cricket coaching. Offered to put a few pennies in his pocket for the kindness too. Graham took his hand off. Anyway, a couple of weeks in, kid goes running to his dad saying that Graham touched him inappropriately.'

Joanne's eyes widened. 'How old was the boy?'

'He's twelve.'

'That's twisted, man.'

'Yes, well, Graham claimed that no such thing ever happened. He said that all he could think was the kid got spooked when he was showing him how to wear a box.'

'What's that?'

'A box?' Harrington gestured to his crotch. 'You know, cricketer's wear them to protect their privates getting walloped by the ball.'

'Oh, sorry, yes.' Joanne frowned. 'So why would the kid suddenly turn on Graham without good reason? There's no smoke without fire.'

Harrington looked her in the eye. 'You *swear* to me this goes no further?'

Joanne reached across the desk and ran the tips of her fingers lightly over the back of his hand. 'Absolutely.'

James swallowed hard. 'You know I've always had a thing for you.'

Joanne was well aware of the fact, but she said simply, 'You have?'

'Don't tease. You damned well know I have.' He withdrew his hand from beneath hers and cleared his throat. 'Graham had the choice of leaving Leicester or facing an official complaint. After that, the only way he was getting in here was to come clean.'

Harrington returned the paperwork to the folder and closed it. 'Off the record, he told me that while he was fiddling around explaining how to adjust the box for best comfort, he might – and he stressed *might* – have inadvertently brushed his hand against the kid's privates. He swore to me that was the extent of it. He said he even made a joke out of it to cover his embarrassment and they both had a laugh.'

'And you believed him? A dirty nonce?'

Harrington shrugged. 'Of course I didn't. But what *I* believe is neither here nor there. I presented his case to the Dean and he was satisfied Graham proved no threat, and said that provided someone kept an eye on him, there was no reason not to grant him a place. If you ask my opinion, the bottom line for The Dean is that incoming money speaks a lot louder than unproven allegations coming from the mouth of a twelve-year-old boy.'

'So if it was never proved, why was he kicked out?'

'I told you, he w*asn't*. He was *invited* to leave and he did so of his own volition. I mean, it's all semantics really. What choice did he have? He could hardly stay on there with a heap of paedophile shit hanging over him. And I'm sure the uni were more than pleased to avoid having to prosecute him and risk an ugly scandal.'

Joanne sat back in her chair. 'Thanks, Jim. I've got to say, I wasn't expecting *that*! I thought it might be drugs or something along those lines. Or maybe, given his past record, bullying.'

'This conversation never took place.' Harrington got up and returned the folder to the filing cabinet.

'I can't look out for him any more, Jim.'

147

'Don't worry. I'm not asking you to. It was wrong of me to ask you in the first place. Knowing what I knew, I mean. I thought a female presence might keep him in check. I'll have a word with one of the boys to keep an eye.' Harrington smiled. 'So, what are your plans for this evening?'

'Working.' Joanne saw his smile waver. 'But that's okay. We'll sort something out.'

Harrington grinned. 'Okay.' He came over and bent to kiss her again, but she dodged him and stood up. 'Easy, tiger. I've got a class to attend. We'll catch up again soon.' She winked at him.

As she left Harrington's office and hurried off along the corridor, Joanne couldn't wait to tell Terence all that she had learned about the despicable Graham Lavis.

But there was something else playing on her mind too.

The triumph over securing the information she had sought was being eclipsed by thoughts of how much she had enjoyed Harrington's kiss. Her visit had only ever been intended to be a honey trap, but it had backfired and she was now wrestling with a gnawing sense of guilt over just how easily her head had been turned by the older man.

PART III

CHAPTER 13

The Christmas of 1979 was the happiest in Terence's memory. Joanne's father had decided to visit his sister in Canada and, although he confessed to being disappointed when she asked if he minded her not accompanying him, he respected her decision. She had good reason to stay behind: Terence had tentatively invited her to spend Christmas at his home in Seatown. She was a little apprehensive about meeting his parents, but when he told her they were eager to meet *her*, she was more than happy to accept.

Emily proved to be the perfect hostess, and even Arthur made an effort to ensure his son's girlfriend felt welcome. They had bought Joanne a gift too; a beautiful woollen scarf stitched with pretty snowflakes. Their bonhomie didn't extend to allowing the couple to share a room, of course; Terence never expected for one moment that it would, nor would he have asked. But Emily had generously cleaned up the spare bedroom at the back of the house and made it nice and cosy for Joanne. And in the small hours of each morning, once he was sure his parents were sleeping, Terence tip-toed through and cuddled up beside Joanne for the rest of the night, being sure to return to his own bed before dawn.

On Boxing Day, while Arthur and Emily were out for the evening visiting the Turners for drinks, Terence and Joanne slipped beneath the blankets and made love for the first time. Their intimacy up to that point had been little more than fumblings, although one night a few weeks earlier Terence had finally – and very timidly – submitted to Joanne's wish to perform fellatio on him. His reluctance had been swiftly eclipsed by pleasure like he'd never known.

As they lay together that Boxing Day evening and he reached climax, Terence whispered to Joanne that he loved her. To his eternal delight, she told him she felt the same. Afterwards, they held each other close, enjoying the primal sensation of propinquity and the reassuring warmth of skin touching skin. It was the happiest day of Terence's life.

The prospect of the new year filled him with a greater sense of anticipation than he'd ever felt before. Since learning from Joanne what Lavis had been accused of at Leicester University, his anxiety had dwindled to nothing. Being armed with the knowledge of Lavis's sins gave him a satisfying sense of superiority over a man he now deemed to be little more than pond scum. Neither Joanne or Terence had breathed a word to anyone about what they knew, but a curious, unspoken understanding materialised between the three of them and Lavis stayed away. On the odd occasion that he did pop into Terence's mind, the memories still made his hackles rise. But mostly speaking, after all this time, he had finally managed to lay his demons to rest.

In Joanne he believed he'd found his soulmate, and his love for her, along with the optimistic prospect of a future together after they graduated, spurred him to double his efforts to succeed academically.

The winter and spring terms came and went in a flash, and the days got warmer as summer approached. One evening, they went to see a disquieting horror picture called *The Brood*, which, much to Terence's surprise, Joanne enjoyed even more than he did. On the way to get something to eat afterwards, Joanne said, 'Do you realise, it'll be a year next week since we first went out together?'

'I know. We should do something special.'

Joanne grinned. 'We could go to the Wimpy.'

'I was thinking something a little more special than that.'

'Something special, eh? Okay, you've got my attention. So where do you reckon?'

'I'll give it some thought. I'm not going to tell you. That will ruin the surprise.'

Joanne's face lit up. 'Oooh, I love surprises!'

153

'And *I* love…' – Terence kissed the tip of her nose – '*…you.*'

In fact, he had far more on his mind than a fancy dinner for two, and the cancellation of his morning class the following Monday due to the lecturer suffering a bereavement moved his plans forward by a couple of days.

It was a beautiful, sunny morning and, having checked his wallet before leaving his room, he strode purposefully off into town.

Three months earlier, he had been passing the window of Ratners jewellers in the town when a banner plastered with the words **50% Off – 1 Week Only** had caught his eye. He left the shop twenty minutes later having put down a deposit on a ring. With a stunning emerald at the centre – green was Joanne's favourite colour – the ornate spray of settings around it each held a tiny diamond, eight in total. Now, as he stood outside the shop again, looking at the display cushions in the window, he knew he had chosen well; there was nothing there that even came close to matching Joanne's.

In addition to having set aside a small amount from the monthly allowance his parents gave him, Terence had drawn on some of his savings from the bank to meet the outstanding balance. Much to his consternation, when he went inside to pay and collect the ring, the woman behind the counter informed him that the 50% off deal had only been valid on fully paid up purchases during the week of the promotion.

She smiled at him sweetly. 'It's still a very reasonable price for such a lovely piece though, don't you think?'

Reasonable or otherwise, Terence simply didn't have the extra funds. Not so long ago, he would have either walked away and come back when he had enough money, or asked if he could choose something else. But one of the many things that had come out of his relationship with Joanne was a new found sense of confidence and determination. He demanded to speak to the manager. A thin-faced man with spectacles perched on the very end of his nose had duly appeared and verified what the sales lady had told him – the ring was indeed back to its original full retail price. When Terence asked angrily why he hadn't been informed that these were the terms when he parted with his deposit, the man could only offer a simpering apology for whoever it was that served him that day having been so remiss. With those words, he had expected Terence to back down. But he didn't.

'Deceiving customers into making downpayments on items they couldn't otherwise afford, based on an ambiguous offer, is both ethically and morally disgraceful,' he exclaimed angrily. 'I shall be taking this matter to the press.'

'Of course, you're perfectly at liberty to do that, sir.' The manager looked at him with bearly disguised amusement. 'But – and it's only my opinion, of course – I'd suggest that the newspapers have much more pertinent things to print than stories about misunderstandings over the cost of an engagement ring.'

'It wasn't a misunderstanding. I think you'll find it was a mispresentation,' Terence countered. 'And as for the newspapers – and it's only *my* opinion of course – I'd suggest you're very much mistaken. My father holds a senior editorial position with *The Times*. I don't think your CEO will be too pleased to have his company's name dragged through the quagmire over fabricated price deals. Do you?' He didn't like lying, it wasn't in his nature. But the supercilious expression on the manager's face was nettling him.

As Terence was speaking, the manager had been fiddling uncomfortably with his tie as his air of superiority was steadily decimated.

The sales lady was standing by with a slightly embarrassed look on her face.

The manager sucked his teeth. 'Alright, I believe on this occasion we can make an exception. You can have the ring for... shall we say eighty percent of the RRP?'

Terence shook his head. 'Let's say *fifty* percent.'

The man winced. 'Seventy-five.'

'Fifty.'

'No, no, no, I'm sorry. Seventy-five is the best I can offer.'

Terence smiled. 'If you'll excuse me, I have a telephone call to make. Mr... Todd, is it?'

The manager instinctively touched the name badge clipped to the breast pocket of his jacket.

Terence smiled. 'Yes, so it is. With two d's. We need to make sure we get the spelling right, don't we?' Tapping his temple to give the impression he was storing away the information, he started to turn away.

'Very well! You can have it at the sale price.' The man didn't look at all happy. 'Sort out the bill of sale, please, Miss Wilkins.'

A few minutes later, feeling extremely pleased with himself, Terence walked out of the shop with the ring tucked safely in his pocket, leaving the manager scratching his head and wondering how he'd just allowed himself to be outsmarted by someone half his age.

As Terence walked back along Tutbury Avenue, it started to drizzle with rain. He inhaled deeply, relishing the warm scent of the freshly mown grass, and picked up his pace. As he hurried along, a movement from behind one of the trees just ahead caught his eye. When

157

he got a little closer, he could see there was a young couple standing talking. The girl had her back to him, but he could see she was wearing a lightweight blue satin shortie jacket with a rainbow embroidered on the back, much like the one he had bought Joanne for her birthday. He couldn't help but smile as he pictured himself getting down on one knee in front of her, imagining how her beautiful green eyes would sparkle when he presented her with the ring.

Then Terence heard the girl laugh. He faltered in his tracks. It *was* Joanne. What on earth was she doing out here at this time on a Monday morning? And who was it she was talking to? Not wishing to be seen – for he certainly didn't want to have to lie about his own presence – he ducked behind a tree. Deciding his best move would be to double back, he peered out from behind the trunk to ensure he'd not been seen.

That was when his world crumbled.

Joanne and the person she had been talking to were now locked in an embrace.

Terence turned away from the sight, his insides gripped by a vice-like wave of nausea. He fought back the need to vomit. It took him a full minute to regain his equanimity, then he gingerly looked out from behind the tree again. The couple had stopped kissing, and Joanne was leaning back against the trunk, idly twirling her hair around her finger. Now Terence could see the other person's face.

It was James Harrington.

His head in a spin, Terence set off back the way he had come. He tried to tell himself that there had to be a logical explanation for what he'd seen. But, as he stumbled along, the irrefutable evidence he'd witnessed with his own eyes was waging war in his head. And whichever way he turned it, there was nothing he could think of that made what he'd just witnessed acceptable.

How the hell could Joanne do this to him? And how far had it gone? Perhaps he was overreacting, after all it had just been a kiss. But even if it was nothing more than that, it was still a betrayal of the love and trust they had built between them.

He cursed himself. There she had been, telling him how much she cared about him while he, the sap, ate up every phoney, hollow word of it. And all the time she had been laughing at him behind his back, waiting for the first opportunity to jump into another man's bed. Harrington probably hadn't been the first interloper she'd spread her legs for either. Or even the second. Exactly how long had she been sleeping around behind his back and making a mockery of him? In his mind's eye he could see her naked in Harrington's muscular arms, her moans of pleasure becoming hoots of laughter as she thought about that naïve simpleton Terry Hallam sat at home oblivious to her deceit.

The more he thought about it, the more things started to make sense. There had been that morning last month when he'd not been feeling well and told Joanne he wouldn't meet her for lunch; he'd felt better when lunchtime came round, and got to the dining room to find her chatting and laughing with Harrington. And then there was the evening just last week when he had some work to finish and cried off a date to see the Peter Sellers film *Being There*; Joanne had asked if he minded her going with Harrington as he'd mentioned wanting to see it – and Terence had stupidly given her his blessing.

What a short-sighted buffoon he'd been.

It was crystal clear to him now that Joanne had been playing him for a fool. Deep down in his soul, he'd always felt that relationships with the opposite sex weren't conducive to happiness – he'd once heard marriage referred to as "the passage to hell". Yet still, against his better judgement, he'd dropped his guard and allowed this spiteful harlot into his life. *You reap what you sow, you bloody fool. You reap what you damned well sow.*

By the time he got back to Ratners, his tears of shock and hurt had been replaced by those of pure blind rage. It took him two minutes to get his money back on

160

the ring, then he stormed back to the university, where he locked himself in his room and sat down at his desk, trying to decide on his next best move.

He decided that he would send Joanne a letter. Taking a piece of writing paper from the drawer, he picked up his fountain pen and started to write. He got as far as *Dear Joanne*, then stopped and tapped the pen lightly on the paper... then harder and harder until suddenly the nib buckled and the end of the shaft shattered, squirting ink all over the page.

With a distraught howl of anguish, he swept his arm across the desktop; books, the pages of his latest essay and the framed photograph of himself and Joanne that his father had taken on Christmas Day spilled onto the floor. He jumped up and kicked the books aside. Retrieving his antique silver ink blotter beside the skirting board, in a frenzied rage he hurled it at the door. He stamped on the picture frame, splintering the glass, pulled out the photo and ripped it in half. But, as he spun round to pick up one of the books, his foot slipped on the scattered paperwork and he fell backwards, cracking his head on the floor.

CHAPTER 14

'Terry? Terry, are you in there?'

The muffled voice coming from outside the door brought Terence round. There was something sticking in his side just above his hip. It took him a moment to realise he was laying on his back on the floor and the thing pressing into him was the bottom corner of a hardback copy of *Business Pyschology: A Theoretical Evaluation* by one of the university's alumni.

Terence sat up and glanced at his watch. It was almost one-thirty in the afternoon. His head was banging, but he vaguely remembered something about Joanne suggesting they meet for lunch.

What was he doing laying here on the floor? He was about to call out when his surroundings came into focus. As he took in the books strewn all over the floor and the broken photograph frame, the awful events of the morning came flooding back to him. He started to sob, but quickly stifled the noise by biting down hard on his hand.

He sat motionless, listening closely until, after what seemed like an age, a folded piece of paper appeared underneath the door and he heard the sound of receding footsteps. He crawled across the floor on his hands and knees and picked up the note. What pathetic excuse for her transgression would it hold, he wondered. Would it be full of contrition and begging for absolution from her sins? There was one thing for sure: she wasn't going to get it. Not from him. Not today. Not ever.

He unfolded the piece of paper. Anticlimactically, it read simply: *Missed you at lunch. Working tonight. See you tomorrow xx*. The addition of the twin x's on the end made Terence bristle. Not more than two hours ago he probably couldn't have been further from her thoughts, yet now here she was imparting frivolous affection like bait to the gullible fish. It was patently obvious she didn't care; all she was interested in was herself.

Getting up off the floor, he felt a wave of dizziness descend on him. He gingerly touched the back of his throbbing head, and when he looked at his fingers they were smeared with blood; he'd evidently gone down much harder than he realised.

Opening the door an inch, Terence peered out to make sure Joanne was definitely gone. He wanted her to stew for a few days, perhaps wonder about him, maybe even reflect upon what she might have done wrong. Then he would confront her. There would be tears, of course, and she would beg him to take her back. But he wouldn't. At least not immediately.

All these thoughts were running through his mind as he went along the corridor to the bathroom. He locked the door behind him and set about cleaning the cut on his head.

The confrontation with Joanne came sooner than Terence had expected. He was on his way back from class the following afternoon, when he rounded a corner to cross to another block and there she was, her arms full of books, coming along the path towards him.

Her face filled with relief. 'Terry! Where have you been? I've been so worried about you!'

She looked more beautiful than he had ever seen her. 'Have you?'

She looked a little confused by his response and rested the books on the low wall running alongside the path. 'Of course I have! Have you been ill?'

'No.'

'Then what's going on? I came to your room yesterday afternoon and again first thing this morning, but you weren't there.' A thought suddenly entered her mind. 'Oh, God! It's not your Dad, is it? I'm *so* sorry. I know he wasn't well last week. Did you have to rush home?'

As she moved to put her arms around him, Terence took a pace back from her.

'No.'

She frowned. 'Well *what* then?'

'What do you think?'

Joanne shook her head. 'I've no idea. Why are you behaving like this?'

'Why am *I* behaving like this?'

She was starting to look genuinely bothered now, but at that moment two girls came along the path and passed by. When they were out of earshot, Joanne said, 'Please don't talk in riddles.' She looked at him imploringly. 'What's going on?'

'You tell me.'

'For heaven's sake, Terry. If you've got something to say, just spit it out!'

'Well, let's have a think, shall we?' Suddenly he stepped up to within inches of her. 'Let's think *really* hard.' He prodded her in the middle of her forehead with his index finger, leaving a small white mark.

'*Oww*!' She stepped back. 'Don't do that! What the *hell's* got into you?!'

'Perhaps we should be asking what's got into *you*. Or rather *who's* got into you!'

Joanne shook her head, but the look of alarm on her face had discernibly lessened. 'I honestly have no idea what you're talking about.'

'No? Well maybe we should ask James. I'm sure he might be able to shed some light.'

'James?'

'Yeah. Or Jim. Or whatever name you cry out when he's screwing you!'

Joanne didn't respond. Her face blanched and she just stared at him dumbfoundedly.

'Ah,' Terence said calmly. 'So the penny finally drops with a bloody great clang.'

'This is nonsense. It isn't what you think.'

Terence actually laughed. 'It? *It*? Exactly *what* isn't what I think? Please do tell. I'm intrigued. Enlighten me.'

'We're just friends, that's all. Come here, silly.' She stepped forward and tried to put her arms around him, but he batted her away.

'I saw you.'

'Saw me what?'

'I saw you with your tongue down his throat!'

'*When*?'

'When? You're not going to try denying it then.' She was putting on a bold face, trying to brazen it out; Terence had to give her that.

'I…'

'Yesterday morning. Among the trees on Tutbury Avenue.'

'That's ridiculous. You couldn't have seen me there. You had a class yesterday morning.'

'I imagine that's what you were counting on. Dumb, trusting old Terry, sat in a classroom studying while you were running around cheating on him. But I *didn't* have a class, you see. It was cancelled. I went into town

166

and on the way back I saw you together. How long's it been going on?'

'Terry, I told you, it's…'

Terence exploded. 'You dirty, disgusting little whore! You think I'm a complete fool? You meant *everything* to me. But, oh no, that wasn't enough, was it? You reeled me in, chewed me up and spat me out.' His tone softened. 'We could have had a future together. I was going to ask you to marry me.' His eyes were misted with tears. 'Well, more fool I, eh?'

'You were going to ask me to *marry* you?'

'I was,' Terence said quietly. 'I even bought a ring.'

For the first time ever in his presence, Joanne's dazzling green eyes darkened and turned cold. 'What on earth makes you think I'd want to get married?'

'You told me you loved me.'

'What's that got to do with it? I *did* love you for a while. I mean, I suppose I still do. A bit anyway. But *married*? That's the last thing in the world I'm thinking about right now. I have a career ahead of me. I want to travel the world a free agent. Why would I want to get tied down to a life of humdrummery? I'm living in the moment and loving every minute of it.' She looked at Terence sadly. 'Look, we've had fun, Terry, and I wish it hadn't come to this. But okay, yes, I admit it. I've got a thing going with Jim.'

'How long?'

'Since just before my birthday. He makes me feel so alive. If you want me to say sorry, I'm afraid I'm not going to. I didn't mean to hurt you, but I'll never be sorry about Jim. When we're together...'

Terence put his hands over his ears. 'I don't want to hear it!'

'Okay. Well, I guess that's all there is to say then.'

Terence scowled. 'You really are a heartless bitch, aren't you? It was all just a game to you, wasn't it? I was a challenge, the little shy kid, a notch to be added to your slimy bedpost. How could I have not seen that sooner? Well, I just hope Harrington sees it before you do the same thing to him.'

Joanne bent and picked up the stack of books from the wall. 'Are you finished?'

Terence sighed. 'Yes.'

'Well, so are we. Don't come near me or speak to me ever again.'

That evening, for the first time in his life, Terence went out and got stinking drunk. He spent most of the following day sleeping or with his head in the toilet being ill.

When Joanne walked away from him, she'd taken with her his motivation to study. Nonetheless, with the date by which he needed to hand in his dissertation rapidly approaching, he pressured himself to get on with it. He crossed through all the upcoming uni social events on his calendar, primarily for fear that he might bump into Joanne, but also because the joie de vivre that being around her had instilled in him was now a shrivelled husk.

As the weeks passed in an indistinct blur, there were a couple of occasions that he caught sight of her around the university, and he tooks steps to avoid an encounter, either ducking into a doorway or simply turning round and walking away. There was one occasion when they almost collided before he saw her coming and their eyes met. She half-smiled, but without acknowledgement he brushed past her and hurried to his class.

For several weekends in succession he didn't go home, giving his mother the excuse that he needed to keep his head in his studies. When she asked after Joanne, he offered up sufficient flimflam to satisfy her, then quickly changed the subject.

The day he handed in his dissertation, he knew it wasn't his best work. But when it was returned to him as a fail, what ought to have been a wake-up call had the opposite effect. He spiralled into depression and began questioning the point of continuing at Warwick. Maybe a change of direction was called for; a fresh start elsewhere. It wasn't too late, he was still young enough to turn things around. He even began to wonder

169

if Joanne cheating on him had in fact done him a huge favour. He made an appointment to speak with his tutor, Mr Abbott the following week.

However, mired in uncertainty, he started to drink.

There was a small pub not far from the university called The Knight's Horse. Despite the knowledge that it had a bit of a reputation for trouble, he and Joanne had been in there one night several months earlier. It was a tiny, dingey establishment, frequented mostly by skinheads – one of whom came on to Joanne while Terence was at the bar ordering – so after only one drink they had left. But now it seemed to Terence to be the perfect watering hole. It was rare to see any other students in there and he was confident he could drown his sorrows with zero fear of Joanne showing her face.

On his first visit since the night he had been there with Joanne, he took a seat near the door; all the better for making a quick exit if something kicked off. But aside from a few derogatory glances, the unsavoury clientele paid him little attention. After that, he returned there every evening, never leaving without having had a skinful.

It wasn't long before he had frittered away most of the money he'd saved for Joanne's ring on alcohol-fuelled trips into oblivion. He started eating less so that he had more disposable cash to spend in The Knight's Horse, and managed to scrape together some additional

170

funds by selling his fountain pen and the antique silver blotter. The man in the thrift store had offered him a pittance for them, claiming that they had nominal resale value. Terence knew he was being jipped, but he wanted the money, so he reluctantly agreed.

He might have continued on this downward spiral were it not for a wake-up call provoked by an incident one Monday evening late in May.

Pint in hand, Terence had taken his usual seat in the pub when a group of three skinheads came in and took up residence at the adjacent table. One of them gave him a filthy look, but otherwise they ignored him. Yet a little later, when he returned from the bar with his third pint of Strongbow, one of the trio was sitting in his seat eating peanuts. His face stubbly and peppered with an unsightly outbreak of acne, he grinned up at Terence. 'You alright there, chief?' he said, spraying the table with flecks of chewed nut. The accent was thick Birmingham.

'I'm fine.' Terence cast a look around the room to see if there was a vacant table he could move to, but there wasn't. 'I believe you're in my chair.'

'*Am* I?' The young man feigned surprise. His two friends were watching from their table. One of them sniggered.

'Yes. I've been sitting here all evening. And I think you'll find those are my peanuts you're eating.'

'Nah, you're mistaken, chief. These are mine.' He emptied the remains of the packet into his palm and stuffed them into his mouth.

Terence really didn't want any trouble, but he'd be damned if he would let this ape pick on him. His days of being an underdog were over.

'Be that as it may,' he said wearily, 'this is definitely my table and that's my chair you're sitting on.'

'Is that so?' The man stared at him menacingly for a moment, then he smiled. 'Well, please accept my apologisations.' He stood up and examined the back rest and then flipped the whole chair over to look underneath. 'I can't see your name on it mind.' He uprighted the chair again. 'But if you say it's yours, who am I to call you a liar?' He theatrically dusted off the seat and, resting his hand on the back, gestured for Terence to sit.

As he went to do so, the man pulled the chair to one side and Terence almost took a tumble, slopping his drink on the table.

'Oops, careful there, chief!'

The man's friends burst out laughing. Instead of rejoining them, he pulled over his chair from the next table and plonked himself down on it. He stared at Terence with a grin on his face that was far from humorous; in fact, it was distinctly intimidating.

'Can I help you with something?' Terence asked wearily.

'As a matter of fact, you can. I was hoping you might be able to settle an argument for me and my mates here.'

'I very much doubt it.'

'You haven't heard what it is yet, chief. You see, Danny here...' – he pointed to one of his friends – '...he reckons you look like a shirt-lifter. And Rich...' – he pointed to his other friend – '...he tends to agree.'

'Deffo an uphill gardener,' the man called Danny said. He had a Birmingham accent too.

'But *me*,' the man continued, 'I think you're more the pillow-biting type.'

Terence frowned. 'What?'

'Don't pretend like you don't know. A pillow-biter.' He formed a circle with the thumb and index finger of his left hand and thrust the index finger of his right in and out of it. 'You like taking it up the jacksie.'

'I have absolutely no idea what you're talking about. Now would you kindly go away, you uncouth little man.'

'Not before you settle our argument.' The man grinned again. 'Come on, chief, don't be shy. Which is it? Are you a giver or a taker?'

Without pausing to think through the repercussions of his answer, Terence blurted out, 'Why, are you offering?'

The two at the next table cackled with laughter.

The cocky grin faded from the man's face and he leaned forward threateningly. 'I've busted smart-arse geezers' jaws for way less than that.'

Terence sighed. 'Go on then.'

The man squinted at him venomously. 'Did you hear what I said? I've busted...'

'I heard you. You get your jollies hitting people, blah blah blah.' Terence locked eyes with him. 'So if you're going to do it, just get on with it. But for God's sake, just stop *talking*!' He closed his eyes, steeling himself for the pain; however hard the man hit him, it couldn't possibly make him feel any worse than he already did.

But then he heard the explosion of laughter and he opened his eyes again.

The man had a broad grin on his face. 'No-one's ever spoken to me like that before. At least not no-one that's still walking around with all their organs intact. I like you, chief. You got balls. What's your name?'

'Terry. I mean, Terence.'

The man slapped him on the shoulder. 'I'm Chas. They call me Cobra.'

'What a nice name.'

'Yeah.' Oblivious to the note of sarcasm in Terence's voice, Chas rolled up his sleeve and held out his forearm for him to see. On it was a faded tattoo of a cobra's head bearing its fangs. 'It's cos I strike like one.' He pointed to his friends. 'That's Rich and Danny.'

'So you said just now.'

'You really have got a sarky mouth on you, haven't you?' The man laughed. 'What you drinking there, Tel?'

'I'm fine. I've had enough for tonight.'

'Bollocks. Come and drink with us.'

Terence shook his head. 'I think not. Another time perhaps.'

'Don't be cunty, Tel. I ain't asking, I'm insisting.' Chas stood up and hooked his arm around Terence's neck. 'Come on, we're dying of thirst here. And it's your round.'

CHAPTER 15

After the landlord of The Knight's Horse called last orders, Terence accompanied his unlikely new companions down to the woods. Had his head been in a sound place, he wouldn't have dreamt of doing such a rash and potentially dangerous thing. But Chas – Terence couldn't quite bring himself to call the man Cobra – had proven to have a wicked sense of humour, and an unexpectedly genial evening combined with seven pints of Strongbow had emboldened him. Hidden away among the trees, they sat and talked and smoked marijuana, which, much to the amusement of the others, made Terence vomit several times. All three of the men seemed to hate everyone and were very outspoken in their opinions about hard justice being served upon – in Danny's words – 'any fucker who don't belong here!'. Curiously, Terence hadn't been shocked, in fact, in his inebriated state, he couldn't help agreeing with most of what they had to say.

He finally crawled into bed just before three the following morning, woke at noon and was sick again.

As much as he had enjoyed his night out, it began to worry him that he had precious little recollection of events after he left the pub and no idea whatsoever how he'd found his way safely back to the university. As he lay on his bed with his head pounding, it occurred to him how reckless it had been to go off into the woods in the middle of the night with three strangers; men who looked like they would stick a knife in him, rob him and leave him for dead just as soon as look at him. The break-up with Joanne had put him through the wringer and left him in a terrible place, but drinking himself into a semi-comatose state every night wasn't the answer. He might be heartbroken, but he wasn't a fool. What were the words to that miserable Squeeze song again? *The devil came and took me from bar to street to bookie.* He needed to pull himself together, and the drinking had to stop before it got out of control and he ended up going down the same route as his Aunt Clara. It was time to sort himself out and address the matter of resubmitting his thesis.

His moment of resolve didn't last long. Terence sat down at his desk with all good intent, but as he stared bleary-eyed at the blank page in front of him, the glimmer of incentive to knuckle down promptly vanished. More worrying than that, he realised he was craving a drink.

He debated whether to go for a little walk and pop into the pub for a quick half, then he could come back ready to tackle his work refreshed. As he was thinking it over, a note on his desk calendar caught his eye: 1.30

– *Mr A*; he realised the appointment with his tutor had completely gone out of his head.

Glancing in the mirror on the back of the door, he was startled to see the face staring back at him, unshaven and with its hair in frightful disarray. His eyes were red-rimmed and puffy and there was a nasty cut on his chin too, the cause of which he had no memory. He was still wearing the same shirt he'd had on the previous night and, as well as some small patches of blood on the collar – which had presumably come from the mystery cut – the front was streaked with yellowish-brown stains; he cautiously lifted the bottom of it to his nose and inhaled, identifying them as vomit. A sniff of his armpits made him recoil.

He checked his watch: Almost one-fifteen. There wasn't much he could do about the cut or the accumulation of stubble now, but he quickly changed his shirt, ran a comb through his hair and set off for his meeting.

In all Terence's years within the education system, Mr Abbott was one of the nicest men he had studied under. He appeared to like Terence too, and always insisted students call him Phillip. Terence never did; in his opinion, addressing an elder by their Christian name was a level of familiarity which needed to be earned over time.

178

It was a measure of the man that, when Terence walked into his office he didn't raise an eyebrow, nor once mention the state of his young undergraduate's appearance. He listened patiently while Terence talked about the reasons why his months of hard work had resulted in an ungraded paper, and how he felt that a move away from Warwick might benefit him.

When he had finished, Abbott praised him to the hilt for his tenacity and exemplary work prior to his relationship problems and even went so far as to reveal that his own career had almost been wrecked in the wake of a messy divorce. He finished by saying he still had high hopes for him, and set up another appointment for ten days' time to ensure he had got himself back on track.

When he left the meeting, Terence was feeling better about himself than he had done for weeks. He decided to stop by the common room for a cup of coffee to mark his new found reason for sobriety.

Collecting his hot drink from the vending machine, he took a seat in the corner near a bookcase and scanned the titles on the shelf. There wasn't much of interest, but one caught his eye and he pulled it out; it was a tattered paperback edition of Irwin Shaw's *Rich Man, Poor Man*. Terence hadn't read it, but in that moment the title spoke to him. He smiled. He knew exactly which of the two he intended to be, and that would only happen if he applied himself.

As he returned the book to the shelf, the sound of a familiar laugh drew him out of his thoughts. He looked up and saw Joanne entering the room. She had stopped to hold the door open for someone coming in behind her. She looked beautiful.

Terence felt his heartbeat quicken. Maybe now was the time to make peace with her. He wouldn't make the mistake of falling back into a romantic relationship, of course, in fact he wasn't sure that he would open his heart to another woman ever again. And if she were to make a move for something more intimate, he would shut it down. But he had said some terrible things to her when they parted and now he finally had his mind straight in terms of his academic aspirations, an apology wouldn't go amiss. What harm could it do? They might be able to get along as friends, perhaps go to see the odd movie together. Who knows, she might even apologise to *him*.

As all this was running through his head, the person for whom Joanne had been holding the door came into view.

Terence felt his stomach convulse. It was Lavis. And it quickly became apparent that he and Joanne were together. Feeling his blood rise, Terence's eyes followed them as they walked to the vending machine and bought drinks. He had barely started his own coffee, but he knew if he took so much as a sip right now, he'd bring it back up again. After all that they had learned about Lavis, what the hell was she doing associating herself with him?

As the two of them found a table on the other side of the room, Terence made his move. Keeping his eyes averted, he made a beeline for the exit, but Joanne spotted him and called out. He ignored her, but she was on her feet in an instant and caught up with him at the doors.

'Terry! Wait!'

Terence stopped and she stepped up beside him.

'Hi.'

Terence avoided making eye contact. 'Hello.'

'I haven't seen you for absolutely ages. I was hoping we might bump into each other. I wonder if we could talk for a couple of minutes?'

'I'm busy.'

'Just for a minute then.'

'About what? That shit James Harrington stealing you away from me?' The moment the words left his mouth, Terence hated himself. He reached for the door handle, but Joanne quickly moved round in front of him and positioned herself between him and the way out.

'Just wait, would you? I wanted to say sorry about the way things ended between us. I know you think I'm a heartless bitch, and maybe you're right. But I never meant to hurt you.'

Terence raised his eyes to meet hers. 'You failed miserably then, because you did.'

'I know.' Joanne sighed. 'And if it's any consolation at all, Jim and me are finished. It was just infatuation for both of us.'

'And that's supposed to make me feel better, is it?'

'I guess not. But I just wanted you to know.'

'And what about *him*?' Terence nodded his head in Lavis's direction. 'You've developed a thing for paedophiles now?'

She looked at him sadly. 'I was wrong to tell you what I heard about Gray. He came into The Rose & Crown a couple of weeks ago and we got talking. What with us giving him the cold shoulder, he'd figured we must have somehow found out about Leicester. But he explained it to me and it really was a genuine misunderstanding.'

Terence gave her a look of pity. 'Well, he *would* say that, wouldn't he?'

'I believe him.'

'So now you're mates.' He glanced over at Lavis. He was watching them with interest. 'A piece of advice, Jo: If you ever have any kids, don't invite Lavis round for dinner.'

'That's a nasty thing to say!'

Terence shrugged. 'He's a nasty man.'

Joanne looked at him as if she was only just registering his appearance. 'You look terrible, Terry. What happened to you?'

Terence glared at her. '*You* happened to me. I gave you my heart and you ripped it out and trampled all over it!'

'And I've said I'm sorry. I know it doesn't mean much. But…'

'You're right, it doesn't mean a bloody thing!'

'Hear me out. I was going to say, whether you accept my apology or not, please don't let what happened between us ruin your future.'

'My future?' Terence glared at her. 'Well, that hasn't got anything to do with you any more, has it?' He could see the hurt in Joanne's eyes, but as far as he was concerned her allegiance to Lavis had crushed all hope of them ever being friends again. So why not just twist the knife a little more? It actually felt rather good. 'Go on with you now. Scuttle back to your new best friend. Best make it quick though, before he loses interest in you and goes looking for someone half your age to molest.'

Before Joanne could utter another word, he pushed past her and disappeared through the doors.

It had been Terence's intention to return to his room following his celebratory coffee, but his encounter with Joanne had got his blood up and he was starting to question whether he had ever really known her at all. How much *did* he actually know about her? The longer he dwelt on it, the more obvious it became to him how little she had ever revealed about herself. It was true, he had never pressed her; he had been reticent to divulge much about his own past, so the fact she had never been particularly forthcoming herself had been fine with him. Of one thing he was certain though: She was a deceitful bitch and the type of person for whom the grass was always greener, eager to leech onto anyone who caught her fancy, before eventually tiring of them and jumping ship as soon as a better prospect came along. And he, Terence the buffoon, had been nothing more than a challenge for her. How she must have been laughing at him behind his back.

And then there was the business with Lavis. It was *she* who had come bleating to him about his dirty little secret, yet, now here she was, cosying up to him. Hardly the behaviour of a rational person. Had she seen him as a challenge too? To lure a twisted pervert who ought to be behind bars into her bed? What a coup that would be for her.

184

Lost deep in his thoughts and without even realising where he was going, before he knew it Terence found himself standing outside The Knight's Horse.

Like a moth to the flame.

He put a hand on the door handle and hesitated. He had come to a fork in the road.

Go left: Kiss goodbye to his future, step inside and drink until he could no longer remember what day of the week it was.

Go right: Walk away and never return.

'Hallam?'

Terence hadn't noticed the man approach him. He turned around.

'I thought it was you, but I wasn't sure. You don't look too well.'

Terence looked at the man standing in front of him. Aside from the whisps of hair above his top lip – the type of moustache that Terence had once heard his father dismissively describe as bumfluff – he had a clean, fresh complexion that suggested he was too young to need to shave. He was a good three inches shorter than Terence and had a shaggy mop of black curly hair, which hung just above inquisitive eyes that were partially hidden behind a pair of spectacles; at some point they had got broken, and there was a sticking plaster bound around the bridge by way of a makeshift repair.

'Do I know you?'

'I should hope you do,' the man answered cheerfully. 'We've only been in the same Business Strategy class for the past six months. Not that I've seen you there for a week or two.' From the expression on Terence's face, the man could see he still didn't recognise him. 'It's me, Pinnock. I sit at the desk just behind you.'

Terence shook his head. 'I'm sorry, I don't… As you observed, I've not been too well.'

Pinnock grinned. 'Yeah. Cards on the table, man, you look like shit.' He cocked a thumb at the pub. 'Do you drink here too?'

'Occasionally.'

'Bit of a dive, isn't it?' Pinnock chuckled. 'Still, the beer's cheap and that's what counts when you're a penniless student, eh?'

Terence nodded. 'Indeed. Well, good to have bumped into you, er…?'

'Pinnock. Robin.'

'Robin, yes, of course.'

'So you're not going in for one then?'

'No. Not today.'

'Looked like you were thinking about it to me. Maybe I could join you?'

'I've changed my mind. If you'll excuse me.'

186

Terence started to turn away, but Pinnock put a hand on his shoulder. 'Listen. I know how tough it is, man. I'm living it too.'

Terence frowned. 'What do you mean, *living* it?'

'The pressure. Everybody says "yeah, go to uni, yap-yap, get yourself a degree yap-yap, it'll set you up for life, yap-yap". I suppose we must believe it or we wouldn't be here, eh? But nobody tells you how fuckin' *hard* it's gonna be. Sometimes I wonder whether I'm here for myself or because my parents pushed me.'

'What's your point?'

'My point? I haven't got a *point*. But what I *have* got is something to help ease the pressure.'

Terence sighed. 'Is that so?'

'It is.'

'I assume you're talking about drugs.'

Pinnock's smile vanished. 'Shhhhhh. Not so loud, man.' He glanced furtively about him and then moved a little closer. He spoke out of the corner of his mouth. 'What I'm talking about is a few sweeties to take the edge off. Calm you down a bit. Help you focus.'

'What are they?'

Pinnock stepped back. 'Not here. If you're interested, come and see me tonight.' Rummaging in his pocket, he pulled out a pen and a piece of folded paper. He tore off a corner, jotted something on it and handed it to Terence. 'Eight o'clock tonight. Be alone. Or else.'

'Or else *what*?'

'You'll have climbed five flights of stairs for jack.'

Terence looked at the scrap of paper. Scrawled on it in spidery handwriting was an address for one of the halls of residence and a room number. 'I'm not sure about this.'

Pinnock gave him a thin smile. 'Yes you are.'

Terence's eyes narrowed. 'You're very sure of yourself, aren't you? What makes you think I'd be interested in...' – he lowered his voice – '...helping fund a grimy drug-running scam?'

'Because you're still standing here talking to me. And I assure you it's not grimy, nor is it a scam.' Drawing a cross over his heart, Pinnock turned and started to walk away. 'See you tonight. And remember: Alone.'

At spot on eight o'clock that evening, Terence knocked on Pinnock's door. On the way in he had passed a young couple necking inside the front entrance; it made him think of Joanne and a fleeting pang of sadness that he would probably never experience that level of intimacy again shot through him.

A scuffling sound came from inside the room, then the door opened an inch and there was a clank as the safety chain pulled taut. Through the small gap, Pinnock peered out at him.

'You alone?'

'No, I brought the Royal Philharmonic Orchestra with me.'

The eye flicked left and right.

Terence huffed. 'For God's sake! Of course I'm alone.'

The door closed, there was a rattling noise as Pinnock unhooked the safety chain, then it opened again. He stuck his head out and looked up and down the corridor. Satisfied that his visitor had come alone, he ushered Terence quickly inside, closed the door and put the chain back on.

The curtains were drawn and the only light in the room emanated from the flicker of an incense burner on the window sill. Terence detected the vague aroma of something floral. It reminded him of his Aunt Clara.

'Who's this then, Rob?'

The voice came from over in the corner, and as Terence's eyes adjusted to the darkness he saw that there was a woman sitting there in an armchair. A second woman was perched on her lap, with her long, slender legs dangling over the side. They were both wearing t-shirts and denim cut-offs.

'Eyes off, you,' the one underneath said, giving the one who had spoken a playful shove. 'I saw him first.'

Before Terence could say anything, Pinnock appeared at his side. 'Girls, meet Hallam. Hallam, this is Carrie and Sam.'

'It's Samantha!' the one sitting on top said tetchily. She rolled her eyes. 'How many times?'

Pinnock laughed. 'Don't worry about them, Hallam. They don't bite. Although, that said, Sam might.' He chuckled and dropped his voice. 'She has a rather low tolerance of human beings in general – and some pretty radical ideas about dealing with anyone who crosses her. So best play safe and not piss her off. ' He saw the look on Terence's face. 'Fear not, mon brave. They aren't interested in the likes of you. Or me for that matter. They're just here for the sweeties.' He had an apple in his hand, which he spun in the air. He caught it and took a big bite out of it.

'Can we just get this done?' Terence said brusquely.

'What's the rush?' Pinnock said, crunching on a mouthful of fruit pulp. There was juice running down his chin. 'Chill. Stay for a beer. All good things come to...'

Terence grabbed the shorter man by the scruff of his neck and pushed him back against the wall. 'I didn't come here to chill!' he said angrily. 'Have you got what you offered me, or not?'

190

'Easy, man! No reason to get heated!'

Terence let go of him.

'Of course I have.' Pinnock straightened his collar. 'You think I invited you here for my health?'

'No, you asked me here because you want my money.'

'You got that right, man. Okay, have you ever taken anything before?'

Terence didn't see the point of mentioning his recently dalliance with cannabis. He shook his head.

'Alright. I'd suggest bennies then.'

'What are they?'

'Bennies, man.' Terence was frowning at him. 'You know, benzos? Benzodiazepines. They're tranqs.'

'They make you feel really mellow,' Carrie said.

Terence ignored her. 'Alright. How much?'

'Two quid for a dozen.'

'Too much. I don't want a dozen.'

Pinnock shrugged. 'What can I tell you? That's the price. Non-negotiable.'

'Everything is negotiable.'

'Not *everything*, man. And certainly not my bennies. I'm not forcing you, but if you don't want them, it's time you left.'

They had reached a stalemate. Terence thought for a moment, then pulled out his wallet. 'Very well.'

Pinnock smiled. 'Sweet. Hold that thought.' He went through to the bedroom.

Terence waited, trying not to look at Samantha and Carrie, who had completely lost interest in him and were now wrapped up in each other.

A moment later, Pinnock returned. 'These will take the edge off.' He thrust a small envelope into Terence's hand. 'One at a time.'

Terence handed over two pound notes. Pinnock shoved them into his back pocket and went over and unhooked the safety chain on the door. 'Nice doing business with you. If you need anything else, you now know where to find me.'

CHAPTER 16

If he'd been honest, Terence hadn't expected much for his outlay. But the single tablet he took later that evening did indeed, as Carrie had suggested, make him feel "mellow". *Good word*, he thought. He said it aloud: 'Mellllloooow'. Chuckling to himself for no particular reason, he took a seat at his desk and spent the next two hours glued to the task of revising his thesis. By the time he decided to call it a night, he really felt as if he'd achieved something.

There was an organised visit to the Houses of Parliament coming up – he'd seen the poster on the common room wall the previous week – and, as he climbed into bed, he decided he would drop into the office the next morning to register his interest.

He slept well and woke later than he'd intended. Without bothering to wash or shave, he threw on some clean clothes, took another tablet, and then made his way across the campus to sign up for the trip to London. As he walked along to the secretary's office at the end of the corridor, the door opened and Lavis appeared.

Terence stopped in his tracks, but Lavis didn't notice him; he crossed to staircase opposite the office and took off upstairs, taking the steps two at a time.

When Terence walked in, the secretary with silver-white hair pulled back tight and held in place with bobby pins looked up at him over the top of her half-moon spectacles. 'Good morning.'

Terence beamed at her. 'Good morning to you too. I'd like to register for one of the upcoming trips, please.'

'Of course.' The woman opened her desk drawer and withdrew a folder. 'Which one would that be?'

'London. The Houses of Parliament in a couple of weeks' time. I forget the precise date.'

The woman didn't even open the folder. She looked at him apologetically. 'I'm sorry, all the seats on that trip have been allocated. I just took someone's name for the last one.'

Lavis!

Struggling to retain his composure, Terence said: 'Was it my friend Graham, by any chance?'

'Yes, as a matter of fact it was. Graham Lavis. He signed up for the last place not two minutes ago.'

Terence could hardly believe it. Why was it *so* difficult to steer clear of Lavis? No matter what he did to avoid him, be it intentionally or inadvertently, the man just kept showing up, infecting Terence's life like some sort of inescapable, cloying stench.

'The early bird catches the worm.' The woman smiled, but it faded as she saw the look of annoyance on Terence's face. 'I can put you on the reserve list if you like,' she added helpfully. 'We often get a last minute cancellation.'

'Don't concern yourself,' Terence grunted. 'It's suddenly lost its appeal.'

'Are you sure? You'd be first on the list if someone drops out.'

'I said forget it,' Terence snapped, and walked out.

By the following evening, he could no longer ignore the burning need for a drink. He had only been seated in The Knight's Horse for ten minutes, when Chas, Rich and Danny walked in. Terence actually felt pleased to see them. They spotted him and came straight over.

'Watchya, Tel.' Chas dropped into the seat beside him. He looked up at Rich. 'Thanks for asking, mate. I'll have a pint of Skol.'

Rich made a face. 'I *didn't* ask.'

'No, but you was *going* to, weren't ya? And get our new best mate Tel another of whatever it is he's necking there.'

'Strongbow,' Terence said. 'A pint.'

Rich and Danny went off to the bar and Chas eyed Terence up. 'What gives then, Tel? You ain't looking so hot. Not still suffering from the other night, are you?' He guffawed. 'The state of you when you left us! I ain't never seen no-one looking that green before.'

'I'm just tired. Problems at uni.'

'Yeah? Spill.'

'I'd rather not talk about it. There's nothing can be done.'

Chas shook his head. 'No such thing as an unsolvable problem, chief. Take tonight, for example.' He picked up his pint and took a swig, then matter-of-factly said, 'We sorted out a couple of queers on the way over just now.'

'When you say "sorted out"…'

'Gave them a good kicking. Beat the shit outta them. Problem solved.'

'That sounds rather drastic. How exactly were they causing a problem?'

Chas frowned. 'You winding me up, chief? They *exist*! It ain't fucking natural. You tell me with a straight face it ain't wrong to wanna exterminatrate pervy fuckers who get off on dirt-mining?'

Terence's eyes widened. 'I thought you said you bashed them up, not killed them!'

Chas laughed. 'Don't be a twat. Course we didn't *kill* them. We made sure they won't be walking straight for a while though. One of them was married too. Begged me not to hurt him for his kid's sake. Dirty cunt. He's gonna have some explaining to do to the

196

missus tonight.' He winked at Terence. 'Like I told you, chief. No such thing as an unsolvable problem.'

Danny reappeared and set down a tray of drinks on the table. He pulled over a chair and sat down.

Chas looked around for Rich. 'Where's that twat gone now?'

'He's washing his hands. He's still got blood on them.' Danny laughed. 'He's fucked up his new shirt too. He ain't a happy bunny.'

Chas guffawed. 'Silly fucker. I was just saying to Tel here, there's no problem that can't be solved. Ain't that right, Danno?'

Danny nodded. 'Problem solvers, us.' He bumped fists with Chas.

'He was telling me *he's* got a bit of a problem.'

'Yeah?' Danny looked at Terence. 'What's that then, mate?'

'It's nothing really.' Terence said. 'Just stuff.' He changed the subject. 'What have you chaps been up to since the other night? I mean, besides getting into an altercation with the…' – the word stuck in his mouth – '…er, queers.'

'What *haven't* we been up to more like.' Chas grinned. 'Thinning out the surplus population of Warwick, chief. Tell him, Dan.'

'Yeah.' Danny swallowed a mouthful of his beer and belched. 'We sent a bunch of pakkis home last

197

night. Way too many of the bastards lording it about round here like they own the fucking place. They're taking over.'

Rich appeared, muttering under his breath. 'That bog roll is fucking useless. My finger went right through it.' As he sat down he saw his cronies looking at him in disgust. '*What*?! I washed my hands for fuck's sake!'

Terence emptied his glass and picked up the fresh one from the tray. 'Thank you.'

Chas grinned. 'Get it down you, chief.'

'So, we've established that you're not too discerning when it comes to citizens of the Pakistani and homosexual communities.' Terence took a sip of his drink. 'Is there anyone you *do* like?'

'Well we fucking hate uni students for a start,' Danny said. He burst out laughing.

Rich frowned at Terence. 'Why do you talk like that?'

'Like what?'

'All la-di-da.'

'Never mind them,' Chas said. 'To answer your question, Tel, no, not really. Pakis and queers – and obviously lezzers, that goes without saying; they're top of the list. But we hate chinks, brillo pads, greasy wops, ay-rabs and kikes. Ragheads too.'

'And frogs,' Rich said. 'Smelly, snail-gobbling turd-burglars.'

'And don't get us started on kiddie-fiddlers,' Danny chipped in. 'Evil fucking nonces. Oh, and trannies. Here, Cobra, tell him about that weirdo geezer you shivved when we was over at…'

Chas pulled a face and drew a line across his throat. Danny fell silent and Terence saw a look pass between them.

'Anyway, Tel,' Chas said. 'You ought to come out with us later. There's this cunt lives above the chippy. He got a bit gobby last weekend when we was outside enjoying our grub. We wasn't bothering no-one or nothing, but he come out and give us a right old earful. Word on the street is, he's a bit too friendly around the local kids. So we thought we'd pay him a little visit after closing time. You in?'

'I don't think so.'

'Why not?'

'Because it's not right.'

'Are you honestly telling me you never once thought about kicking the shit out of some cunt that deserved it?'

The image of Lavis sitting in the common room with Joanne popped into Terence's mind. He shook his head. 'It depends on your definition of deserved.'

199

'I tell you, chief, it's a fucking rush putting your boot on someone's head and giving it a bit of pressure. You've got their life in your hands and they know it. And they know *you* know they know it. The fear in their eyes is a power rush and there ain't another feeling in the world like it. You should come with us. You don't have to do nothing if you don't want to, but it might open your eyes to what's going on out there beyond your iver tower.'

'You mean *ivory* tower.'

Chas shrugged.

'I assure you that I *don't* live in an ivory tower,' Terence continued. 'And I'm certainly not desensitised to the appalling level of misconduct and contravention going unpunished in the world today.'

'There he goes talking all la-di-da again,' Rich said.

Terence ignored him. 'Doing what you want when you want without consideration for others is a contagion that's rapidly spiralling out of control. Somebody needs to step up and start dealing with it before anarchy rules, though in many respects it's already too late. If you ask me, Parliament passing Sydney Silverman's bill to abolish the death penalty back in 1965 was the thin end of the wedge. Mind you, Silverman was Labour. Need I say more?'

Danny and Rich were staring at Terence blankly.

'Whatever,' he continued. 'The point is, although there are clearly cases for which the death penalty should still be considered appropriate, there's no justification for terrorising someone because of their race, or their sexual persuasion, or their religious beliefs. There just isn't.'

Chas had been listening intently. 'You talk a good case, Tel. I mean, you're *completely* fucking wrong, and I don't agree with a word you just said, except maybe that stuff about doing away with the death penalty. All I'll say to you is, there's a lot of shit walking about out there on the streets that don't deserve to be.'

Terence didn't subscribe to Chas's one-rule-for-all neanderthal assertions, but not everything about the man's philosophy had been wrong. There *were* people whose behaviour needed addressing. God knows, he had crossed paths with enough rotten souls in his time; people who seemed to think it was fine to treat him badly and then walk away unpunished. The idea of seeing Lavis – and other reprobates like him – held accountable and served their just desserts certainly held a level of appeal.

He nodded. 'Very well. I shall come. As long as you promise I don't have to get involved.'

Chas grinned. 'Absolutely, chief. But if you happen to get caught up in the moment and feel like putting the boot in, we won't hold you back.'

'I guarantee that won't happen.' Terence felt in his jacket pocket and pulled out the envelope Pinnock had given him. He popped a tablet in his mouth and swilled it down with some cider.

Danny looked interested. 'What you got there, mate?'

'Just something to help calm my nerves.'

Danny held out his hand. 'Give us one then.' It was less a request than a demand.

Terence hesitated. 'They were a bit expensive.'

Chas punched him on the arm. 'Don't be cunty, chief. Share them round.'

Reluctantly Terence handed over the envelope. Chas took out two and swallowed them, then passed it around to his cohorts.

Terence started to say, 'One is all you need for maximum…' But they weren't listening. He sighed inwardly as he watched half of his expensive purchase vanish in one fell swoop. He decided he would have to pay Pinnock another visit the following day.

They didn't make it to closing time. Having consumed several pints of barley wine, Danny got into a heated dispute with the barmaid over the change from his round. Terence kept his head down, but Chas and

202

Rich waded in and then the girl screeched that Danny had touched her. Amidst the commotion, the landlord appeared. He was a mammoth of a man; solid muscle and built like a tree trunk. He ejected the three skinheads, with a growl: 'You're all barred!'

Terence quickly finished his drink and went outside to join them.

Chas was laughing. 'That's the fourth time Tiny Dave has barred us this year! It'll all be forgotten again in a week.'

'*Tiny* Dave?' Terence chuckled. 'What does *Big* Dave look like?!'

'There ain't a Big Dave. Everyone just calls him Tiny cos he ain't.'

Terence rolled his eyes and was about to explain that he was making a joke when Chas cut him off.

'Come on, this way. Let's go give that fucker a hiding he won't forget.'

Twenty minutes later, as they approached the chip shop, Terence was beginning to regret having agreed to tag along, and he was quietly pleased to see that not only had the shop closed up for the night, there were no lights on in the overhead flat. He hung back with Chas and Danny while Rich went into the alleyway at the side of the premises and scooted up the wrought iron staircase and banged on the door. Aside from the sound of him knocking a couple more times, everything was deathly quiet. There wasn't even any traffic about.

Two minutes later, Rich reappeared. 'I don't think he's in there.'

Terence felt a wave of relief wash over him. 'Ah, well, c'est la vie.' He glanced at his watch; it was approaching midnight. 'I suggest we'd best call it a night then.'

Chas shot him a dirty look. 'You're having a laugh, ain't you?' His eyes were glittering in the light from the street lamp and for a fleeting moment it occurred to Terence that he was looking into the face of evil. 'The night ain't over until we've heard the sound of cracking ribs. Ain't that right, boys?'

Rich and Danny bumped fists with him.

'Course,' Chas continued with note of sarcasm, 'if it's past diddums' bye-byes time...'

'I'm here aren't I? What exactly are you planning to do? I can understand you may have had a grievance against this man, but surely you're not just going to wander off and victimise some random stranger?'

'We'll head up towards the woods, kick about until some raghead comes along. Anyone out this time of night is fair fucking game far as we're concerned.'

'And what if *nobody* does come along?'

'Someone will. There's enough of the cunts live up that way.'

'So you'll simply target someone on his own?'

'Or *her* own. We don't care.'

'But it's still three against one. Not very equitable odds.'

Chas looked at him as if he couldn't quite believe he was having this conversation. 'What the fuck's the matter with you, Tel? All's fair in blood and violence. And besides, it'll be *four* against one if you fancy getting stuck in.'

'I won't be getting involved. My presence will be strictly in an observational capacity.'

Chas grimaced. 'Whatever. If you're coming with us, stop fucking gabbing and start walking.'

He and Terence took the lead in silence, while Rich and Danny brought up the rear, play-fighting like children and trying to trip each other over.

The search for a target didn't take long.

'Knock it off, you fucking benders,' Chas said, as the rumble of a bus engine sounded. 'Out of sight, quick.' He ushered everyone to get off the path.

All four of them ducked swiftly into the trees lining the avenue and they watched the bus pass by and pull to a halt at its stop fifty yards up the road. The doors hissed open and a lone figure carrying a briefcase alighted. Even from this distance, Terence could see the man was wearing a turban; all that was needed to make him prime pickings for Chas and his buddies, he thought. His gorge began to rise, but it was quelled as he became aware that they were standing in more or less the same spot where he had seen Joanne kissing Harrington.

The man started off up the path in the opposite direction and, as the bus pulled away, Danny took off like a jackrabbit and charged after him.

As he got closer, the man heard the beat of footsteps fast approaching from behind and his pace faltered. But he knew better than to stop or look back.

'Scuse me, mate,' Danny shouted. 'I don't s'pose you could spare me 20p?'

The man kept walking. 'Sorry,' he called back over his shoulder.

Danny caught up and slowed to a trot beside him. 'Come on, mate, it's just 20p,' he said breathlessly. 'I'm skint and I need it for my bus fare home.'

The man stopped and turned to look at him. Evidently Sikh, beneath the turban was a handsome face with an immaculately trimmed beard. 'Then you are out of luck, my friend. That…' – he pointed at the receding bus – '…was the last one tonight. I hope that you don't have too far to walk.' He nodded a polite goodnight and started to turn away.

'Why does your lot always stink of curry, eh?'

The man was taken off guard. If he hadn't already suspected trouble was imminent, all his senses were now on alert. He looked back at Danny. 'Excuse me?'

'You heard. And what's in that case?'

The man started to walk again. 'That would be none of your business. You are a very rude man. Now kindly leave me alone.'

Danny made a lunge for the case. The man struggled to keep hold of it, but lost his grip.

'Give that back!' he demanded.

That was when Chas and Rich decided to make their move. Grabbing Terence by the arm and hauling him after them, they moved rapidly up the path.

Danny was taunting the man now. He held out the case towards him. 'What, this?'

Seeing the other men approaching, the Sikh tried to take it, but Danny stepped smartly back, holding it out at arm's length in front of him, but just beyond the man's reach.

'Please, just give it back.'

As Chas, Rich and Terence came up behind him, Danny suddenly swung the case and struck the man hard across the side of his face.

He cried out and staggered back.

Chas darted forward – 'Why don't you fuckers go back where you come from, Gurinder?!' – and kicked the man's left knee with the steel-capped toe of his Doc

Marten boot. There was a sickening crack and the man screamed as his leg buckled and he went down. In an instant Rich was astride him and bent over, his fists pounding in a blur of ferocious rage.

Standing several feet back from the unfolding horror, Terence looked up and down the street, but there wasn't a soul to be seen. As much as he wanted to run like the wind, he simply couldn't tear his eyes away.

Rich was still punching the man, whose face was now awash with blood. His turban had come loose and, with a whoop, Chas whipped it off his head and got down on his knees beside him. Rich ceased his assault and stood aside, and Chas wrapped the turban twice around the man's throat. His face darkened as he wound the ends around his clenched fists and pulled tight.

The helpless man was barely conscious now, but survival instinct kicked in and as he started to choke, his hands scrabbled at the material in a feeble attempt to loosen it.

All the while, Danny was scampering around them in circles, laughing dementedly and whirling the briefcase around his head.

A white car rounded the bend up ahead and Terence watched it approach, turning quickly away to hide his face from the headlights. Almost as if they knew there was no threat, the other three didn't even bother to look up. As the car drew alongside them, it slowed to a crawl. But then, presumably deciding it best not to get involved, the driver put his foot down and it sped away.

The Sikh had finally stopped fighting and lay still.

Chas yanked the turban free from the man's neck, stood up and stepped back. 'That'll teach the cunt not to mess with the Cobra.' Dropping the turban, he bent and put his hands on his knees to catch his breath. 'Fucking hell, that was a rush.'

'You killed him!' Terence exclaimed.

'Nah, he ain't dead.' Chas stood upright and kicked the man's prone body in the ribs.

The man stirred slightly and made a weak gurgling noise.

'See?'

'You knew him.'

'Nope.'

'But I heard you address him as Gurinder.'

Chas laughed. 'They're all called Gurinder, you muppet. Or Gurjeet. Or Ganesh. Or whatever the fuck!' He held out his hand to Danny. 'Give me the case.'

Danny did as he was asked and stood back with Rich to watch as Chas knelt down and tried to open it.

Terence looked at him aghast. 'Surely you're not robbing the poor man?'

209

'I'm pretty sure he ain't no poor man, and besides, he's got no use for it any more.'

Terence stared at him in disbelief. 'This isn't right!'

'But you're okay with watching us kick seven shades of shit out of him?'

'Whether I agree with what you all just did to that man is beside the point. That's what you *came* here to do. Robbing him is another matter entirely.'

'Fuck me, you've got a twisted idea of right and wrong, Tel.' Chas was fiddling irritably with the latches. 'Bollocks! It's locked.' He hurled the case aside. 'Come on. We'd better make ourselves scarce in case that driver calls the filth.'

On his way back to the halls of residence, Terence threw up in the gutter. His heartbeat was racing and he was sweating profusely. He still couldn't quite process everything he'd just witnessed. The torrent of unharnessed hatred had been startling. But perhaps not quite as startling as his reactions had been as he had stood and watched. To his bewilderment, he'd been transfixed by a cocktail of shock, enthralment and – much as it frightened him to admit it – intense arousal.

He fumbled in his pocket for the Benzodiazepine; there was one left. He tried to swallow it dry, but it only made him vomit again.

He definitely needed to revisit Pinnock the next day.

CHAPTER 17

Following a sleepless night, it was just after six o'clock the next morning that Terence slipped on his jacket to go out again. He put a hand in his pocket and jingled the loose change. He knew Pinnock wouldn't appreciate a visit at this time of the morning, but he was desperate.

It wasn't quite seven when he rapped on Pinnock's door. After a moment, there was the requisite sound of the safety chain being put on, the door opened and Pinnock's face peered out warily through the crack.

'Hallam? Christ, man, I thought you were the fuzz. What time is it?'

'I need some more pills.'

Pinnock rubbed his right eye with the base of his palm and yawned. 'Come back later.' He started to close the door, but Terence put his full weight against it to stop him.

'I need them now.'

Pinnock's brow furrowed. 'I only sold you a dozen two days ago. You're supposed to take one at a time.'

'I shared them with friends. Now let me in. I have money.'

'Okay, hang on.' Muttering under his breath, Pinnock closed the door and released the chain, and as he opened the door fully, Terence barged past him into the room.

'Come in, why don't you?'

Pinnock closed the door and Terence spun to face him.

'If you thought I was the police, why did you open the door?'

Pinnock laughed. 'Seriously? We're five floors up. Where exactly am I gonna run to?' Pulling the belt tight on his towelling dressing gown, he looked Hallam up and down. 'You look worse than you did the other day, man.'

'Never mind what I look like!' Terence snapped. 'What about the Benzodiazepine?'

Pinnock squinted, raised a hand and rubbed his thumb back and forth across his fingers. 'What about the money?'

Terence ferreted around in his jacket pocket. He pulled out a handful of coins and Pinnock watched cagily as he crossed to the window. Opening the curtain a little to get some light, Terence started counting out on money on the sill.

'Who is it, Rob?' A woman's sleepy voice came from the bedroom.

Pinnock went to the door – 'No-one, go back to sleep.' – and pulled it shut. Scratching his crotch through the gown, he yawned again. 'So did you really share them with mates?'

Terence nodded.

'Charitable kind of guy, are you?' Pinnock said, his tone suggesting he didn't believe him.

Terence didn't answer. He was still counting. He stopped and muttered something, then started again.

'I'm guessing they must have had the desired effect for you though?'

Terence finished counting. 'I'm thirty-four pence short.'

Pinnock sucked air through his teeth and shook his head. 'Not much I can do for you then, mon brave.'

Terence looked at him desperately. 'Can't you just sell me ten?'

'No can do, man. I told you last time, it's two quid a dozen.'

'Alright, but can I owe you the thirty-four pence?'

Pinnock shook his head again. 'I don't do credit.' Seeing the desperation in Terence's eyes, he smiled and rested his hand on his shoulder. 'Look, I like you, man. I really do. And if I could help you out, I would. You know that. But you don't seem to understand. I'm not actually registered as a charity. I can't just *give* you the stuff.'

'Please, just this one time.'

'You're not listening to me, man. It's time for you to leave.'

Terence glared at him. 'I'll report you.'

Pinnock gave him a thin smile. 'No you won't. You'll toddle off and find that extra thirty-four pence, then you'll come back and we'll do business.' He crossed to the door and held it open.

'Okay,' Terence said. 'I've got the money back in my room.'

'You better go and get it then.'

'You'll be here when I get back, won't you?'

Pinnock nodded. 'Sure.'

Without another word, Terence pushed angrily past him and headed for the staircase.

Pinnock's mocking voice echoed down the corridor behind him. 'See you soon, man.'

Seething with rage, Terence returned to his room. He knew full well he didn't have the additional money; his recent lifestyle choices had come with a price and his disposable funds had dwindled to almost nothing.

The idea of going home to Seatown filled him with dread, but he had spoken to his mother a few days earlier and promised he would come for the weekend. He couldn't actually remember the last time he'd visited; five weeks, Emily had informed him. It suddenly occurred to him that this would be an ideal opportunity to ask his parents for a little more pocket money. There would undoubtedly be awkward questions to answer about Joanne, but he would take those in his stride. Right now, he needed money.

With no lecture to attend until the following Monday, he crammed some clothes into a suitcase, checked his annual rail pass was still in date and set off for the station.

CHAPTER 18

The journey home took far longer than it should have. There was a signal failure outside Leamington Spa that left the train stranded and they went nowhere for almost two hours. The result was that Terence didn't walk through the door of the cottage until late afternoon.

Emily was pleased to see him and mockingly admonished him for having stayed away for so long.

She hugged him. 'It's good to see you, Terence.'

'Where's Dad?'

'He's upstairs taking a nap. His breathing has got worse. The consultant at the hospital prescribed him an oxygen tank a few weeks ago, but he's parked it behind his armchair and refuses point blank to use it.' She saw the look on Terence's face. 'Don't worry. You know what he's like. And he'll be down for dinner. He'll be pleased to see you.'

Terence seriously doubted that.

Emily picked up her washing basket. 'Would you be a dear and lay the table for dinner while I get the washing on the line?'

As soon as she'd gone out into the garden, Terence checked to ensure she couldn't see him, then he went to the kitchen cupboard.

When he was a boy, they used to keep emergency funds tucked away in a cocoa tin. There was no reason it shouldn't still be there. He had every intention of asking them for an increase in his weekly allowance later, but he had no confidence that he would get it.

There were a number of tins stacked in the cupboard and he had to move them aside to get to the back. But there, as he'd hoped, was the old cocoa tin. Smiling, he pulled it out and, retrieving a knife from the cutlery drawer, jemmied the lid off. As he pulled out the two bundles of notes inside, a noise sounded behind him.

Terence whirled round to see Arthur standing in the doorway.

'What the hell do you think you're doing?'

'I thought you were upstairs asleep. I…'

'I bet you did!' Arthur stepped forward. 'How *dare* you steal money from us!' He grabbed Terence's arm. 'Put it back!'

'Get off me!' Terence said angrily, yanking his arm free.

Arthur glared at him. 'You should be bloody ashamed of yourself.' He looked at Terence contemptuously. 'You can be *anything* you want to be. All you had to do was keep your head down and work hard. Like your grandfather did, and his father before him. Just like *I* do. But here you are, creeping about with someone else's hard-earned money clutched in

217

your mucky little paws. You're no better than a common thief!'

'Maybe I am. But one day I'll be better than you or your father or anyone else. I'll show the lot of you what success really means.'

Arthur's ire subsided a little. He shook his head. 'Not on the back of my money you won't.' He held out his hand. 'Give it back. Now.'

There was a pause during which Terence appeared to be weighing up his options. Then, with a huff, he handed over the bundles of notes. 'Bollocks to you then.'

Arthur's face turned to thunder. He spoke quietly through gritted teeth. 'I'll let you have that one. But don't you *ever* speak to me like that again!' He pushed the money back into the tin and Terence watched him return it to the cupboard. 'I'm not going to upset your mother with any of this. But in the morning you're going to apologise to her and say that something has come up and you have to leave early. Then you pack up your things and get the hell out of my house.' Arthur closed the cupboard door. 'But right now, you can make yourself useful and go help your mother with the washing.'

When they sat down to dinner, Emily immediately detected an atmosphere between her husband and her son. 'I was saying to Terence, dear, it's nice to have him visit again.'

'Is it?' Arthur grunted. 'Haven't you noticed the state of him? He looks like he's been sleeping in a hedge. And when did he last get a haircut? Or even bother to wash it for that matter?'

'Please don't go on, Dad,' Terence muttered. 'I'm not in the mood.'

Arthur rolled his eyes. 'Hark at him, Em. He's not in the mood.' He grimaced. 'What happened to your self respect, boy?'

Emily tried to steer the conversation away from her son's unkempt appearance. 'How are you and Joanne getting along, Terence? We were thinking perhaps she might like to come and stay for a few days over the summer.'

'We're finished,' Terence said sourly.

'Don't tell me she jilted you?' Arthur shook his head. 'Well, looking at the state of you I can't say I blame her. I couldn't understand what she saw in you in the first place. She was probably ashamed to be seen out with you.'

Emily looked at Terence sadly. 'I'm so sorry, dear. What happened?'

'I don't want to talk about it.'

'But you seemed so happy together.'

'I said I don't want to talk about it!' Terence snapped.

'Don't take that tone with your mother!' Arthur said angrily. 'You're not too old to receive a slap, you know!'

Terence glared at his father. 'From *who* exactly?'

'Terence!' Emily exclaimed. 'Don't talk back to your father like that. What on earth has got into you? Apologise immediately!'

Terence buried his face in his hands. 'I'm sorry. Everything seems to have been going wrong recently. Joanne didn't dump me. I finished with her. She was seeing someone else...'

Emily shot Arthur a look that dared him to utter a word. 'There are plenty more fish in the sea,' she said, trying to sound comforting. 'There'll be time enough for girls later on. When you've graduated.'

'*If* I graduate. I fouled up big time on my thesis.'

Both Arthur and Emily had been astounded on the day Terence had called to tell them he'd failed his paper and they hadn't attempted to conceal their disappointment in him. Arthur had gone as far as to read him the riot act. Now Emily tried to inject a note of positivity.

'We know you tried your best. There's a lot of pressure on youngsters nowadays and not everyone succeeds first time. It's just a blessing that you have the option to resubmit.'

'I'm not sure I'm going to.'

His parents exchanged stunned glances. 'What do you mean, "not going to"?' Arthur exclaimed. 'If you think we've invested all this money into your education just so you can waltz away when things get a bit difficult, you've got another damned think coming!'

'I just can't focus. I've tried *so* hard, but I feel like I wasn't cut out for uni. I have no friends and I spend most of my time alone. I've got no money either. I can barely afford to eat. I…'

'What do you mean, you can barely afford to eat?' Arthur interjected testily. 'Six pounds a week is a more than generous allowance if you budget wisely.'

'It just goes,' Terence said dejectedly.

Arthur wrinkled his nose. 'Well, whatever else you're spending it on, it's clearly not deodorant. You stink!'

Terence sat up. He sniffed and pretended to wipe a tear from his eye. 'Talking about money, I was wondering if you might consider letting me have a little more.'

To his surprise, Arthur smiled at him. 'Sure! How much would you like? Fifteen a week enough?'

Terence smiled gratefully. 'That would be good.'

221

'Or twenty perhaps?' Arthur continued. '*Fifty*? I know, let's just make it a round hundred, shall we? Will that be sufficient for you?'

Terence's smile faded. For a moment he'd been naïve enough to actually believe his father was going to grant his request.

Arthur's smile had vanished too. 'I know crocodile tears when I see them, boy. I have no idea what you're spending your allowance on and I'm not going to ask; I'm in no doubt you'd spin me lies anyway. But if you think I work six days a week to fund your indolent lifestyle then you're dead wrong. You'll not be getting another penny out of us until you buck your ideas up. In fact, unless you've got something to say that will convince me you genuinely intend to sort yourself out and get back on track with your studies, as of right now your allowance is terminated.'

'Oh, Arthur!' Emily gasped. 'You can't do that.'

'Don't undermine me, woman!' Arthur had worked himself into a frenzy. 'I can and I damned well will!'

'But what's he going to survive on?'

'I don't know and frankly I don't care,' Arthur said breathlessly. 'Enough is enough. He'll have to go out and get himself a job.'

Terence's expression had hardened. 'So that would be a definite no then.'

'Too bloody right it's a no.'

'I see. Well, it's no less than I expected.'

Arthur scowled. 'I'm not in the business of helping people who can't help themselves, be it my son or anyone else for that matter.'

Terence stood up. 'I'm going to my room.'

'But we haven't had dessert yet!' Emily exclaimed.

'I'm not that hungry.'

'Says the boy who just claimed he can barely afford food,' Arthur said sarcastically. 'Don't bother showing your face down here again until you've had a long hard think about your attitude.'

Emily looked at her husband tearfully. 'Please, Arthur, haven't you said enough?'

'No.' He looked after Terence as he disappeared up the stairs. 'And while you're at it have a wash and put some clean clothes on. You're a bloody disgrace!'

Closing his bedroom door, Terence squatted down at his bedside cabinet. He felt a twinge of sadness at the sight of the framed photo sitting on the top; it had been taken at Christmas, and there was Joanne laughing and playfully waving a sprig of mistletoe over his head.

Rifling through the drawer, buried beneath all manner of childhood ephemera that should have been consigned to the dustbin years ago, he found the china piggy bank he'd received for his seventh birthday. Giving it a shake, his spirits lifted slightly when he heard the rattle of coins. It was a transitory moment, for when he prised the rubber cap off its belly, the contents totalled a paltry seventeen pence.

He was sick of university, sick of his parents, sick of everything. The thought of having to spend even the one night in Seatown now held even less appeal than it had before he arrived. If there was one thing about his father that Terence had learned over the years, it was that he was capable of taking stubbornness to the point of ridiculous; there was nothing he would be able say or do now that would convince the man to change his mind. He could maybe work on his mother, but he was fairly certain that – even though she would probably make all the right sympathetic noises – ultimately her allegiance would rest with his father.

For as long as he could remember, it seemed to him, that while the world around him enjoyed the party of life, he'd been left to watch resentfully from the sidelines; an outsider looking in, lacking the confidence to put his head above the parapet. Sure, there had been Joanne, and he had been momentarily fooled into thinking there might actually be a place for him at the party after all; but look at how that had turned out.

He reached for the picture frame and turned it face down.

What to do next then? He decided he would wait until his parents were asleep, then he would sneak back downstairs and get the money.

He sat and waited until just after one o'clock, then crept out onto the landing barefoot. The house was in darkness and there wasn't a sound to be heard except the rhythmic ticking of the grandfather clock in the hallway downstairs. Moving stealthily, he went down to the kitchen and opened the cupboard.

Stuffing the two bundles of money into his back pocket, he was about to head back upstairs when he saw the light through a crack in the living room door. He crossed the hall and peered cautiously in.

His mother had mentioned some time back that Arthur's sleep patterns had become erratic and he often ended up falling into a slumber and spending the night in his chair. And sure enough, there was Arthur now, sound asleep with his newspaper on the floor at his feet.

Suddenly an idea came to him. It was sheer madness, but in that moment it seemed like the solution to all his problems. Everything that his parents owned – the house, the money in the bank, the proceeds from the inevitable sale of Hallam Toys – would all be his. But not while they were still breathing. He looked at the man sleeping peacefully in the chair. If Terence had ever felt any love for him whatsoever – and he couldn't actually remember a time when he had – it was dead and buried now; in its place, abject hatred.

His heart pounding, he crept quietly across the carpet to the bureau and opened the lid of the cedar hardwood humidor sitting on top of a pile of paperwork. Extracting one of the Montecristo Especials, Terence pressed it between his lips, then picked up the box of Swan Vestas laying beside the humidor. Carefully removing a match, he tried to strike it, but it snapped.

Arthur made a noise somewhere between a snore and a grunt and Terence froze. Suddenly aware that he was holding his breath, he softly exhaled. He waited a full minute and then, satisfied that Arthur was still sound asleep, he struck a second match. There was a flash as the potassium chlorate tip flared into life. He held the flickering orange flame to the end of the cigar and sucked gently until it began to glow. As the smoke filled his mouth he felt an overwhelming urge to cough. He put a hand to his face and stifled it, hissing out the smoke between his fingers. Then he shook out the match and slipped it along with the broken one into his pocket.

If his father were to wake now there would be no explanation in the world that could rationally account for what he was doing.

Arthur's hand was resting on the arm of the chair. Holding his breath again, Terence carefully lifted the tips of the fingers, just enough to be able to tuck the cigar in underneath, then lowered them back down. Arthur didn't stir. He stepped back and exhaled quietly. Striking a third match, he bent to the patch of material that his mother had sewn over the damage following the accidental fire the previous year and held the flame to it until it started to burn. Shaking out the match, he dropped the box back onto the bureau, then crossed swiftly to the door, pausing only to glance back and ensure the flame hadn't died. It would only be a minute or two before Arthur's lungs would fill with choking carbon monoxide and then there would be no chance of him waking to see another dawn.

Feeling sick, Terence ran back upstairs. He slipped on his shoes and was about to grab his suitcase when he thought better of it; it would be simple to explain his absence from the house when the fire started – 'I've been having trouble sleeping you see, officer, so I went for a walk.' – but why would he have had his case with him?

Deciding that a few bits of old clothing were a small sacrifice to make, he left the case where it was and went back out onto the landing. Leaning over the banister, he could see there was already smoke curling up from the living room. He stopped outside his parents' bedroom door and rested the flat of his hand on it. 'I'm so sorry, Mum,' he whispered. Then he hurried back downstairs. Crossing the kitchen, he went out into the garden and closed the door softly behind him.

Moving swiftly, he opened the ornamental wooden gate at the side of the house and walked down the path to the front garden. He paused for a second outside the living room window. Through a crack in the drawn curtains he could see dense black smoke and the bright flicker of flames as they leapt up the wall. As he watched, the bottom of the curtain caught light and a line of flame shot up its length towards the ceiling.

For one horrible moment, he was engulfed in regret; but it passed as quickly as it had come and he walked across the flowerbeds and out onto the footpath that ran past the front of the cottage.

He looked up and down the lane. There was nobody around, but he would have been surprised if there had been at this time of night in their quiet corner of Seatown.

Slowly, he strolled down the path towards the public telephone callbox on the corner. As he pulled open the door, there was an almighty explosion from behind

228

him. He spun round to see the whole lefthand side of the cottage erupt in a ball of fire. It took him a moment to comprehend what had happened, but then the answer came to him; of course, the oxygen tank that his mother had told him about was hidden away behind the armchair!

He stepped into the phone box. Breathing quickly and deeply in and out a dozen times, he picked up the receiver and dialled 999.

A woman's voice came on the end of the line. 'Emergency. Which service do you require?'

'Fire!' Terence gasped breathlessly.

'Please hold.'

There was a click followed by static. No more than ten seconds elapsed, then there was another click and a man spoke. 'Fire Service. How can I help you?'

'There's been an explosion in my home!' Terence applied just the right level of pitch to his voice to make himself sound distraught. 'It's on fire and I think my parents are still inside! Send help quickly!'

The man asked Terence to calm down and provide him with the address, and when he had all the details he needed, he told him not to attempt to go into the house and that a fire engine would be dispatched immediately.

'Thank you,' Terence said. 'Please, *please* hurry!'

He hung up the receiver and the expression of panic dropped from his face. Stepping back out of the phonebox, he could see the cottage was fully ablaze now and neighbours from the homes opposite were gathering in the street.

Readopting the expression of shock, he ran back up the pavement towards his burning home.

CHAPTER 19

Sirens wailing, two fire engines and an ambulance arrived simultaneously, followed a matter of minutes later by a police car.

Terence was sitting on the kerb outside the house opposite his childhood home, watching the inferno that had once been a beautiful thatched roof blazing merrily against the cloudless, inky black night sky.

There weren't many houses in the immediate area surrounding the Hallams' cottage. Mrs Baker – who, along with nearby neighbours the Conliffs and the Reeds – had been woken by the explosion. She had seen Terence charging up the street towards the house and had cried out to him to stay back. When it appeared he hadn't heard her, or simply wasn't listening, she ran forward and intercepted him at the gate, grabbing his arm and pulling him away. He'd instantly sunk to his knees in the gutter, sobbing inconsolably.

Mrs Baker had always been fond of Terence and she disappeared into her house and returned a minute later with a blanket, which she draped over his shoulders.

Making a show of wiping the tears from his eyes, he thanked her and she stood at his side while the squad of firefighters went into action.

Three members of the team had donned breathing apparatus, but it quickly became apparent that even with all the hoses pumping at full power, the blaze was too fierce to attempt entry to the building.

One of the men removed his mask and turned to the one next to him. 'If there's anyone in there, there's no way they're coming out alive.' He caught sight of Terence sitting on the kerb staring at him and realised he had spoken louder than he'd intended. With a sheepish expression on his face, he disappeared around to the far side of the engine and busied himself assisting with the pumps.

A pair of paramedics who had arrived in the ambulance came over and spoke with Terence, quickly establishing that there was no evidence of physical harm. But one of them suggested he was showing classic signs of delayed shock, and they requested that he come and sit in the back of the ambulance. Muttering almost incoherently, Terence stubbornly refused.

Two police officers – a man and a woman – approached and helped Terence to his feet. They told him they had a couple of questions to ask and suggested he come and wait in the back of the police car. He didn't respond, but allowed them to lead him over to the vehicle, which was parked up behind the ambulance.

When he was seated comfortably on the back seat, the female officer climbed in beside him, while the male stood beside the open door. She asked Terence where he had been when the explosion occurred. He didn't answer. Staring blankly at his shaking hands, it appeared that he hadn't even heard her. She looked up at her colleague.

'I think the paramedics were right. Poor kid's in shock.'

Mrs Baker had been loitering nearby. Overhearing what was said, she came over. 'I've got the kettle on. Do you think some tea might help?'

The policewoman smiled at her. 'Thank you, love.'

Five minutes later, with his fingers wrapped around a mug of steaming hot tea, Terence blinked and shook his head as if he were coming out of a trance. He took a sip of the tea and, wincing, handed it to the policewoman. 'I can't drink that.'

'It'll do you good, love. Just another sip.'

Terence shook his head. 'I feel a bit sick.'

Giving Mrs Baker a grateful smile, the officer passed the mug back to her. 'Thanks anyway.' Then she turned back to Terence and asked him again what had happened.

Terence turned his head and looked at her blankly. 'I… I'm not sure.'

The policewoman decided not to press him any further, but the male officer looked down at him sympathetically and apologised in advance for any upset it might cause, saying that there was one question he really needed Terence to answer if he could: Was he able to confirm who was in the house at the time of the explosion?

'My Mum and Dad,' he replied miserably, making sure he choked on the words. Then he started to sob again.

The two officers exchanged glances and the woman shook her head sorrowfully. She rested a comforting hand on Terence's knee and he flinched, so she quickly withdrew it again. 'I was just going to ask, is there somewhere you're going to be able to stay tonight, love?'

Before Terence could answer, Mrs Baker, who was still eavesdropping, spoke up. 'He can stay with me,' she said firmly. 'I've plenty of room'

As the downstairs clock chimed eleven the following morning, Terence was standing in the window of Mrs Baker's front bedroom, surveying the charred, smouldering remains of his parents' cottage. If he felt the slightest hint of remorse for what he'd done the night before, there was no sign of it on his face. In truth, he had slept better the night before than he had

234

done in a long time, and the only thing on his mind as he tried to visualise where his bedroom had once been, was what the insurance payout might amount to. And how long he would have to wait to receive his inheritence.

There was a soft tap on the door.

'Are you decent?'

It was Mrs Baker's voice.

Terence had to put a hand over his mouth to stop himself sniggering aloud. Of the many things someone might be called for robbing their parents blind and immolating them while they slept, he was certain that "decent" wasn't among them.

'One moment,' he replied. Stepping away from the window, he scooped up the scattering of banknotes from the bedspread; he'd counted them out a few minutes earlier and discovered that his foray into robbery had been fruitful to the tune of more than three hundred pounds. He stuffed the money out of sight under the pillow and sat down on the end of the bed.

'I am now.' Terence congratulated himself on the impressively mournful inflection he'd managed to convey with his short reply.

The door opened and Mrs Baker poked her face in. 'I didn't like to wake you earlier, but I heard you moving about. I hope I'm not disturbing you now, but there's a man downstairs who'd like to speak with you.'

'Oh? What man?'

'He did say, but I've got a brain like a sieve. I think he said a liaison support officer, or something like that. Does that sound right?' She looked at him apologetically. 'Sorry. Anyway, he's one of the fire people. And he's got a police officer with him.'

Terence stiffened. 'Really?'

'Yes. It's that nice lady who spoke to you last night.'

'I'll be right down.'

The man who had come to see Terence spoke quietly and solemnly. He told him that the fire investigation unit had entered the premises a couple of hours earlier and, he was very sorry to say, had recovered the remains of two people. He explained that the officer in charge had initiated an investigation to ascertain the cause of the fire, and that someone would be in touch once they knew more; most likely that afternoon. He concluded by offering his sincere condolences.

The policewoman echoed his commiseration and asked Terence if he minded her asking him a couple of questions, specifically relating to what, if anything, he could tell her about the tragedy.

Mrs Baker appeared from the kitchen and handed round mugs of tea.

'If you need me for anything, I'll be in the garden.'

'No,' Terence said. 'Please stay.'

Mrs Baker looked to the policewoman for affirmation that it was alright to do so . She nodded.

'Just pretend like I'm not here,' Mrs Baker said, taking the armchair near the door.

'So,' the policewoman said. 'What *were* your movements last night, Terence?'

Taking a breath, he gravely began to spin his carefully rehearsed tale:

'I've been having some difficulties at university, you see, and I've been sleeping really badly. I thought I'd take a walk to clear my head. I often do. It's so peaceful around here at night. Very calming.'

'What time might that have been?'

Terence looked thoughtful. 'I'm not sure exactly. Somewhere between half eleven and midnight.'

The policewoman looked at him questioningly.

'I'd heard the clock downstairs chime half eleven,' Terence added. 'So... maybe twenty-to, or eleven-forty-five?'

The policewoman made a note on her pad. 'Did you speak to your parents before you left the house? I'm guessing as it was late they were already in bed sound asleep?'

Almost imperceptibly, Terence's eyes narrowed. Surely that had to be a leading question. She had to be aware that Arthur's body had been discovered downstairs. Was she suspicious he'd been involved? Was she trying to catch him out? Suddenly, Terence didn't feel so confident.

'As a matter of fact, Dad hadn't gone to bed. I'm not sure about Mum, but I would think she probably had.'

'Where was your father?' The policewoman put down her pen. She was smiling at him disarmingly.

'In the living room,' Terence said. 'He often stayed up after Mum had retired. He liked to do his crossword in peace.'

'So you did speak to him?'

'No, no. I saw the living room light was still on through a crack in the door. I could hear him snoring.'

'You didn't go in?'

Terence was starting to feel uncomfortable. 'No, I didn't disturb him.'

'I see. Was he a heavy sleeper?'

'Why are you asking all these questions?'

'It just crossed my mind that he might have heard you go out and woken.'

'Oh. Well, no. I went out the back way.'

'Why not the front?'

'Because it was locked up for the night.'

238

'And the back wasn't?'

'It seldom is.'

'I see.' The policewoman scribbled another note. 'So how long were you out for?'

'Well over an hour. An hour and a half perhaps. No more than two.'

'I see you made a call to the emergency services at…' – the woman riffled back a couple of pages in her notebook – '…one-fourteen.'

Terence nodded. 'If you say so. I'm sorry, I've no idea what time it was. It's all a bit hazy.'

'That was the time the call was logged, yes. So the explosion in the house would have occurred a couple of minutes prior to that.'

It was more a statement than a question, but Terence answered anyway. 'Yes, I was just coming up the road when it happened. If I'd have got back a minute or two earlier I'd have been inside.'

'You were very lucky.'

Was there a trace of suspicion on her face? Had he said something that didn't quite add up? Terence berated himself for being paranoid. He nodded forlornly. 'Very.'

Something unspoken seemed to hang in the air for a moment, but then, the policewoman smiled.

'Well, I think that's everything.' She closed her notepad. Terence's account appeared to have satisfied her; for the time being at least.

The call from the fire service came through later that afternoon. Mrs Baker handed Terence the receiver and hovered in the background, dusting the ornaments on her mantlepiece while he listened, stony-faced, to what the man on the line had to say.

After he'd been appraised of the findings of the investigation, Terence thanked the man for calling and hung up.

'What did they say?' Mrs Baker asked, trying not to sound nosy, but failing dramatically.

'He said the case is still open, but they've ascertained that the fire started in the living room, most likely the result of a cigar.'

Mrs Baker's eyes widened. 'Oh, dear Lord, no! That's happened before, hasn't it? It was only a little while back your Mum was telling me your Dad had fallen asleep with his cigar still burning and set fire to the chair!'

Inwardly, Terence did a little jig. There was no reason that the cause of the fire should appear fishy, but *if* questions did happen to arise, there was someone right here who would corroborate any statement he chose to make with regard to Arthur's historic indifference to the inherent dangers of smoking while tired.

'But what about that awful explosion?' Mrs Baker continued.

'He said it was Dad's oxygen tank going up.'

'Oxygen tank?' Mrs Baker looked genuinely shocked. 'What on earth did he have an oxygen tank for?'

'He hasn't been very well. Mum told me he did nothing but grumble about it though. The man said that although oxygen itself isn't flammable, the tank can overheat and explode because of the compression, or something like that. If it does, even a small fire can quickly spiral out of control. He said Dad would have been killed instantly.'

There were tears in Mrs Baker's eyes. 'That's some small mercy, I suppose. Did they say anything about your poor Mum?'

Terence nodded sadly. 'The combustion was so intense she would likely have been asphyxiated. He said she more than likely wouldn't have been concious enough to realise what was happening.'

'Oh, Terence, it doesn't bear thinking about! Come here.' Mrs Baker put her arms around him and gave him a hug. The scent of her perfume was overpowering; it reminded Terence of Parma Violets.

241

He grimaced – he had always loathed Parma Violets – and disengaged himself from her embrace.

'Let's have some tea,' Mrs Baker said. 'You didn't eat at lunchtime, you must be starving.

She rustled up a round of cheese and pickle sandwiches and a pot of tea and they sat down to eat.

'What are you going to do now?'

Terence selected a sandwich from the plate. 'I don't really know. There's nothing more I can do here at the moment, not until the investigation is closed. I suppose I may as well head back to Warwick tomorrow afternoon. If nothing else I need a change of clothes. I didn't bring much down with me, but what I did have is gone. I know there will be a funeral to arrange soon enough – and that's probably only the tip of the iceberg. I haven't a clue where to start. Hopefully someone will be able to point me in the right direction for advice.'

'They will. You're never as alone as you think you are. You know if there's anything I can do to help, you only have to ask.'

'Thank you.'

Mrs Baker smiled. 'It's a sad thing to have to say, but by the time you reach my age, organising funerals gets to be par for the course. My parents passed when I was still quite young. Not quite as young as you are mind, but not a great deal older.' A faraway look appeared in her eyes. 'I'd only been married to my Percy for a year. What with mine and his, I've had to bear the loss of two sets of mums and dads. But then, that's the natural way of things, isn't it? No parent should see their child go before them. It happens, of course, but it's a tragedy when it does. And then I lost Percy, of course, year before last.'

'You've been ever so kind to me, Mrs Baker. I shan't forget it.'

The old lady smiled warmly. 'It's the very least I could do, dear. I liked your Mum and Dad very much and I'll miss them. They were good people.' Her face brightened. 'Here, I've just had a thought. Your clothes. There's a box full of Percy's old stuff in the cupboard under the stairs. I meant to give them to the church jumble months ago, but you know how it is, you hang on and hang on. Having them there makes it feel like there's still part of him around. Daft really, isn't it?'

'Not at all,' Terence said. He placed his hand over hers and gave it a little squeeze. 'I imagine such things provide one with a modicum of solace.'

Mrs Baker nodded. 'They do. But if you wanted to try some of them on, you're more than welcome take anything that fits.'

Terence shuddered inside as he recalled some of the frightful garments he'd seen Percy Baker wearing in years gone by. 'That's a very magnanimous offer, but I'll be fine. I have plenty of clothes back at uni.' He finished his sandwich and helped himself to another.

'Just something to travel back in then. Some fresh undies maybe. You look about the same size as my Percy. I'm sure there are some Y-fronts in there that could be put to good use.'

Terence's almost choked on his sandwich. 'No, really, I'll be fine.'

'They're perfectly clean!' she added hastily, seeing the look of alarm on Terence's face. 'I put everything through a boil wash before I stored it away.'

'That's very kind, but no.'

'Well, the offer stands if you change your mind.' She reached for the teapot. 'Another cup?'

CHAPTER 20

'A little birdie tells me you missed out on the London beano.'

It was the Wednesday following the events at Seatown and Terence had been enjoying a spot of lunch in the uni dining room. He looked up from his plate of meatballs and spaghetti to see Lavis standing beside him with a lunch tray in his hands.

'Go away.'

They were the first words to have passed between them in months.

'Don't be like that, Hallam.' Lavis smirked. 'I just saw you sitting here on your own and thought I might join you for lunch. Have a little chat.'

Terence looked at him with disdain. 'You can't be serious!'

Demonstrating that clearly he was, Lavis hooked his foot around the leg of a nearby chair, dragged it over and sat down. Straightening his tray in front of him, he picked up a spoon and stirred his bowl of soup, peering at it doubtfully.

'This is supposed to be pea and ham. I think they could be had under the trades description act where the ham is concerned.'

Terence set down his knife and fork and looked at Lavis impatiently. 'What exactly do you *want*?'

Lavis broke off a piece of bread and dipped it in the dark green sludge. 'I was just wondering if that was right?'

'If *what* was right?'

'What I heard. The Westminster trip.' He popped the engorged piece of bread into his mouth.

'I'm not sure why a lowlife like you would even be interested in participating in something as edifying as a visit to the Houses of Parliament.'

Lavis tensed up. 'Lowlife, is it? You might talk a bit posh, Hallam, but what makes you think you're better than me?'

'Quite a number of things since you ask.'

Lavis appeared to relax again. 'Whatever. But just ask yourself who nabbed the last seat on the coach. I admit I'd forgotten all about it, but luckily Jo gave me the heads up that places were running low. It's going to be *so* bloody good.'

'I'm delighted for you,' Terence said sourly.

'Listen, Hallam. I know we haven't always seen eye to eye, but…'

'But what? There is no *but*, Lavis. You crawled into my life like some scurvy little cockroach, grabbing every opportunity to spite me. I thanked God that I'd seen the last of you the day we left Bagshott, but more fool me. You went and showed up here and it started all over again.'

Lavis nonchalantly spooned some soup into his mouth. 'Bit harsh. I seem to recall I extended an olive branch.'

'Oh, yes, that's right,' Terence said sarcastically. 'And you started reminiscing about the good old days when you used to torment me like it was all some sort of joke.'

'You should have lightened up a bit. I told you, it was only ever meant to be a bit of fun.'

Terence felt his blood rise. 'Your *fun* was my purgatory. You and your nasty little friends systematically persecuted me, and for *what*? I did nothing to you. *Nothing*! But still, you went out of your way to make my life a complete misery.'

'But we're adults now,' Lavis said, setting down his spoon. He smiled and held out his hand. 'I thought we might bury the hatchet. Let bygones be bygones and all that shit.'

Terence could hardly believe what he was hearing. He wouldn't have thought it was possible to despise this man more than he already did, but that moment proved him wrong.

He looked at Lavis's outstretched hand with disgust. 'There's nothing on God's earth that you can say to make amends for the hell you put me through. You're a vile bully. And, from what I'm given to understand, a deviant sexual predator.'

The smile dropped from Lavis's face. 'You what?'

Terence stood up and raised his eyebrows. 'Oh, I'm sorry, have I spoken out of turn? Touched a nerve? Well, I guess your friend Joanne can't be trusted to keep a confidence, can she?' He smiled thinly. 'You might want to have a word with her about that.'

Abruptly, Lavis jumped up out of his chair and grabbed Terence by the collar of his shirt. 'You're a toffee-nosed cunt, Hallam! You always were and you always will be.'

'Everything alright, lads?'

Neither of them had noticed Mr Abbott approach.

'Absolutely.' Lavis loosened his grip and made a show of straightening Terence's collar. 'Just a minor disagreement. Isn't that right, Hallam?'

Terence batted his hands away. 'Indeed.'

Abbott looked at them both suspiciously for a moment. 'Just make sure your remember that we resolve our disagreements with words, not fists. Do I make myself clear?'

Lavis and Terence both nodded.

'Very well.'

As Abbott walked off to get his lunch, Lavis leant in close to Terence.

'You might have lost a bit of weight, Hallam, but you're still the same pathetic mummy's boy you always were. And just for the record, you were right about Jo: nice tits, loose lips. I hear your cock is still like a baby's thumb.' Seeing the hurt in Terence's eyes, he grinned savagely and slapped him on the shoulder. 'See you round, mate.'

Leaving Terence struggling for words, Lavis picked up his tray and moved over to another table to finish his soup.

By the time he got back to his room, Terence was fuming. Why in God's name wouldn't Lavis just leave him the hell alone? The man had been a thorn in his side for so long now, it was difficult to remember a time when he *wasn't* there, skulking in the background, biding his time until the chance arose to chalk up another triumph in his relentless persecutory campaign. It felt as if the man was an envoy of some unearthly agency, sent to punish him for an unknown misdemeanour, slowly and irrevocably driving him to the brink of madness.

Well, Terence wasn't going to tolerate it any more.

He pulled out the bundles of banknotes that he'd purloined from his parents and counted out thirty pounds in fives and ones. Shoving them into his wallet, he set off to see Pinnock.

249

One of the young women he'd seen on his first visit answered the door. She was wearing a T-shirt and underwear and her hair was hanging in messy tangles. To Terence, she looked as if she'd only just crawled out of bed.

'Rob's sleeping,' she said lazily, confirming Terence's observation.

He scowled. 'In the middle of the day?!'

'What are you, his mother?'

'I need to see him urgently.'

The woman eyed him up and down. He was pasty-faced and sweating freely. 'You don't look so good, honey.'

'Neither do you.' Terence pulled out his wallet and extracted a one pound note. He lowered his voice. 'Be a good girl and go find me two dozen Benzodiazepine.' He held the money out in front of her face. She reached for it but Terence whipped it away. 'Uh-uh. *When* you get me the benzos.'

'Who is it, Sam?'

Looking past the woman, Terence saw Pinnock, dressed only in his pants, emerging from the bedroom.

He caught sight of Terence. 'Oh, it's you.' He grinned. 'I thought you'd deserted me.'

'I told you I'd be back.'

'Yeah, but I thought you meant straight away, not five days later. I hope you've brought enough cash with you this time.'

Terence raised his wallet.

'Hey, what about my pound?' the woman protested.

'For a service you didn't actually provide.'

'You sod!'

Pinnock chuckled. 'Just let him in, Sam.'

Samantha stepped aside to allow Terence to pass. He pushed the door shut behind him.

'You can't keep just showing up here when it suits you, man,' Pinnock said. 'I deal by appointment only.'

'Do you want my money or not?'

'That's not the point.'

'I assume you've heard the saying that the customer is always right?'

'Ah, so we're debating the niceties of bullshit customer-vendor protocol now, are we? In that case, I should point out that I, being said vendor, have the prerogative to adjust the price as I see fit. It just went up.' Pinnock saw a look of indignation appear on Terence's face. He shrugged. 'Supply and demand, mon brave.'

'So how much is it?'

'Two-fifty a dozen.'

Terence returned the one pound note to his wallet and withdrew two fives. He held them out.

251

Pinnock looked at the money greedily and his tongue flicked out across his lips. 'I'll sell you what you want today. But in future we do things my way.' He became aware that Samantha was slumped in an armchair listening to the conversation. 'Carrie must be getting cold in there on her own.' He cocked a thumb towards the bedroom. 'Make yourself scarce and go warm her up. I shan't be long.'

He waited while the girl strolled into the bedroom and when she closed the door he turned his attention back to Terence.

'Right. A dozen benzos then.'

'Two dozen.'

Pinnock laughed. 'You jest, man. They aren't smarties, you know.'

'Make it three. You get to keep the change and we'll have no more of this appointment only business.'

Pinnock thought for a moment. 'What appointment business is that?' He winked. 'Wait here.' He disappeared into the bedroom and returned a minute later with an envelope. 'Three dozen benzos for my new favourite customer. Use them wisely.'

'I intend to.' Terence relieved him of the envelope and tucked it into his trouser pocket.

Pinnock squinted at him. The Hallam standing before him was worlds apart from the one he'd sent packing a few days earlier. 'There's something different about you. You've changed.'

Terence handed over the cash and crossed to the door. 'A pleasure doing business with you.' He paused, his hand resting on the handle. 'Mon brave.'

It had just turned seven-thirty and The Knight's Horse was almost empty when Terence walked in. He spotted Chas and Danny huddled together at a table near the bar; they noticed him at the same moment and cheered.

'Here he is!' Chas exclaimed. 'Haven't seen you for days.' He stood up and held out a clenched fist. Terence bumped knuckles with him. 'Thought you'd deserted us.'

Terence's face dropped. 'Desert my friends? Not at all.' He hadn't berated a word to anyone about the death of his parents and he wasn't about to tell these idiots.

Chas roared with laughter and slapped Terence on the back. 'Pulling your plonker, chief. Drinks are on you.'

'Of course they are.'

Terence went to the bar and bought a round, then he joined them at the table.

'No Rich tonight?'

'Ponce got roped into doing some work for his Dad,' Danny said.

'What line of work would that be?'

'Fuck knows.' Chas grinned. 'But you can bet it's something dodgy if Jack Anderson's involved.' He took a mouthful from his pint of Skol and swallowed. 'So where have you been spending your nights?'

Terence sighed. 'Here and there.'

Danny picked up his glass. 'You look like you've got the weight of the world on your shoulders, mate. What's up?'

'This and that.'

'Here and there. This and that. You don't know your arse from your elbow, chief.' Chas chuckled. 'You on something?'

'Funny you should say that,' Terence said, pulling out the envelope Pinnock had given him. 'I've brought something for you fellows.'

Chas and Danny looked at each other and grinned. They both held out a hand and Terence handed over two pills to each of them.

'Sweet,' Danny muttered.

Terence spoke conspiratorially through the side of his mouth. 'There are plenty more where those came from.'

Chas guffawed. 'It's like Christmas fucking morning!'

Both men swallowed the pills and washed them down with their drinks.

'So come on then, chief. What gives?'

Terence made a show of appearing reticent to say. 'Oh, it's something and nothing really. Hardly worth mentioning.'

Chas slapped him on the shoulder. 'If there's something bothering *you*, chief, it bothers *us*. Ain't that right, Danno?'

Terence smiled inwardly. 'It's just this guy at uni who's been pestering me.'

'Shirt-lifter, is he?' Chas took a swig of his drink.

'You could put it that way. But I learned something about him recently that's been playing on my mind.'

Danny sniggered. 'Don't tell us he nicked your homework!'

Chas guffawed, spraying a mouthful of lager over the table and the two men bumped fists.

'It's no laughing matter,' Terence said sternly. 'As a matter of fact, it's rather disturbing.'

Chas set down his glass and leaned forward. 'Keep talking, chief.'

'He behaved inappropriately with a young boy.'

Danny frowned. 'What the fuck does *that* mean?'

A shadow passed over Chas's face. 'He's saying this twisted wanker fucked a kid!' He looked at Terence. 'That's right, isn't it?'

How typical that this gorilla should jump to the worst possible conclusion, Terence thought. It hadn't been his intention to gild the lily, but if Chas wanted to think that, why not let him? It could only serve to strengthen the man's hostility towards Lavis.

'I have reason to believe so, yes,' he lied.

'Dirty fucking cunt! Nonces make me puke!'

'Me too,' Danny chimed in. 'They should have their bollocks chopped off!'

'With a rusty cleaver!' Chas added.

Terence lied again: 'The thing is, he's going around bragging about it! He should be behind bars, but he behaves as if it's something to be proud of.' He was really starting to enjoy his little fabrication. 'You should have seen the self-satisfied smirk on his face when he recounted what he'd done. He seems to think he's above the law.'

Chas grimaced. 'Well he ain't above getting a fucking good smack from the Cobra.' He looked at Danny. 'What say we go give this fucker a hiding he'll never forget?'

Terence sat back and held up his hands. 'I couldn't possibly get involved in anything like that.' Not that his stooges noticed, but there was wiliness in his eyes now. 'I couldn't risk jeopardising my place at the university.'

256

Chas grinned. 'Then let us take care of it, chief. You just point him out to us and we'll give his bollocks such a sound kicking he'll be pissing blood for a month.'

'Are you sure?' Terence said, trying to sound uncertain, whilst simultaneously allowing himself an internal cheer of jubilation. 'I probably shouldn't have said anything.'

'Course you should.' Chas raised his glass. 'I guarantee that by the end of the evening there'll be one less cunty nonce walking the streets. Where do we find him?'

'He'll be where he usually is. He drinks at a pub where his...' – Terence choked on the word – '...*girlfriend* works the bar. He hasn't got any other friends.'

Chas grinned. 'Leave him to us.'

Hook, line and sinker, Terence thought. *Hook, line and sinker*.

'There's only one thing,' Danny said, emptying his glass.

Terence's heart skipped a beat. 'What's that?'

'Rich is gonna be so pissed off that he missed out.'

CHAPTER 21

None too subtly, Terence continued to sow the seeds of hatred for the rest of the evening. Chas and Danny were more than happy to let him foot the bar bill and when they staggered out of The Knight's Horse just before closing time, they were more than ready for a fight.

After only a couple of pints of cider, Terence himself had switched to orange juice and sodas; he intended to be sober for what was to come and he sustained the ensuing ribbing with a genial smile.

As they set off in the direction of The Rose and Crown, from the way the two skinheads were laughing and weaving about, he started to think he'd miscalculated the number of beverages required to keep them tightly wound up; after all, he'd pretty much had them in the palm of his hand at "inappropriate behaviour". Fortunately, by the time they reached their destination, Chas at least appeared to have calmed down a little and Terence was content that they would be fit enough to carry out the job.

As the door of the pub opened and a cluster of people came out laughing, the three of them took refuge in the shadows across the street.

Chas looked over at the sign hanging above the pub door and belched. 'That place is a fucking shithole. You sure this cunt drinks in there?'

'He has an acquaintance who works the bar here.'

'Not *another* fucking nonce!' Danny exclaimed.

'No. I told you, a young woman.'

Chas frowned. 'I thought you said this geezer was in to little boys!'

The truth of the matter was that Terence had no idea what the extent of Joanne and Lavis's relationship was. He had hoped against hope that it was nothing more than a platonic friendship, but the crude remark Lavis had made that afternoon had been like a punch in the gut, and the idea that they might be romantically involved pained him too much to dwell upon.

'I said girlfriend, but I think they're just mates,' he said.

'If she's mates with a nonce, she's just as bad as him.' Chas made a snorting noise and spat out a glob of muscus on the pavement.

Danny nodded. 'Agreed. We'll give them both a fucking good pasting.'

'Absolutely not!' Terence said angrily. 'You aren't to touch the girl.'

Chas gave him a filthy look. 'I thought you said you didn't want to be involved.'

'And I don't,' Terence said.

'Then why the fuck are you still here?'

'In case you'd forgotten, you haven't the first clue what Lavis looks like. I'm here to identify him.'

Danny frowned. 'Who's Lavis?'

Terence sighed. 'The man I've been telling you about all evening.'

Danny looked unsure, but he nodded. 'Ah, yeah, right.'

Chas grimaced. 'Well, just stop telling me what I can and can't do. And soon as you've pointed him out to us you'd better fuck off.'

As Terence had anticipated it might, the mood had suddenly become tense. Deciding to nip the air of hostility in the bud, he felt in his pocket for his wallet and pulled out a few notes. 'This here says you don't lay a finger on the girl.'

'You got a hard on for this bitch or something?' Chas sneered.

'Whether I have or I haven't is no concern of yours. She is *not* to be harmed. Do we have an accord?'

Chas snatched the money out of Terence's hand and greedily counted it. 'Seven quid?' There was a touch of scorn in his tone.

'There's another two pounds for each of you, but only on the proviso you leave the girl out of it.'

The affability returned to Chas's face. 'Whatever you say, chief.' He handed two pounds to Danny. 'It's your party.'

Seemingly unconcerned by the inequality of the financial split, Danny shoved the notes into his back pocket.

Terence's plan had been to guide the two men to Lavis and leave them to it. But now he wasn't sure he trusted them not to drag Joanne into it. He would have to accompany them, at least until he was satisfied Joanne was safe.

'Assuming they leave together,' he said, 'and I suspect they will, we'll follow them back to the campus. After Lavis drops her off, that's when you take him.'

Chas nodded. 'Like I said, it's your party, chief.'

They didn't have long to wait. At spot on eleven-thirty, the lights inside the pub winked out and Lavis and Joanne stepped out onto the pavement.

'See you Friday,' she called out and a voice responded indistinctly from inside.

Terence ushered Chas and Danny further back into the shadows, and they watched in silence as she linked her arm through Lavis's and together they strolled off up the street.

'Being spotted isn't an option,' Terence whispered. 'We stay *well* back. Understood?'

261

Neither of the skinheads looked too happy at being ordered around, but for now they both nodded compliantly.

'Okay, let's go,' Terence said quietly.

To give himself the best vantage point of remaining unseen should Joanne or Lavis look back, he positioned himself behind the two men and they set off. They managed to maintain a safe distance and went unnoticed until, as they neared the campus, their quarry stopped to cross the road.

Lavis turned to look back the way they'd come and his gaze lingered for just a second too long; for one heart-stopping moment, Terence was convinced they'd all been spotted. But then Joanne said something – they were too far away for Terence to hear what – and Lavis burst out laughing. He gave Joanne a jovial shove and they crossed over and walked through the gates into the grounds of the university.

'You can't risk being seen on the campus,' Terence whispered. 'Wait here.'

The two men looked at each other uncertainly.

'Where the fuck are you going?' Chas said suspiciously.

'I need to see something.'

'How can you be sure that cunt is coming back?' Chas said. 'I say we've left it too late. We should have jumped both the fuckers soon as they left the pub.'

'Lavis doesn't room here,' Terence muttered irritably. 'He's just seeing his friend back to her room. There's an alleyway over there...' – he pointed across the street – '...he'll go down there to get back to his lodgings. Now *please*, just wait here. I'll be right back.'

Without giving either of them a chance to argue, Terence ran swiftly up the pavement and across the open ground towards the dormitory block. Confident he couldn't be seen in the darkness, he ducked down behind a bush about twenty yards away from the doors.

As he stared bitterly at Lavis and Joanne kissing goodnight, a little piece of him died inside. When he saw her hand drop down and squeeze his crotch, he couldn't stand it any more. Tears brimming in his eyes, he turned and crept away.

'So are we doing this or aren't we?' Chas said impatiently as Terence approached them.

'One hundred percent. And I want to watch.' Terence handed each of them two five pound notes. 'Just make sure he doesn't get up again. If you've an ounce of doubt, keep thinking about what he did to that poor, innocent little kid.'

Chas grinned. 'Don't you worry your little head about that, chief.' He tucked away the money. 'Far as we're concerned, the only good nonce is a dead nonce.'

'He'll be coming back this way any minute. Go and wait for him in the cut and be sure you keep quiet. I'll follow him in.'

'Right you are.'

Chas grabbed Danny's arm and they scuttled across the road. No sooner had they disappeared into the darkness of the alleyway than Terence heard the sound of whistling and Lavis came out through the campus gates. But then, much to his dismay, he didn't cross over to the alley. Instead, he turned left and sauntered off in the opposite direction.

Where the *hell* was he going? Before he even had time to think, Terence heard himself calling out: 'Lavis! Wait!'

The man stopped and turned round. He squinted at the sight of Terence hurrying towards him. 'Hallam?'

Terence caught up with him. 'I thought it was you,' he puffed.

'What are you doing here this time of night?'

'Oh, just out walking. I got a bit bogged down with my dissertation. Needed time to think.'

'On your own?'

'Yes, I told you, I wanted to clear my head.'

Clearly not convinced, Lavis looked up and down the road distrustfully. 'And you just happened to be passing Jo's dorm block.'

Terence let the question slide. 'I'm actually quite pleased to see you,' he continued. His mind was racing. 'I felt I needed to apologise for the way our little téte-a-téte broke down this afternoon.'

Lavis looked at him with amusement. 'Is that so?'

'Yes. I was in the wrong. You were trying to patch things up between us and I was being a bit of an arse.' He rolled his eyes. 'As usual.'

Lavis didn't smile. 'More like a cunt actually.'

Terence winced internally, but he nodded. 'Yes, that too. Anyway, listen, I'm sorry.'

'Okay.' Lavis still didn't sound convinced. 'Apology accepted.'

'Listen, what do you say I make it up to you? We could go and get something to drink. Have a proper chat. You know, like you said, bury the hatchet.'

Lavis shook his head. 'Pubs are closed.' He started to walk away.

'I know somewhere we can get something.' It was a bare-faced lie and a poor one at that, but thinking on the hop had never been Terence's strong point.

Lavis hesitated and looked back. 'Yeah?'

'Yes. Friend of mine. He keeps an open house.'

Lavis clearly wasn't buying it. 'Nah, not tonight. I'm tired.'

'Oh, come on, Gray.' Calling Lavis by his Christian name was almost a pleasantry too far and it stuck in

265

Terence's throat. But despair was setting in. 'Come on, what have you got to lose?' He was praying he didn't look as desperate as he sounded. 'It's just down there.' He pointed to the alleyway. 'Two minutes walk.'

Lavis appeared to be considering it. 'Two minutes, eh?'

'That's correct. I promise you we'll end the evening the best of friends.'

'I doubt that.'

Terence chuckled. 'Well, in the very least you'll have had a few free beers.'

'Yeah. Yeah okay.'

Got you, you bastard!

'But let's not go that way.'

Terence felt his stomach tighten. 'Why?'

'Because it backs a row of houses and there's a bloody big dog lives at the one at the end. Barks for England.'

Terence had to bite his lip not to laugh. 'You're not telling me you're scared of a dog?'

'Yeah. I mean no. He's just loud, that's all. Plus other people let their dogs shit down there too. I walked through a turd the size of your head the other night and ruined my best trainers. We'll take the street out and round.'

'It adds a good ten minutes if we walk round. Come on. There's safety in numbers. We'll be quiet as mice.'

Lavis reluctantly conceded and they made their way back to the alley. No sooner were they out of the sight of the street than Terence stopped in his tracks.

'Actually, Lavis, there was one other thing I wanted to say to you.'

The man turned back to look at him. 'Can't it just wait 'til we get there, Hallam?'

'No.'

As his eyes adjusted to the darkness, Lavis saw Terence staring at him defiantly. He suddenly felt uncomfortable. 'Just spit it out then.'

'Rot in hell,' Terence said quietly.

Nothing had been said beforehand, but almost as if those three words had been a pre-arranged cue, Chas and Danny emerged from behind some dustbins a few yards ahead.

'Oi. Nonce!'

Startled, Lavis spun round to see who had spoken. Glimpsing Chas and Danny advancing on him, he looked back at Terence with confusion on his face. But then he saw Terence's expression and the confusion vanished as, in that moment, he realised he'd been duped.

Before he could react, Chas and Danny were upon him.

Eyes wide and panting with excitement, Terence took a few paces back and watched as Danny wrestled

Lavis into a headlock. He was holding him so tightly that he was struggling to breathe.

'Who are you?' Lavis managed to gasp.

That was when Chas set about him. He landed a punch below the ribs and Lavis grunted with pain. 'Your worst nightmare, you fucker. We hear you like shagging little boys.'

'*What*?! That's not true!' Lavis spluttered.

'A filthy nonce *and* a liar.' Chas punched him again – twice.

Groaning, Lavis tried to squirm free of Danny's arm, but the skinhead had too strong a hold on him. 'I've done nothing I tell you!' he gasped. 'You've made a mistake.'

'It's you who made the mistake, sunshine. You think you can ponce around here happy as Larry after what you done to that kid?' Chas booted Lavis's right kneecap and he let out a cry as his leg gave out beneath him.

Danny supported the weight effortlessly.

Although Terence was standing several yards back, Lavis locked eyes with him. 'Please, Hallam!' he cried out hopelessly. 'Tell them!' But even as the words came out, he knew he was wasting his breath.

Terence's heart was beating so hard, he wondered how he hadn't passed out. *That's right, go on, Beg!*, he

268

thought. *Beg me to save your pathetic little life.* There was spittle on his lips and he feverishly licked it away.

Danny's mouth was right alongside Lavis's ear. 'Shut your hole, you worthless fucking piece of shit,' he whispered, then sunk his teeth into the lobe and bit it off. Lavis let out a high-pitched squeal and somewhere off down the alley, a dog started barking.

'Quickly!' Terence cried. 'Get it done before someone comes!'

Danny spat out the remnant of Lavis's ear and grinned. There was blood on his mouth.

Chas scrabbled at his back pocket and withdrew a knife. He glanced back at Terence as if he was seeking permission.

Terence's eyes flashed with anticipation. 'Do it!' he hissed. At the same moment, he felt his loins stir and a wave of pleasure engulfed him. It was so intense that he had to put a hand against the wall to steady himself.

'Nighty-night, you cunt,' Chas snarled and Terence watched wide-eyed as he drove the blade up into Lavis's crotch and twisted it hard.

Lavis's face contorted and his mouth yawned wide, but no sound came out.

Terence could hardly believe what he was seeing and feeling. There was no shame, just a glorious tingling sensation coursing through his entire body. And, as Danny released his grip and Lavis crumpled to the ground, Terence surrendered himself to the moment of all-consuming sense of euphoria.

'Come on, chief, we need to go!'

Terence opened his eyes and blinked. He felt as if he were waking from a beautiful dream. He could hear a dog barking in the distance and a man's voice angrily shouting at it to be quiet.

Chas was tugging frantically at his arm. 'What the fuck's the matter with you? Come on, we've gotta get out of here now.'

Terence looked down and saw Lavis's body splayed out on the ground. His wits flared and the reality of where he was and what had just happened cascaded through his head like a tsunami.

'You're on your own then.' Chas let go of his arm and started to run. Danny was right behind him.

His heart racing, Terence turned around and took off in the opposite direction.

CHAPTER 22

There's a saying that a killer always returns to the scene of the crime. Terence had always considered it a contrivance adopted by the writers of fiction; a cliché for an investigating detective inspector to sagaciously mutter to his sidekick. The very idea of it being a truth was risible. After all, what murderer in his or her right mind would unnecessarily revisit the spot upon which they'd stolen a life? Simply being seen in the vicinity would be taking a risk that no reasoning could justify. All the same, the following morning, the compulsion to take a walk past the alleyway and bear witness to the tumult surrounding the inevitable discovery of Lavis's corpse was too powerful to ignore. And maybe, Terence thought, it might generate a little more of that delectable feeling of elation into the bargain.

Initially, the sight of no less than four police cars parked out on the road opposite the campus gates needled him irrationally; the death of his parents had warranted just one, whilst a worthless speck of excrement like Lavis appeared to have attracted half the Warwick constabulary! He consoled himself with the thinking that his parents' demise had been admirably staged as a terrible accident, whereas cold-blooded murder on a university campus was no trifling matter.

He smiled to himself contentedly as he recalled the last glimpse he'd had of Lavis before fleeing the scene.

He wondered how quickly the body had been discovered, and by whom. He thought about the man with the barking dog. If it hadn't been him, maybe someone else walking a dog. He remembered Lavis grumbling about his shoes and had to stop himself sniggering; if only he had known that a soiled trainer was the least of his worries. No, Terence thought, it was more likely to have been the first passer-through of the morning, which would probably make it one of the students with off-campus digs heading to an early class.

There were a lot of youngsters standing around in little groups, all looking inquisitively towards the alley and talking in muted tones. There were one or two faces among them that Terence recognised, but, deciding it wouldn't be prudent to linger and draw unnecessary attention to his presence, he strolled past without acknowledging them.

Nevertheless, when he reached the end of the alley – now cordoned off with blue and white police tape fluttering gently in the breeze – he couldn't resist pausing to speak to a woman with a dog who was standing observing the activity.

The dog was a little poodle and its likeness to Harvey was uncanny.

'Is it alright if I stroke him?' Terence asked.

The woman smiled. '*He* is a she. But that's fine, she's friendly.'

Terence squatted and ran his hand through the soft curls on the dog's head. Its tail started wagging and it licked his hand. 'Lovely little thing. What's her name?'

'Penelope.'

Ruffling the little dog's head again, Terence stood up. 'I had a poodle when I was a boy.' He gestured to the alleyway and, endeavouring to sound only casually interested, said, 'Any idea what's going on?'

'One of the students over there said somebody has been shot.'

'Shot?!' Terence almost exploded with laughter. Struggling to maintain a straight face, he said, 'That's awful! Did they say who the victim was?'

The woman shook her head.

A man standing close by had overheard what she'd said and spoke up. 'I heard someone say it was a strangling.'

The woman looked at the man haughtily. 'Shot is what I heard.' She pointed towards two students who were standing nearby talking. 'Ask them over there.'

How utterly delicious misinformation and tittle-tattle can be, Terence thought.

Deciding to leave them to it, he slipped away. He was disappointed that the feeling of the excitement he'd experienced watching Lavis die had failed to

273

rematerialise, and for a moment he considered following the road round to the far end of the alley to see if there was any activity there worth feeding on. But then he thought better of it. Best not to chance his arm and get noticed showing undue interest. He was satisfied enough knowing that Lavis was gone.

Suddenly he felt hungry. A visit to the uni dining room for some breakfast might pay dividends; there was sure to be a bit of buzz with regard to the discovery of a dead body worth tuning in to there.

As soon as he walked in, Terence caught sight of Joanne at a table near the window. Sitting with her was another girl; Pauline, was it? Or Patricia? Terence was sure it was something beginning with a P. She was one of Joanne's extensive circle of friends and he had spoken to her once or twice, but now he wouldn't have been able to state her name with any certainty if his life depended on it.

Paying for a coffee and a round of buttered toast, and making sure that Joanne didn't notice him approaching, he edged his way over to the vacant table adjacent to hers and sat down within earshot with his back to her. He needn't have worried; Joanne was completely wrapt in conversation with her friend.

It immediately became apparent to Terence that she knew Lavis was dead.

'I just can't believe it, Terri.'

That's it!, Terence thought. *Teresa. Not something beginning with P at all.*

Teresa slipped a comforting arm around Joanne's shoulders. 'I can't either, sweetie. It's dreadful.'

'The thing is, Gray wanted to come up when he dropped me off last night. If I'd just said yes, it might never have happened.'

Teresa gave her shoulder a squeeze. 'You couldn't have known. You mustn't blame yourself.'

Joanne blew her nose on a scrap of tissue. 'I know I shouldn't. But I feel far worse about what I've been thinking.'

Terence's ears pricked up. *What have you been thinking?*

Teresa echoed his thoughts. 'What have you been thinking?'

'Karma.'

Teresa frowned and removed her arm from her friend's shoulders. 'I don't understand.'

Joanne lowered her voice and Terence had to strain to hear what she was saying. 'Between you and me,' she said quietly, 'I can't help thinking it was only a matter of time.'

'What do you mean?'

'If I tell you, you must promise to keep it to yourself.'

275

'Of course.' Teresa drew the sign of a cross on her chest.

'Gray was a paedo.'

'*What?!*' Teresa looked dumbfounded.

'Yeah. He was accused of messing around with some kid at Leicester uni. That's why he transferred here.'

'You're *kidding* me!'

Joanne shook her head. 'No. I mean, yes, he was accused. But he swore to me it was all a big misunderstanding.'

'And you believed him? You're not making sense. How could you be friends with a creep like that? Did he do it or didn't he?'

'I *thought* he was telling me the truth and I honestly wanted to believe him. But I've always had these niggling little doubts. And now I can't help wondering if he really did do it.'

The expression on Teresa's face was one of incredulity. 'And you think somebody attacked him because of what he did?'

'I don't know. The policeman I spoke to was a bit evasive when it came to details, but he did say Gray had been stabbed in the groin. It crossed my mind what an apt way that would be to get revenge on a paedo.'

So, Terence thought, *you've already come forward and given the police your story.*

276

'Wow!' Teresa exclaimed. 'That's some depraved shit.'

'It is. But there's something worse than that and I feel terrible about it.'

'Worse?'

'I can't help thinking that if it *was* karma, he deserved it.' Joanne looked her friend in the face. 'Does that make me a bad person?'

Too damned right it does, you traitorous, Janus-faced bitch!, Terence thought. *And to think I was going to ask you to marry me!*

'Absolutely not, sweetie!' Teresa stroked Joanne's arm. 'He was a disgusting perv and you're better off without him in your life.'

'Yeah?' Joanne blew her nose again.

'Yeah.'

Terence had heard enough. Leaving his coffee and toast untouched, he stood up and stepped over to Joanne's table.

'Excuse me.'

The two women looked up. Joanne's face radiated surprise. 'Terry!'

Terence locked eyes with her. 'I'd just like to say you're the most deceitful and all round malicious person it's ever been my misfortune to meet. Lavis was an evil bully, but at least he was straight up about it and I knew where I stood with him. You, though, you're a

277

real piece of work. You're beyond contempt. I'm almost sorry that Lavis is dead.' Terence congratulated himself on the little tremor he imbued those final words with. A subtle disassociation with Lavis's murder could only be beneficial.

There was shock on Joanne's face. 'Gray's *dead*?!'

Terence's heart leapt into his throat. 'Isn't he?!'

'I don't know! *You* just said he was!'

Terence suddenly realised how foolish his impetuous decision to confront Joanne had been. 'I thought…' he started. 'What I mean is…'

'I knew he'd been stabbed and lost a lot of blood. But he was alive when they took him to hospital!'

CHAPTER 23

The far-reaching effects of his split with Joanne continued to eat away at Terence's soul. If he spent any time thinking about it, it became ever more obvious that the day he'd seen her cheating on him with Harrington had been a turning point in his life. However indirectly, so many significant events since then could be traced back to that morning. His parents' death; his ungraded thesis; his growing dependence on pills and alcohol; his alliance with dangerous individuals whose mad dog moral values had led to the removal of the canker that had been Graham Lavis. None of these things would have been cause to celebrate for the old Terence Hallam. But what he'd once been was now long gone, in his place a stronger, shrewder, more confident man, albeit one with questionable moral values of his own.

There are those who would suggest that the cost involved in cultivating this new individual was indefensible. For Terence, however, they had all been necessary casualties in his emergence from his shell.

The only frightening dent in his new-found confidence was the seed of doubt that had been planted by Joanne's assertion that Lavis was still alive. In the days that followed, it transpired that she had been right:

the owner of one of the properties backing the alleyway had been woken just before midnight by a courting couple who had stumbled upon Lavis's body on their way home from the movies, and an ambulance and police were on site twenty minutes later. Although Lavis had been alive when he was admitted to the emergency unit at Warwick Hospital, he died eleven hours later without ever having regained conciousness.

Warwick University went into mourning, while Terence went out and celebrated. On the day of the funeral, all lectures were cancelled. Terence had briefly considered attending the burial, purely for the thrill of seeing his archenemy lowered into the ground, but, at the last moment, he'd decided against it. He later learned that he wasn't the only absentee of note; it didn't really surprise him, but Joanne hadn't bothered to show up.

Meanwhile, the murder investigation that had been ongoing came to an abrupt dead end, and the police had resorted to appearing on television, appealing for witnesses. None came forward.

There was one other funeral that Terence did attend: Arthur and Emily's. He fretted beforehand that he would struggle to summon a convincing enough level of grief, but when the day arrived, genuine tears fell from his eyes. Thinking on it afterwards, he put it down to an outpouring of relief that the stress of the arrangements were over, for he certainly wasn't lamenting their loss.

Two weeks later, a letter came in the post from Arthur's solicitor, Duncan Meyer.

The man had been a personal friend of Arthur's and, on the occasions that he would come for lunch, he would always bring a bag of liquorice allsorts with him to bestow upon Terence; as a child, Terence had liked his "Uncle Dunc" a great deal.

He had been eagerly anticipating the arrival of the letter, which would furnish him with the details of his parents' last will and testament. Their entire fortune, including the house – Terence ground his teeth, but consoled himself that there would at least be the insurance payout to look forward to – had been bequeathed to him. Just the same, things were not quite as straight forward as he had been expecting.

The documentation made it clear that, should Arthur and Emily pass away before Terence graduated with his degree, all monies were to be held in trust and would be released to him upon that date. Of greater concern were the conditions that had been put in place should he fail to graduate: the money would still *ultimately* be his, but essentially he would have to find gainful employment under his own steam, with no handout until he reached his 30th birthday. Arthur, knowing in his heart that

281

Terence would never follow in his shoes, had made provision, that in the event of his death his fifty-one percent of Hallam Toys should be made available for purchase by his partner, Paul Crawford; the man had jumped at the opportunity. The substantial proceeds of the sale were added to Terence's inheritence pot.

Most distressing of all, however, there had been no consideration given to his tuition fees; it was an evident oversight, but one that would soon impact him massively.

Anyone normal would have taken all this on board as incentive to knuckle down and obtain the requisite qualification. But, rather than it giving him the motivation to succeed, Terence found himself plummeting into a downward spiral of drink and drugs. The amount of money he'd stolen from the house wasn't insubstantial, but neither was it finite. He pawned whatever he could to keep it topped up – the antique silver blotter was one of the first things to go – but it was tantamount to arranging deckchairs on the Titanic.

His visits to Pinnock had become increasingly more frequent and he'd started spending more and more of his time in the company of Chas, Rich and Danny. Most of that was passed drinking in The Knight's Horse, the upshot of which being that it wasn't long before the money dwindled away to almost nothing.

Occasionally, Terence would accompany his dubious acquaintances on one of their hate-generated sprees. It gave him a thrill to watch voyeuristically from the sidelines as they rained down their alcohol-fuelled venom upon some unsuspecting innocent, but nothing he witnessed managed to engender quite the level of ecstasy as Lavis's murder had. He craved to feel it again and, after each of these nights on the street, he would return to his room and quietly relish the memory of Lavis's dying moments. It brought him negligible but temporary pleasure.

And so, as the days became weeks and the weeks became months, before Terence knew it he was half way through his final year at Warwick.

With the realisation that he would soon be in dire financial straits, Terence bit the bullet and sought out part-time employment. The job in the offices of a stationery supplies company – two hours a day, from eight until ten every morning – suited him well; he seldom had a lecture to attend now before ten-thirty, and if he did, he skipped it. However, his first experience of the working environment wasn't a happy one and it didn't last long. His immediate superior was a short-tempered shrew named Vera Pryce and she was always pulling him up on what she perceived to be his inadequacies. Terence had no problem with that per se,

283

in fact he rather admired the woman. She had a no-nonsense code that he aspired to himself. No, it was the relentless round of tea-making and filing that wore him down. He started to become a no-show, and on those days when he did deign to turn up, he would often still be suffering the after-effects of a night on the sauce. Eventually, Ms Pryce handed him an ultimatum: smarten up his ideas or she'd sack him. Terence didn't wait around to be fired.

Leaving turned out to be a timely move. He managed to secure a similar position with a finance company in the heart of Warwick. Harper & Vigo furnished him with like-for-like hours and fifty percent more pay.

Terence had only been with them for a few weeks, when his attention was drawn to the availability of a full time probationary position at their Birmingham office. After much consideration, and given the fact he'd had it up to the back teeth with uni, he decided to draw a veil over the notion of getting a degree. He knew in his heart he would fail, so why prolong the agony? It rankled him that a consequence of dropping out meant his inheritance would be beyond his reach for eight years, but he had unexpectedly discovered that working life agreed with him, and the pleasure of taking home money he'd earned through hard graft gave him a sense of self-worth he'd never felt before.

He spoke at length with his tutor, Mr Abbott, who tried to convince him to change his mind – after all, despite the fact he was struggling, why would he throw away four years' hard work? – but Terence remained steadfast.

His withdrawal from Warwick uni came at a cost. He was instructed to vacate his room immediately. The daunting prospect of having to seek new lodgings was obviated when Rich and Danny offered him a bed at their flat. Without giving the pros and cons a second thought, Terence accepted. That was a mistake.

The block of flats where the two skinheads resided was an insalubrious hellhole. The walls were daubed with graffiti, the corridors stank of urine and faeces, and many of the safety barriers on the exterior walkways had fallen into disrepair. But the bed was rent free and, for a while at least, Terence was willing to endure it.

At Harper & Vigo in Birmingham, Terence felt as if he'd found his vocation. It meant a daily commute, and part of his initial remit still comprised the hum-drum routine of filing and making the coffee. But there was one man working there, Donald Phillips, who took Terence under his wing and nurtured him. He had acute business acumen and, nearing retirement, he saw in Terence something of his younger self.

Terence had been rather surprised to find that another young man started in the Birmingham office at the same time as himself: Johnny Berman. It was made clear to both of them on their first day that they would be vying for one position and, at the end of three months, one of them would be let go. Terence had every intention of being the surviving candidate.

He began to ease off on his drinking and curtailed what had become an untenable reliance on depressants; he anticipated having a struggle on his hands with withdrawal symptoms, but he discovered in himself a level of willpower he never knew he had, and he all but kicked the habit overnight. He handed the remainder of his stash of Benzodiazepine to Chas, who practically bit his hand off.

One morning, Donald Phillips called Terence into his office. 'Can I have a word, son?' He looked inordinately tired.

'Of course, sir.'

'I've told you before, don't call me sir. Only my dentist and the milkman call me sir. It's Don, okay?' He smiled. 'Close the door and take a pew.'

'Okay.' Terence sat down.

'As you know, I'll be retiring at the end of the week. I'll no doubt have to endure the requisite gather-around, slap on the back, 'here's a carriage clock for your trouble' sort of nonsense. But I don't like fuss and I won't be making any speeches.'

Terence wasn't sure where this was going. 'I'll be sorry to see you go.' He liked the man and he meant it.

'I just wanted to take a moment now to say to you personally what a pleasure it's been having you around these past few weeks.'

'Thank you, sir.'

Phillips raised an eyebrow.

Terence corrected himself. 'Sorry. Don.'

'We've had a lot of nippers come and go at H&V. I was one of them, except of course I came and didn't go.' A wistful expression appeared on his face. 'I started here forty-two years ago. A bloody lifetime.' He cleared his throat. 'Anyway, the thing is, I see potential in you, young Terence. Great potential. You probably haven't realised it yourself yet, but you can trust me when I tell you that I know potential when I see it. Keep your head down and work hard and you have all the hallmarks of a success story in the making.'

Nobody had ever spoken to Terence so encouragingly before, not his tutor at university, not even his own father. He nodded. 'I'll do my best.'

'Just remember two things as you travel through this great cesspool they call life. All's fair in love and finance, and there's no shame in taking a hard-nosed approach to achieve your aims. No one will thank you for shafting them, but fuck 'em. Nobody comes into this business to win friends.'

'I'm not sure I follow.'

'I'm just saying that stacking the odds in your favour is paramount, and it's okay if the methods you use to attain what you want aren't entirely ethical. You'll encounter a lot of shit-eaters in life. Some of them will be insignificant and not worth worrying about. But – and trust me on this – there will be others who'll see you as an obstacle in their own narrative. They'll want what you've got and they'll stoop as low as low gets to take it from you. You need to be able to discern the worthless shit-eaters from the dangerous ones. Take your little mate Berman.'

'He's not my mate,' Terence interjected.

'But you rub along well enough. And there's no reason you shouldn't, he's a likeable kind of guy. But be sure you don't lose sight of the fact that two weeks from now one of you will be gone. I've seen Berman's sort before. He's a snivelling little toady and come judgement day, he's going to want this job. You just have to want it more. As I say, your MO doesn't matter, you just need to do whatever it takes to keep the odds stacked in your favour. *Now* do you follow?'

Terence nodded. 'I think so, yes.'

'Good. Thus endeth the lesson for today.'

'You said I need to remember *two* things.'

288

'I did. The other is never let the bastards grind you down.'

Terence smiled. 'That I *do* understand.'

'Good lad. Now, how about a coffee?'

'Absolutely, Don. The usual? Black, no sugar?'

Donald Phillips never made it to his retirement gathering that Friday. The same day that he spoke with Terence, he went home, put a shotgun in his mouth and blew his brains out.

A few days later Terence heard he had been recently diagnosed with stage four cancer and had only weeks to live.

Harper & Vigo operated two offices. The one in Birmingham, where Terence was now situated, was the dominion of Sidney Vigo. The other in Warwick, where he had started out, was overseen by Sherman Harper.

Vigo had a secretary, Denise Randall. She always wore her mousey brown hair pinned back in a tight bun, which gave her a very prim and proper air. But whenever she had cause to speak with Terence, she would turn into an incorrigible flirt. She didn't speak to anybody else that way, or not as far as he was aware, and it became increasingly apparent that she had a soft spot for him. She would seldom pass up the opportunity to make a suggestive remark. Whenever Terence took her a cup of tea, she would chuckle and with tiresome inevitability say, 'Don't put any sugar in yours, my lovely, you're sweet enough already.' And then, equally predictably, whinny at her own wit. Once, when she noticed Terence yawning, she thrust out her chest and said, 'I've got plenty here to keep your mind off sleep.'

Terence began to foster a deep dislike for her. Firstly, he estimated her to be somewhere in her mid-fifties and therefore, in his opinion, far too old to be making eyes at someone as young as him. His experience with Joanne had been sufficient to put him off women for life, and the fact Denise was married – he had noticed she wore a plain gold band on her ring finger, so the assumption was reasonable enough – only compounded the untrustworthy nature of the female of the species in his eyes.

One day, she made a lewd remark that the size of a man's feet were widely said to be a guide to the size of his manhood, observing with a wink that Terence's feet must be 'size elevens at least!'. At that point, he'd had enough. He was contemplating whether to report her for misconduct, but then something happened that gave him pause for thought. She was usually careful to make sure nobody else was in earshot when she was in top flirt mode, but this time Berman overheard.

He sidled up to Terence. 'She's wet for you, mate.'

'I beg your pardon?'

'You play your cards right, you could be drinking from the furry cup.' He stuck out his tongue and waggled it rapidly up and down.

Terence scowled. 'Don't be so disgusting.'

Berman laughed. 'No, really mate, I've seen how she looks at you.'

'I have no idea what you're talking about,' Terence said tersely. 'I've more important things on my mind than loose trollops. Besides which, she could do far worse than to learn a little decorum.'

'*Seriously* mate?'

'Seriously.'

Berman gave him a funny look. 'You're looking a gift horse in the mouth. Even if you wouldn't, I would.'

Terence tapped his fingers on the ledger laying on the desk in front of him. 'If you'll excuse me, I've been asked to check through some figures.'

'Guess I'll have to have your share.' With that, Berman sloped off.

Fat chance, Terence thought. But the man's parting shot started to play on his mind and he recalled Donald Phillips's words to him: *'Do whatever it takes to keep the odds stacked in your favour.'*

It occurred to Terence that, with Phillips gone and less than two weeks of the probationary period

291

remaining, having somebody batting for him – especially somebody as close to one of the bosses as Denise was – might prove expedient. She had often mooted how nice it would be if they could go out for an after-work drink. When, the next day, she coincidentally raised the subject again, he agreed.

He spent a miserable evening watching her get drunk and listening to her bemoan her barren sex life. She told him that her husband, Neville – who she irritatingly insisted on referring to as "Nevvy" – was some sort of telecommunications executive and was away on overseas business trips more often than he was at home. She frankly and unashamedly also revealed that she had a high sex drive and 'the gears aren't being oiled, my lovely.'; Terence winced internally.

It was tipping with rain when they left the bar and, when she offered Terence a lift home, alarm bells went off. And not only because she was seriously over the limit. Against his better judgement, he went along, and when she suggested they stop by her house for a nightcap, what choice did he have?

They ended up sleeping together that night and it was even more unpleasant than Terence had anticipated; Denise's personal hygiene left a lot to be desired. Additionally, she was a smoker and when she kissed him he almost gagged at the stench of halitosis, and she drooled into his mouth. Nevertheless, the self-sacrifice ultimately paid off.

As they lay in the dark afterwards, completely out of the blue, she said, 'That was wonderful.' She lit a cigarette. 'I'm going to have a word with Sid tomorrow and make sure the office junior job is a one-horse race.'

She was as good as her word and, to ensure she didn't have a change of heart, Terence gritted his teeth and endured the humiliation of Denise's slobbering love-making on three more occasions over the next ten days.

As soon as it was announced that he was H&V's new permanent office junior, he enhanced his jubilation at watching Berman clear his desk by paying a visit to the personnel office, where he filed a complaint over unwanted sexual harrassment in the workplace.

It transpired that Terence hadn't been Denise's first office paramour; she had been served with two previous disciplinaries. Implementing the three strikes and you're out rule, she was summarily dismissed.

CHAPTER 24

It wasn't long before Terence's life began to change. The evenings spent out with Rich, Danny and Chas became less frequent and he grabbed every opportunity he could to spend time away from the flat. Going out with his work colleagues became his new social life and he felt a lot more comfortable associating with them; he soon came to realise that it was in those circles that he truly belonged. There was no doubting his ulterior motive was to mingle and make contacts that would ultimately benefit him, but he also craved the intelligent conversation that was patently absent when he spent any time with the trio of dysfunctional skinheads. There were regular after-work meet-ups for drinks with his colleagues and, as time moved on, some of H&V's client base too. He was even getting invited along to the occasional dinner party, and enjoyed one particularly memorable evening at a soiree to celebrate Sherman Harper's birthday.

This change in lifestyle didn't go unnoticed by Rich and Danny. They were rarely present at the flat when Terence arrived home though and, if his increasing absence from The Knight's Horse was ever mentioned, he would blame long days at work as his reason for refraining to join them.

He had been grateful for the room they had offered him; it benefited him at a time when he really needed it. And, by way of a small repayment, he didn't mind treating his hosts to a four-pack of lager from time to time, or occasionally feeding the electricity meter when the money ran out and the flat was plunged into darkness.

But the arrangement wasn't without its pitfalls. The worst of these was the fact that, since none of the skinheads were employed, they had no cause to go to bed at a reasonable hour. Chas lived in an adjacent tower block with two other men, but spent more time at Rich and Danny's flat than he did his own. It wasn't an infrequent occurrence for the three of them to return late from a night at the pub with a few motley friends in tow, whereupon they would resume drinking, continue talking loudly and play music into the early hours.

Getting only two or three hours sleep every night was beginning to take its toll on Terence, and coasting through the working day on fumes was becoming increasingly unsustainable. He was earning good money – more than enough to rent his own place – and it had already occurred to him that the insalubrious environs of the misleadingly-named Juniper Heights was no place for an up and coming, career-minded young man such as himself to be living.

Yet before he had a chance to make a move, things came to a head when he fumbled an assignment at work and lost a potential client. The man concerned, Jake McFarlane, was harshly confrontational, berating Terence by telling him that he had no confidence in either him or, by virtue of association, 'the Mickey Mouse outfit you work for'. Then he took his business elsewhere.

Sid Vigo wasn't so much annoyed as he was disappointed. Although securing the account had been important to Terence – if only because Vigo had shown faith in him and he'd let his boss down – the loss hadn't been an important one for H&V. In fact, McFarlane was a very small minnow in their pond. And Vigo had only handed Terence the opportunity to deal with his first solo account to test him and see if he was up to the task.

When Vigo called Terence into his office the morning after the McFarlane account crumbled, he was almost apologetic. That made Terence feel worse than had he received a sharp rebuke.

'I expected too much of you far too soon, young Hallam. I tried to get you to run before you could walk.'

'I can't apologise enough,' Terence said glumly. 'I know its no excuse, but...'

Vigo raised a hand to silence him. 'The whys don't matter, my boy. Lesson learned. I certainly won't make the same mistake twice.'

Vigo's final remark wounded Terence more than if he had been stabbed. If it hadn't been for the devastating fatigue preventing him from focussing, he was confident the McFarlane account would easily have been his. He felt crushed and shamed. There and then he made up his mind that it was time for him to leave Juniper Heights.

He wrestled with ideas over the best way to break the news to Rich and Danny. He certainly didn't want to come across as unappreciative. But he was actually a little afraid of them and, as much as he had been drawn to and thrilled by their brutality and blind hatred, the idea of being on the receiving end of a beating made him guarded.

And then there was the whole matter of Lavis's murder. There wasn't much chance that either Chas or Danny would get caught so long after the fact, but it wasn't beyond the realms of possibility. Even though Terence hadn't been involved in the physical murder, he was certainly an accomplice, and should he handle his departure in the wrong manner, the notion that they might finger him to save their own skins – or purely out of spite – terrified him.

Eventually deciding that a non-confrontational departure would be the best option, he booked a handful of appointments to speak with two different lettings agents and, over the course of several days, viewed seven properties, all of them within sensible reach of his workplace.

On the day that he signed the papers for a three year lease on a bijou ground floor flat in Edgbaston, he arrived back at Rich and Danny's to find it empty. Pleased, he immediately started packing his bag. There wasn't much to take; aside from his minimal wardrobe, there were only a small number of personal effects and his toiletries to worry about, and everything fitted comfortably into one medium-sized suitcase.

When Terence had attended Sherman Harper's birthday party, all the guests had departed with a goodie bag that included a bottle of Glenfiddich Single Malt. He briefly considered leaving it for Rich and Danny as a parting gift. He even got as far as scribbling out a short note:

Please accept this small token of my heartfelt
appreciation for your hospitality. T.

But then he decided it was too good for them, stashed the bottle in his case with his other belongings and screwed up the note.

It was only just after nine o'clock, but as he took a quick look around to ensure he'd left nothing behind, he heard the sound of laughter, followed by the rattle of a key in the lock. The door to the flat opened and Danny, closely followed by Rich and Chas, stumbled in.

Chas saw Terence standing in the doorway of his bedroom and grinned. 'Tel! Long time no see.' Then his eyes fell upon the suitcase and his expression changed. 'You going somewhere, chief?'

Terence cursed himself over being unprepared for a verbal farewell, but he hadn't really considered it a possibility; it was rare, if ever that his flatmates returned home before eleven.

'You fellows are home early,' he said, avoiding Chas's question.

Danny laughed. 'Yeah. Tiny Dave kicked us out because *someone…*' – he cocked a thumb at Rich – '…called him a tubby bum-boy cunt for refusing to let him have a pint on tick.'

'He fuckin' knows I'd be good for it,' Rich grumbled.

Danny rolled his eyes. 'You never have two pennies to rub together, you twat. Mind you, neither have any of us. The dole don't pay shit.' He frowned and nodded towards Terence's case. 'So what's in the bag, mate? You *do* look like you're going somewhere.'

Rather than bluster his way through an unprepared excuse, Terence decided to come clean. 'It was good of you fellows to let me stay with you, but the fact of the matter is, the time has come for me to move on.'

Danny squinted at him. 'Move on?'

'Yes. You know how it is.'

'Why don't you tell us *how it is*, chief.' Chas's dark eyes were tinged with venom.

'In essence, an opportunity has come up and I'd be foolish not to take it.'

Rich scowled. 'Would that be one of those opportunities where you've got yourself a bunch of new posh mates and your old mates – you're *real* mates – who gave you rent-free lodgings aren't good enough for you any more, so you do a moonlight flit without even saying goodbye?'

Terence had never credited Rich with much savvy, yet he'd just hit the nail square on the head. 'I wouldn't exactly call it a moonlight flit,' he muttered.

'What *would* you call it *exactly*?' Chas took a pace forward. It probably wasn't meant to be threatening, but Terence spontaneously took a step back.

'There's no reason for us to fall out over this. When opportunities arise, one has to grab them. As I said, you know how it is.'

'Yeah, I think we do actually,' Danny said. 'You *do* reckon you're too good for us now.'

Terence felt a trickle of sweat run down the back of his neck. 'Not at all. I had every intention of informing you of my plans.' He endeavoured to force an amiable smile but a muscle at the corner of his mouth was twitching.

'When was that then? You'd already packed your bags and you were on the way out the fucking door.' Danny was looking at him reproachfully. 'You're a bit of an ungrateful cunt actually, aren't you? We put you up for months and this is how you repay us?'

All three of the men were now looking at Terence with tangible contempt.

He gave up trying to maintain the pretence of a smile. 'Listen. You fellows have been really good to me and I couldn't hope to repay your kindness.'

'You could fucking try,' Rich snarled.

Terence ignored him. 'But you don't honestly think I'd just disappear without a word, do you? I'd like to think you know I have more integrity than that. And I *did* intend to leave a note.' A thought suddenly flashed through his mind. 'Oh, and this, of course.' He quickly set down the suitcase, flipped the clasps and pulled out the bottle of Glenfiddich.

Chas reached out and took it from him and his face brightened. 'Oooh, very nice.'

'It's a single malt,' Terence added, smiling. 'Nothing but the best for my friends.'

Danny leant over and glanced at the bottle. 'As parting gifts go, that's not unacceptable.' He nodded

301

approvingly. 'Go get some glasses, Ricardo. I think it would be appropriate that we see our old mate Tel off with a glass or three of the good stuff.'

The mood in the room had changed completely and, as Rich went to get the glasses, Terence breathed an inward sigh of relief.

The four of them clinked glasses.

'To lifelong friendship,' Chas said.

'To lifelong friendship,' Danny and Rich repeated in unison.

Terence mumbled something incoherent in close enough proximity to the same words.

Chas downed his measure of Scotch in one. 'Shit. *That* is fucking smooth.'

Terence beamed. 'Like I said, nothing but the best for you fellows.'

'So, this fantastic opportunity, chief.' Chas poured himself another measure of whisky. 'Spill.'

'The company I work for need me to be on call twenty-four-seven post haste,' Terence lied. 'They've set me up in a flat closer to the office. It's all been a bit of a whirlwind really. And I assure you I'd have been in touch to let you know.' Another lie.

Danny grinned. 'You'll have to have yourself a housewarming party, mate.'

'Yeah,' Rich chipped in. 'Make sure you invite your best pals along.'

Terence shook his head. 'Regretfully there won't be a housewarming party. It's a very small flat.'

Chas raised his eyebrows. 'Don't be cunty, Tel. You've *gotta* have your mates round for a piss-up!'

Terence had no intention of doing any such thing, but he said, 'I'll tell you what, fellows. If I do decide to have a little get-together, you'll the the first to hear about it.'

Three lies in two minutes. Terence smiled inwardly.

'I'll drink to that!' Danny said cheerfully. Refilling his glass, he did just that.

Being handed the keys to his own place was a wondrous moment for Terence, and something of a milestone. As he stepped through the door into the one-bedroom flat on Wellington Road and sat down on an upturned packing crate in the middle of the empty living room, he felt exalted. Admittedly the place wasn't up to much, but he now had a well-paid job that he enjoyed, influential acquaintances who would hopefully pave the way to even better things and, at long last, a real sense of independence. The knowledge that the flat was no more than a stepping stone, and the day that he would receive his inheritence was getting ever closer, certainly helped.

He had opted to pay an additional three pounds a week for partially-furnished accommodation, but said furnishings amounted to no more than a bed frame, a small electric hob and a refrigerator; it was far from palatial, but there would be time enough to build on it. Besides which, the idea of a minimalist existence rather appealed to him.

The letting agent had generously left a bottle of fizz and two glasses on the kitchen counter with a small card which read: WELCOME TO YOUR NEW HOME. Terence looked at the label on the bottle. He didn't know a great deal about wine, but he'd heard the name Babycham. He peeled off the silver foil to reveal a metal cap, struggled to remove it with his doorkey, then filled one of the glasses to the brim.

Raising it in the air, he said aloud, 'To absent friends.' He swallowed a draft of the sparkling liquid. It was surprisingly more palatable than he'd expected it to be. He smiled and nodded approvingly. 'And long may they remain that way.'

CHAPTER 25

'We have a saying in business that I live by. It goes: if you have an ounce of common sense, never trust a person who smiles all the time.' Sid Vigo leaned forward in his chair and looked at Terence questioningly. 'Why do you think that should be?'

Vigo had called Terence into his office to discuss a semi-informal dinner with a client that evening. Since Terence had messed up on the McFarlane deal several weeks earlier, Vigo had gone out of his way to ensure the next time he handed him an account, he would be one hundred percent ready.

Terence looked thoughtful. 'I would suggest because either that person is a complete idiot, or they're trying to sell me something.'

'Ah, you've heard that saying.'

'Not at all. It just strikes me those would both be good reasons not to trust someone who smiled at me all the time. Especially the latter.'

'Excellent!' Vigo slapped his hand on the desk and roared with laughter. 'I'd like you to come along for the ride this evening. There's a free dinner in it for you – a bloody good one too if I know Matthew Sinclair's wife – and I think you'll learn a thing or two about schmoozing a new client. What do you say? Are you in?'

'I'd be delighted to come along, sir. And I appreciate everything you've done for me recently. I won't let you down again.'

Vigo nodded and smiled. 'I know you won't. The Sinclairs live in Harborne and dinner is at eight. I'll pick you up at seven. Dress smart and wear a tie.'

'I'm actually living in Edgbaston now,' Terence said. 'If you can give me the address I can make my own way there.'

'I'll not hear of it. Just be ready at seven.' He winked. 'It pays to be fashionably early.'

Due to a road closure following a collison between a car and a motorcyclist, the traffic coming out of Edgbaston was nose-to-tail and it was almost seven forty-five by the time Vigo and Terence arrived in Harborne.

'Fashionably late works too,' Vigo said with a smile.

The Sinclair family home was a vast, six-bedroom detached property on Hamilton Avenue. There were two cars parked on the drive and three more out on the street.

Vigo neatly pulled his metallic blue Ford Granada Estate in behind a silver Mercedes-Benz SL and turned off the engine. He nodded at the car in front of them. 'That's *very* nice.'

Terence agreed.

'I can see you behind the wheel of one of those beauties, my boy.' Vigo swivelled in his seat to face Terence. 'Before we go in, there are a couple of things to keep in mind. Matthew Sinclair is a lovely chap, as is his lady wife, Charlotte. But Julius Prendergast – that's his business partner – will be at the table this evening and he's a complete arsehole. Barwick Holdings has been on our books for five years, but they're looking to expand and they're scanning the field to see where the grass might be greener. Fortunately for us, Sinclair is the major shareholder and his mantra has always been "better the devil you know", so whether or not the company remains with us will ultimately be his decision. *Not* so fortunately for us, Prendergast appears to hold considerable sway over Sinclair, so we need to ensure we do everything we can to keep him on side. The Barwick account is a big deal for H&V and we can't afford to lose it, so we do whatever it takes to retain the account, even if we have to get on our knees under the table and fellate the bastard.'

Vigo saw the look on Terence's face. He chuckled. 'Don't worry, Hallam, no blowjobs necessary. All I'm saying is we laugh at his jokes and agree with everything he says, regardless of whether we *actually* agree or not. Prendergast thrives on yes-men. I don't mind admitting, I've only actually met him a small handful of times, but I don't like him one bit. He has a pretty disgusting sense of humour with no tact and he can be very opinionated on topics that get people heated under the collar.'

Terence thought that Prendergast sounded rather interesting and he was glad that he had accepted the dinner invitation. 'What sort of topics?'

'Anything you care to think of that any rational soul would take a civilised stance over. Let me see, examples, examples...' – Vigo drummed his fingers on the steering wheel – 'Well, he's a staunch believer in bringing back hanging for one.' He looked thoughtful. 'What else, what else? Oh, yes, he thinks the social security system symbolises the most gross, short-sighted mistake the British government ever made and encourages lollygaggers to, well... lollygag.' He chuckled. 'And for Christ's sake don't let him get started on the advantages of genocide. In short, he's a not-so-closeted sociopath.'

Despite the fact that Terence was beginning to admire the cut of Prendergast's jib, he furrowed his brow appropriately and said, 'He sounds like rather an unsavoury character.'

'Put it this way: if Prendergast and Hitler had ever gone head to head, Prendergast would have left old Adolf in the dust. But I digress. The thing is, all we're interested in is Barwick Holdings' investment with us. So, like I say, whether you agree with the vitriol spewing out of the man's mouth or not, you just need to be responsive enough to make him *think* you do. Are you ready then?'

Terence nodded. 'More than.'

'Good lad.'

They were greeted at the front door by a short, portly woman wearing an elegant, low-cut, red velvet wrap-over evening gown, held together at the bust-line by a golden brooch fashioned in the form of a hedgehog. Terence estimated she was in her early forties, and something about her aqualine nose reminded him of his parents' old friend, Mrs Turner. He hadn't thought about her since the funeral.

'Sidney, how lovely to see you again,' the woman cooed. She leaned forward and planted a small kiss on each of Vigo's cheeks, making a small "mwah" sound. 'It's been far too long.' She brushed some loose strands from her mop of brown hair out of her face. 'And who's this handsome beast?' she added, eyeing up Terence.

'This is Terence Hallam, our up and coming junior executive,' Vigo said. 'Terence, meet our lovely hostess, Charlotte Sinclair.'

'Delighted,' Charlotte said. She extended a pudgy hand.

Terence politely took it in his own; it was slightly clammy. 'It's a real pleasure to meet you, Mrs Sinclair.'

'Call me Charlie, darling, everybody does.'

'Thank you for inviting me to your lovely home.'

Charlotte looked at Vigo and pursed her lips. 'Oh, Sidney, he's absolutely adorable. I could eat him up alive!' She stepped to one side and beckoned them inside. 'Everyone else has already arrived. We're just having smoked salmon canapés in the lounge, and Jules...' – she chortled – '...silver-tongued devil that he is, has been telling us all how he sweet-talked a thousand pounds off the price tag on his new Merc. I expect you noticed it when you arrived.'

As they stepped over the coconut coir doormat – ostentatiously emblazoned with the words **WELCOME TO OUR HUMBLE ABODE** – Vigo exchanged glances with Terence. 'We could hardly miss it.'

Charlotte closed the front door. 'Isn't it just divine? I'm going to have to be super-nice to Matty, we absolutely *have* to get one. Come on through.'

310

She led the way past a staircase and down a wide hallway lined with laden bookshelves, towards the sound of laughter and voices. At the end, she opened the door into a spacious lounge in which seven people, each holding a glass of champagne, were stood around a long, narrow table. It was dotted with small dishes brimming with peanuts, crisps and olives, and two silver platters bearing the intricately laid-out smoked salmon canapés.

'Everyone, everyone, looks who's here,' Charlotte announced loudly, clapping her hands together. The chatter faded to silence. 'It's Sidney and his young protégé, er… what was it again?' She looked to Terence for help.

'Terence.'

'Of course it is. Sorry, darling.' She chortled and patted the side of her temple. 'Brain not earning its keep this evening. Boys…' – she was addressing Vigo and Terence – '…come and meet everyone.'

All the people in the room were dressed formally; suits and ties on the gentlemen, expensive-looking evening gowns on the ladies.

A tall, good-looking man with a neat moustache and slicked-back black hair that was flecked with grey over his ears stepped forward and pumped Vigo's hand. 'Sidney, good to see you, my friend. You too, Terence.'

311

He held out a hand and Terence shook it. 'Matthew Sinclair.'

Mrs Sinclair motioned to a portly man who was stuffing a canapé into his mouth. 'And you know Jules, Sidney?'

'Indeed.'

Julius Prendergast had a head of thick, unkempt red hair that looked as if someone had dropped a dishcloth on his head. He was wearing tinted glasses and was wedged into a weathered tartan suit, the jacket of which looked at least two sizes too small for him.

'Vigo, you old bum-bandit,' he said with a pronounced Ulster accent, spraying crumbs. Stepping towards Vigo, he threw his arms wide – 'Bring it in!' – and wrapped them around him in a tight bear-hug. Then, with a cry of 'Tezza!', he did the same thing to Terence. He glanced back towards the woman who had been standing with him. 'This is the wife, Dolores. Don't laugh!' He cackled. 'No, I'm kidding you, she's a good sort really.'

Prendergast wasn't tall himself, but Dolores was a good six inches shorter. She had a sad-looking face, the unavoidable focal point on which was an unsightly wart protruding from her chin. She smiled warmly at Terence and Vigo, her expression tacitly apologising for her husband.

312

Charlotte introduced them to an elderly couple she said were her parents, Brian and Henrietta Charles. Neither spoke, but they both nodded politely and smiled.

Terence was amused by the thought that, before she was married, Charlotte Sinclair would have been Charlie Charles.

Last of all were an unassuming couple, who again appeared to be in their mid-forties and who Charlotte introduced as Luke and Rhianna Kirk; 'They're good friends of Barwick Holdings.' She smiled. 'And this pretty little thing is their daughter, Brioni.'

'Keep your hands off, Tezza!' Prendergast sniggered. 'Jailbait, so she is!'

Terence noticed Dolores give her husband a disapproving nudge in the ribs.

Brioni was slender and pale-skinned and her long blonde hair was plaited in doll-like braids. Terence thought she looked to be around eighteen or nineteen-years-old, but the braids were possibly making her appear younger than she actually was. She afforded Terence a shy smile and he smiled back.

'Help yourself to nibbles,' Charlotte said, handing Vigo and Terence each a glass of champagne and picking up her own. 'I was just telling the boys about your new Merc, Julius.'

'She's a beauty, isn't she?', Prendergast said proudly.

'If I recall, weren't you driving a rather spiffy Rolls last time we met?' Vigo asked.

Prendergast grinned. 'Well remembered. Bit of a story there. Took her off the road doing eighty in fog down near Maidstone last February.'

'Good lord!'

'Yeah. Busted up an arm, but what the hell?' He whirled his right arm around in a wide circle, almost knocking his wife's glass out of her hand. 'Good as new now. Not so much the old Roller though. Totally banjaxed.'

'Tell them how you got a thousand off the Merc, Jules,' Charlotte giggled.

'Julius is a bit of a charmer,' Sinclair said, looking at Terence. 'He has an enviable knack for turning situations to his advantage.'

Prendergast guffawed. 'What can I tell yous? There's those that can spin gold and there's those that just get left with a handful of shite. Honestly, talking down a price isn't so hard, guys, especially when you're dealing with a feckin' eejit like the guy at the Benz dealership. Useless testicle.' He shook his head. 'I could easily have taken him for more, but you don't like to take the piss, you know?' He popped some peanuts into his mouth.

Everyone in the room chuckled except for Dolores. 'I preferred the Rolls myself.'

Prendergast rolled his eyes. 'Arrr, hush with you, woman.' He looked at Vigo. 'She can't even drive.'

The door through to the dining room opened and a young, smartly-dressed man appeared and waited patiently for Charlotte to notice him.

'Ah, Gordon. Is dinner ready?'

The man nodded. 'Yes, madam.'

'Come along everybody. The cheese soufflés won't wait and they're absolutely to die for.'

The seating around the large, circular oak table had been predetermined; there were silver-edged place cards on which the guests' names had been neatly inscribed in black ink.

Terence found himself seated between Brioni Kirk and Charlotte Sinclair's mother.

Presented in ornate bone china ramekins, the starters arrived and were as mouth-watering as their hostess had promised, the accompanying crudités equally so.

'Did you all enjoy that, my darlings?' Charlotte said, eager for her guests' validation.

Everyone mumbled their approval.

'I'd say Annette really excelled herself there,' Sinclair said, dabbing at his moustache with a napkin.

'She's only been with us a month,' Charlotte explained to the table. 'She's coming along in leaps and bounds. Wait until you see what we have for the main course!'

There was a generous selection of wines arranged in the centre of the table. Prendergast reached over and helped himself to a bottle of Mateus Rosé. He tutted. 'Not this old shite again, Matt! I keep telling you, it tastes like cleaning fluid. Zinfandel is the only rosé worth a light.' His boorish put-down didn't prevent him from pouring himself a measure, downing it in one and refilling his glass to the brim.

The young man, Gordon, made his way round the table, filling everyone's glasses. Terence opted for a glass of Black Tower white – 'a poofter's choice,' as Prendergast declared loudly when he noticed.

No sooner had the starter plates been cleared by Gordon, than the main course arrived; it was canard à l'orange, served on a bed of wild rice. Terence had never tasted anything quite like it before; the tender braised meat was melt-in-the-mouth delicious.

The conversation became lively and touched upon everything from the Sinclair's disastrous Mediterranean holiday the previous summer (for which they had demanded their money back and were proud to announce they got) to the decline in quality of BBC programming. The Kirks enthused about their lively pair of Bedlington Terriers and Prendergast quickly changed the subject to express his denigrating views on homosexuality ('Mind you, I'd watch a couple of lezzers at it,' he guffawed). Other subjects included the steep rise in vagrancy around Birmingham, the palatability of French cuisine, the defeat of the Argentines in the Falklands War and the outrageous cost of new greenhouses (a matter over which Henrietta Charles was appalled, although Prendergast naturally enough remarked that he would easily have wheedled some discount for her if she had asked).

Terence chipped in occasionally, but mostly he kept his thoughts to himself, instead absorbing and revelling in the convivial atmosphere.

Only Brioni Kirk had remained completely silent, and Terence started to become aware that she kept surreptitiously glancing at him. He decided to try and find out a little about her.

'This duck is very appetising, isn't it?' he began.

Brioni was just forking a small morsel into her mouth. She didn't really look as if she was much enjoying it, but she nodded.

'So, are you at college? Or are you working?'

'I've been at uni for two years.'

Slightly older than I estimated then, Terence thought. 'I see. Whereabouts?'

'Warwick.'

'Magnificent! I went there. What are you studying?'

'Medicine. I want to become a doctor.'

Prendergast had homed in on the conversation. 'I've got a medical joke for you. There's these two blokes in hospital beds having a little chat. One of them says, *What you in for?* And the second one says, *Endoscopy, I've been having digestive problems. What about you?* The first one says, *Camera up my bum...*'

Sinclair raised an eyebrow. 'Keep it clean, Julius.'

Prendergast waved a hand to hush him. 'So the second guy says, *Oh, a colonoscopy, I'm sorry to hear that. You've got a bowel disorder?*' The first guy replies, *No, my neighbour was sunbathing nude and my wife caught me taking a photo!*' Roaring with laughter, he banged his fork up and down on the table like a hyperactive child. 'Get it? The wife shoved his camera up his arse!'

'I'm sure they got it, dear,' Dolores said, clearly embarrassed. Looking around the table, she silently mouthed, 'Sorry everyone.'

Even though it was evident nobody found the joke particularly funny, they responded graciously with small murmurs and awkward smiles.

Terence was finding Prendergast fascinating. He was uncouth, arrogant and obnoxious, yet everybody in the room seemed to treat him with a level of deference that, on face value, he didn't appear to deserve. He had no idea what might be at the root of their reverence, but, speaking for himself, he decided that he despised and admired the man in equal measure.

Gordon efficiently cleared the dinner plates. 'Are you ready for dessert, madam?' he asked.

'Yes please, Gordon,' Charlotte said.

The young man gave her a respectful nod and returned to the kitchen.

'Just wait until you taste the roulade!' Charlotte cooed.

The dishes arrived. The meringue was light and crunchy and filled with decadently rich cream, while the berries were impeccably sweet and tart.

Over coffee, Sinclair smiled at Vigo. 'I think we've kept you in suspense long enough, Sidney. I'm pleased to tell you that Barwick Holdings will be renewing its account with you.'

'Thank you, Matthew.' Vigo smiled warmly. 'You've made the right decision. I assure you that...'

'With some conditions to be discussed,' Prendergast interjected.

'*Possibly*,' Sinclair said. He appeared a little nervous. 'We agreed possibly, Julius. But we can discuss those in the office next week. If that's agreeable to you, Sidney?'

'Of course,' Vigo said, unable to hide the note of suspicion in his voice. He was clearly wondering what Prendergast's conditions might be.

Sinclair looked at Terence and smiled. 'So, young Terence, are you scheming to oust our Sidney from his throne?'

'Not at all. I'm more than happy working for him.'

'Anyone worth spit wants to get to the top of the tree,' Prendergast said.

'Not everyone, Julian,' Sinclair said. 'There's something to be said for happiness.'

Prendergast shot Sinclair a look. 'Happiness is power. And money.' He looked back at Terence. 'What's the matter with you? No ambition? No taste for success?'

'I've plenty of that, sir.'

Prendergast's eyes narrowed. 'Have you though? When you can stand up and say you earned your company a record profit you know you've done well. I brought in close on two hundred and thirty grand to Barwick Holdings last year. And don't you go thinking it's been easy, a guy from Northern Ireland establishing himself in the UK. It's been an uphill struggle all the way. But I never gave up. *That's* real success, son.'

'Terence is coming along very nicely,' Vigo said. 'H&V are proud to have him on board.'

Prendergast shook his head. 'I like you, Vigo, but you're soft. You want to keep this puppy on a tight leash, or he'll steal your job from under your nose and you'll be out on the streets selling matches.'

Terence stirred a teaspoonful of sugar into his coffee. 'May I say, Mr Prendergast, I admire you. I've listened to you this evening and you're clearly a very driven and successful man. But I have to say, I don't like you.'

Vigo visibly winced.

Rhianna Kirk gasped and the room fell silent. For a moment, everybody looked as if they were expecting a murder to take place in front of their eyes.

But then Prendergast burst out laughing. 'You're a cocky little fucker, aren't you?'

'Language, Julius!' Dolores exclaimed.

'Oh, hush, woman, I'm listening to Tezza.'

'I believe I have the requisite drive and aspiration to succeed that you speak of,' Terence continued. 'And making money is unquestionably a constituent of success. But I don't envisage trampling over decent people like Mr Vigo to achieve it. I *do* believe there's a case to be had for the selective extermination of reprehensible obstacles on one's road to the top, but that's another matter.'

Prendergast was looking at Terence with awe. A bead of sweat trickled down onto his brow from beneath his mess of red hair. He wiped it away. 'Reprehensible obstacles, eh? I'm intrigued. Such as?'

'Those who sap the life out of the welfare system for a start.'

Vigo realised where Terence was going. Almost imperceptibly, a smile appeared on his mouth. He took a sip of his coffee and peered at his junior over the top of the cup.

'We pay our taxes to the Government to provide funding for public services,' Terence said. 'And who benefits most from those? Not the hard-working man. He's out there earning a respectable living. No, it's the indolent and the stupid, holding out their grubby hands and leeching off a system that, frankly, should never have been put in place. These people contribute *nothing* and, figuratively speaking, they steal the food out of the mouths of decent people and laugh in their faces while they're doing it. They're a drain on society and, mark my words, they'll bring those public services to their knees and then there'll be nothing left for decent people when they themselves fall on hard times and need it.'

'I think this is getting a bit heavy for dinner,' Sinclair said. 'What say we change the subject?'

'I agree,' Charlotte chimed in. 'I was thinking after dinner we might all play Monopoly.'

Rhianna Kirk smiled. 'That would be fun!'

Prendergast held up a hand. 'Just a minute, I'm interested in what the kid has to say.'

'Mr Vigo is an honest, hard-working man,' Terence continued. 'You must know that. After all, your company has held an account with H&V for years.'

'He can be a bit of a prick,' Prendergast said. He glanced at Vigo. 'No offence.'

Vigo smiled. 'None taken.'

'But I suppose he's a decent man.' Prendergast frowned. 'What's your point?'

'I wonder why you would choose to tell Mr Vigo that you're renewing your account with him, but append it with allusions that there will be conditions attached. You told me that you personally made your company a two hundred and twenty thousand profit last year...'

'Two hundred and *thirty*!'

'I stand corrected. But you did so off the backs of Mr Vigo and Mr Harper. As I see it, H&V doesn't need Barwick Holdings.'

Vigo suddenly realised he was holding his breath.

Terence looked steely-eyed. 'But clearly Barwick Holdings needs *us*. If you didn't, you'd already have upped sticks and moved on to pastures new. I'm just curious, Mr Prendergast, as to why you would risk killing the golden goose by trying to pluck a few extra feathers.'

Prendergast actually seemed to have been taken down a peg. 'It's food for thought, I suppose.' He looked at Vigo. 'You want to hang on to this kid. He's a damned smart one.'

'He is that.' Vigo winked at Terence. 'He *certainly* is that.'

Prendergast looked back at Terence. 'Here's a question for you then, Tezza. If you had an endless sum of money, what would you do with it?'

Terence didn't hesitate. 'I'd do something to fix this broken country.'

Prendergast laughed. 'Good luck with *that!* I mean, I can't say I disagree with your viewpoint, but this country's gone way beyond fixing. Where would you even start? The streets are crawling with the sort of scum you just mentioned – we're kindred spirits on that matter – but at this point I reckon the only way to handle it would be to nuke the fuckin' lot of them!'

'Language, Julius.' For the umpteenth time that evening, Dolores looked around the table apologetically.

There was a pregnant pause and then Charlotte giggled. 'Well, wasn't that enlightening, darlings? Now, come on, who's ready for that game of Monopoly?'

CHAPTER 26

While Charlotte and Matthew were setting up the game board and the other guests were chatting amongst themselves, Vigo quietly pulled Terence to one side.

'Holy Mother of God, Hallam, what the hell just happened in there?' he hissed.

Terence, who had been feeling extremely pleased with himself, felt his stomach turn. 'Please accept my apologies, sir.'

'I thought I'd made it crystal clear how vital Barwick Holdings is to H&V.'

Vigo didn't look particularly angry; in fact, for a moment Terence thought there might be a trace of admiration in the man's eyes. He decided to chance his luck. 'May I speak candidly, sir?'

'You may.'

Terence took Vigo's arm and manoeuvred him over to the French windows, well away from everybody else. The twin doors were slightly open and there was a refreshing breeze filtering through.

He spoke softly. 'I completely understood what you said to me, sir. But, should there be cause to revise the terms and conditions of the contract, surely *we* get to lay them out, not Julius Prendergast. Please don't think I was questioning the validity of your approach to massage his ego; it costs nothing to nod our heads sagely in agreement with everything he says and laugh at his terrible jokes. As you said, we do whatever is called for. But I don't believe it wise that we accede to any deal over which *he* has dictated conditions.'

Vigo was listening to him with curiosity. 'That's extremely presumptuous of you, lad. We don't actually know what those conditions are yet.'

'Granted. But, honestly, who do you think they will benefit the most? I guarantee it won't be Harper & Vigo. Good, bad or indifferent, whatever it might be that he was alluding to, you could see Sinclair wasn't comfortable with it. Prendergast is a gluttonous predator. From every word that came out of his mouth this evening, it's clear to me that his philosophy is to be the victor in any given situation – especially in financial matters. Nevertheless, I can only repeat my apologies if what I said gave you cause for concern.'

'*Concern*? You nearly gave me a bloody heart attack!' Vigo was smiling.

'I saw an opportunity to play Prendergast at his own game and redress the balance of power.'

'You handed him his balls on a plate is what you did.'

'I'd wager Barwick Holdings will be renewing their contract with us, no caveats attached.'

326

'You did good, lad, and I couldn't be prouder.' Vigo placed a hand on Terence's shoulder and gave it a little squeeze. 'I knew my faith in you wasn't misplaced. And all that baloney about exterminating the indolent was the cherry on the cake. The look on his face was priceless. He bought into it lock, stock and barrel.'

'Oh, I was completely serious about that,' Terence said, as if he believed he had made his views clear.

Vigo studied Terence's face, trying to weigh up whether or not he was joking. Then he chuckled. 'Very good. You had me going for a moment there.'

Before Terence could explain that he hadn't actually been joking, Charlotte appeared at his shoulder.

'What are you two boys plotting and planning over here?' She leant in and planted a soft kiss on Terence's earlobe. The corners of her mouth curled into a cheeky smile. 'Well done you for standing up to Jules,' she whispered. 'There aren't many people bold enough to give him a dose of his own medicine.' She took a step back and handed each of them a small glass of golden liqueur. 'This is about the only good thing to come out of that Godforsaken holiday. We brought several bottles back with us.'

Vigo sniffed the contents of the glass. He caught the aroma of cinnamon. 'What is it?'

'It's called Calisay. It's absolutely heavenly. The primary flavouring comes from the bark of the Calisaya tree, but there are other bits and bobs in it too. It's herbal, rather orangey. You'll adore it.'

Matthew Sinclair handed round a box of Cuban cigars and each of the men took one.

Terence wanted to decline, but Prendergast was having none of it. 'Don't be a baby, Tezza. Don't you know these little treasures are hand-rolled on the thighs of young maidens?'

'Pay no attention to him,' Sinclair said. 'That's urban myth.'

Prendergast chortled. 'To be sure it is. But it doesn't half add a thrill to slipping one between your lips. Go on with you,' he urged Terence. 'They're Habanos, the finest money can buy.'

Conceding, Terence took one from the box and handed it back to Sinclair, who produced a cutter and went around clipping the ends from each of his guest's cigars. Then he dutifully circled again with a box of cedar matchsticks, and soon the room was filled with aromatic smoke.

'The first puffs have to be sufficient to ensure you stay lit,' Sinclair said, holding a match to the end of Terence's cigar. 'Don't inhale though. Grip it between your teeth and puff and blow three times in short succession.'

'I'm sure he's had plenty of experience of that!' Prendergast guffawed, motioning his balled fist in front of his mouth and forcing his tongue into his cheek.

'Actually,' Terence said, 'I'm not mad keen on cigars. They were responsible for the death of my father.'

'Really?' Charlotte said, a shocked look on her face. 'Cancer?'

'No, the house was set on fire.'

The room fell silent for a moment and the guests exchanged glances.

'I'm sorry to hear that, lad,' Vigo said.

Terence nodded. 'Thank you.' He did as Sinclair had suggested and immediately started coughing.

'Rookie,' Prendergast scoffed.

'No, you're doing fine,' Sinclair said. 'But you should never inhale. Just keep the cigar clenched gently between your teeth and hold the smoke inside your mouth long enough to savour the flavour. Then blow it out nice and slowly.'

'Very well,' Terence said, uncertainly. He followed Sinclair's guidance and, much to his surprise, he didn't find the smoke harsh at all. 'That's actually rather agreeable,' he said.

Sinclair patted him on the shoulder. 'I'll send you a box for Christmas.' He turned to address the room. 'Right then, shall we get this game going?'

329

Terence said he would prefer to sit it out – in truth, he didn't want to admit that he'd never played Monopoly before – and the game didn't last long anyway; when Luke Kirk rolled the first dice, tensions already seemed to be running high. Prendergast proved to be predictably competitive and, just twenty-minutes in, he threw a minor strop when Charlotte's father purchased Park Lane and smugly tucked the card alongside the one for Mayfair, thereby having laid claim to the two best properties on the board.

'Play nice, Jules,' Charlotte said reprovingly.

Two minutes later, Prendergast inadvertently sent the board flying and the playing pieces and paper money scattered across the thick pile carpet.

'Oh, Julian!' Dolores exclaimed. 'That was really clumsy!'

'Don't harp on, woman! It was a feckin' accident, so it was.'

Nobody in the room believed that for a moment, and Terence, watching from the sidelines, was wholly convinced it had been intentional.

Sensing that the mood was turning pugnacious, Charlotte swiftly diffused it. 'I'm sure you'd have won anyway, Jules. You usually do.' Her remark brought the desired grin to Prendergast's face. 'Anyway, I've got a better idea,' she cooed. 'Let's get the ouija board out.'

'Whoooooo-ha-ha-ha-haaaah' Prendergast cried. 'Here I've got a brilliant joke about a ghost. There was this prozzie, you see, and one of her clients died...'

Leaving them to it, Terence slipped through the French doors and out into the garden. The evening air was cool and invigorating. The vast expanse of lawn stretched away a hundred metres or more to a line of trees.

In the moonlight, Terence could see the shape of a small, Japanese-style pagoda. He sauntered across the grass towards it. Painted white, it was an ornate wooden structure raised about three feet up off the ground. Climbing the steps on to an enclosed area of decking, he took a seat on one of the two padded three-seater benches that were arranged at forty-five degrees to one another.

He stretched back and drew on his cigar, thinking about the way he had spoken to Prendergast at dinner. It had been a calculated risk challenging the man and, had it backfired, Sidney Vigo would most certainly have hung him out to dry. But it hadn't backfired. He'd impressed the boss – he wouldn't be surprised if there was a small gratuity appending his salary at the end of the month – and the adrenaline rush he'd felt as the look of self-satisfaction on Prendergast's face drained away had made his loins stir with excitement. It had given him a rapturous feeling of power.

331

The soft sound of approaching footsteps across the grass disturbed his thoughts and he looked up to see Brioni coming up the steps.

'Mind if I sit with you?'

Terence spread out his hands. 'Take your pick.'

'Thanks.' The obvious place for Brioni to sit was on the opposite bench, but instead she planted herself down on the end of the same one occupied by Terence, leaving an empty space between them. 'I can't stand those ouija things. They're dangerous.'

Terence took a puff on his cigar. 'It's all hokum. Someone very much of this mortal world will be manipulating it.'

'Maybe. But that stuff scares the fucking shit out of me.'

Terence barely recognised her as the same demure young lady who had sat alongside him at dinner. He smiled. 'Take my word for it.'

'I admire you for standing up to Uncle Julius. He can be a bit of a cunt.'

'Mr Prendergast is your uncle?'

'Oh, no, sorry. He's not my *actual* uncle. I just call him uncle. I have done for as long as I've known him – since I was a kid, I suppose. My Dad is a silent partner in Barwick Holdings.'

That expands upon Mrs Sinclair's description of the Kirks as "friends of the business", Terence thought. 'I see,' he said. He wondered if Vigo was aware of Kirk's true involvement, and what importance, if any, it had.

Brioni bit her bottom lip. 'I'm not wearing any underwear, you know.'

Terence looked at her with undisguised shock. 'Why on Earth would you say something like that?!'

Brioni giggled. 'Because it's true.' She shuffled along the bench until her knee touched against his. Her short skirt had ridden up to her thighs. 'Would you like to see my boobs?'

Terence was lost for words, and before he could muster a response, Brioni lifted up her pink, crocheted sweater to reveal that she wasn't wearing a bra. Her full breasts looked pale in the moonlight.

'You can touch them if you like. I don't mind.'

Terence shifted awkwardly on his cushion. 'I think not.'

'What's the matter, don't you like women?'

'That's got nothing to do with it. What do you think your parents would say if they knew you were propositioning a complete stranger like this?'

'Who cares? They probably think I'm still a virgin.' Brioni pulled her sweater back down and nuzzled even closer. 'Besides, we're not strangers. We just had dinner together.' She smiled up at him coquettishly. 'I *really* like you, Terence. I'll give you a blowie if you want.' She caught sight of what she perceived to be a look of alarm on Terence's face. 'Don't worry, nobody needs to know. It'll be our little secret.' Reaching down, she placed a hand on his thigh and squeezed gently. Her breathing had quickened. 'I'm really good at it.'

Terence brushed her hand away. 'What the hell's the matter with you?' He stood up and moved over to the other bench.

Brioni let out an exasperated sigh. 'You *are* a homo, aren't you?'

'Don't be obtuse.' Terence glared at her angrily. 'I was brought up to understand that women are the fairer sex. But, my God, whoever came up with that notion clearly never encountered women like the ones I've known. All women are awful. And you...' – he pointed a finger – '...*You* are something else. We only met a couple of hours ago. You don't know the first thing about me, and yet...'

'I know I fancy you.'

'So what if you do?'

'That's all that matters, isn't it? Women have what men want, men have what women want. If two people really fancy each other, why piss about with all the romantic bullshit? Just cut to the chase and bloody well fuck.'

'Evidently it didn't occur to you that I might *not* be attracted to you.'

Brioni shrugged. 'Nope. But I don't see what that's got to do with it either. There aren't many guys who'd turn down a no-strings-attached blowie – unless they were only into other guys, I guess.'

Perhaps it was the alcohol he had consumed that evening, or possibly the heady effects of the cigar smoke. Or maybe a combination of both. But suddenly Terence was again consumed by that rapturous feeling of power. He looked into the young girl's eyes. 'I don't recall turning you down.' His mouth formed into a thin smile and, reaching for his fly, he unzipped it. 'Come here.'

Brioni gave him a kittenish look and her eyes shimmered in the moonlight. She got down on her hands and knees and crawled across the decking towards him.

As Terence felt her cool fingers encircle him, he rested his head on the back of the bench and gazed up at the night sky. Then, gripping the cigar between his teeth, he put one hand behind Brioni's head and closed his eyes.

Afterwards, when his excitement had subsided, Terence adjusted himself.

'I knew you fancied me,' Brioni said, standing up and smoothing the rumples out of her skirt. 'I never met a guy who didn't want to get me into bed.'

'Well, I'm sorry to disappoint you, but you just did.'

'Liar! You know you enjoyed it.'

'It was acceptable.'

'Oh, I see, just acceptable was it? Cheeky sod!'

In the half-light, Terence could see Brioni was frowning at him. 'You scratched an itch,' he said. 'What do you want, marks out of ten?'

The girl was trying to decide whether he was winding her up. '*Seriously*?'

'You'd better run along,' Terence said, waving a dismissive hand at her. 'Get yourself back inside before your father notices his not so prim and proper daughter has disappeared and comes out looking for her. Oh, and make sure you stop off in the bathroom and tidy yourself up. Your lipstick is smeared.'

Brioni stared at him incredulously. 'You arrogant prick!' Petulantly tossing her hair, she flounced down the wooden steps and set off across the grass towards the house.

Terence eased himself back on the bench and smiled. One of the things to surface from the fallout after Joanne Cormack cheated on him with James Harrington had been a concious decision on his part to never again trust a woman. Nevertheless, whatever his opinions on the gutter-level morals of Brioni Kirk and her kind, the female of the species certainly wasn't without its uses. And Brioni had been right about one thing; she *was* good at it.

Sighing, he rezipped his fly and puffed gently at his cigar. Holding it up to admire the golden glow of burning tobacco at the tip, he exhaled a thin plume of smoke through his clenched teeth.

Very good in fact.

PART IV

CHAPTER 27

Terence received his bonus for having challenged Julius Prendergast. On the day that he and Matthew Sinclair renewed Barwick Holdings' contract, Sidney Vigo called Terence into his office and handed him an envelope containing five hundred pounds in cash.

A month later, Sherman Harper paid the Birmingham office a visit and, along with Vigo, all the members of staff gathered around for an announcement. It was rare for Harper to show his face and everyone feared the worst. When they learned that – with the impending departure due to ill health of Reg Cooper – up and coming wunderkind, Terence Hallam, would be taking over the role as H&V's Financial Risk Manager, nobody was more surprised than Terence himself.

With the higher profile job also came a secretary, Melissa Hills. She had been appointed by Cooper and had been with the company for almost ten years. Terence didn't like her. The occasional clumsy mistake aside, she was proficient enough in secretarial terms. But she was always twittering away about her children, had an irksome giggle and was extremely forgetful.

One day just before Christmas, when she made Terence a coffee – for the umpteenth time neglecting to add any sugar – it was the straw that broke the camel's back.

'You know, you absolutely astound me, Mrs Hills.' Terence's tone was controlled, but there was an unmistakable note of impatience at play. 'How long have you been working under me?'

'Just over four months, Mr Hallam.'

'Four months. So, let's say that's three coffees a day, four on a Monday...' – he made a small mental calculation – '...you've made me something in the region of two hundred and fifty cups in that time.'

Mrs Hills looked at him nervously. 'If you say so.'

'I do say so. I'm keen to know though: what exactly is it that you find so difficult about remembering to put two teaspoonfuls of sugar into the mug?'

'Hmm.' She appeared to genuinely give the question consideration. 'I suppose it's because Mr Cooper used to take his without.'

'But I'm not Mr Cooper, am I?'

'No. I'm sorry, sir. Honestly, I sometimes I think I'd forget my own head if it wasn't sewn onto my neck!' *There was that damned giggle.*

Terence glowered at her. 'As it happens, I've been thinking too. You've heard the expression about a new broom sweeping clean?'

Mrs Hills looked at him uncertainly. 'Yes, sir.'

342

'I've come to the conclusion that you would be happier working for somebody else.'

'Oh, no, Mr Hallam, sir. I love working for you.'

'It's not a negotiable matter Mrs Hills. Clear out your desk and be off the premises in fifteen minutes.'

'But, Mr Hallam...' she stammered. 'It's Christmas.'

'You want me to wish you a Merry Christmas? Very well. Merry Christmas, Mrs Hills. And a Happy New Year to you too.' Terence tapped his watch. 'Fourteen minutes.'

The woman looked at him in disbelief. 'You're firing me just because I forgot to put sugar in your coffee?'

Terence's dark eyes seemed to fill with hatred. 'That too. But mostly because you're incompetent and you'll always *be* incompetent, and I'm sick to death of the sight of your ridiculously chirpy face.'

'But I've worked here for ten years,' she said despairingly. There were tears brimming in her eyes. 'What will Mr Vigo say?'

'Nothing whatsoever. Who I choose to appoint as a secretary is entirely my affair.'

Mrs Hills pulled out a scrunched-up tissue from the sleeve of her sweater and used it to dab at her eyes. Her expression changed to one of derision. 'It seems what

343

they all say about you is right. And after the number of times I've stood up for you.'

'Really? And what *is* it they *all* say about me?'

'That you're a ruthless bastard.'

Terence grinned. 'I shall take that as a compliment.'

'God damn you!' She crossed to the office door. 'I'm a firm believer that what goes around comes around. And you'll get what's coming to you, just you see if you don't.'

Terence tapped his watch again. 'Thirteen.'

Melissa Hills was quickly replaced by a slip of a girl with olive skin and a mane of jet black hair. Patricia Bianchi was of Italian heritage. She was meticulous in her work, efficient, and, most importantly, never once forgot to add sugar to Terence's coffee.

Terence had been learning to drive and when he passed his test, Miss Bianchi bought him a congratulatory card. He had been squirreling away money for years and when he informed her that he was in the market for splashing out on a new car, she mentioned that her boyfriend was a salesman for a local Land Rover showroom and would be able to get him a good deal. Terence couldn't help remembering Prendergast bragging about his new Merc.

The following week, he proudly drove a five-door Range Rover 4x4 off the forecourt of Green's Motors.

Two years later, an opportunity presented itself to purchase the flat in which he was living in Egbaston. Terence was able to meet the asking price effortlessly. He moved into a three bedroom property in Harborne within striking distance of Matthew and Charlotte Sinclair's home. He had the flat gutted and redecorated and started renting it out to a young Asian couple. It became the first component in what would, over the course of the next ten years, become an extensive rental portfolio.

The money poured in.

In 1990, on his thirtieth birthday, a letter arrived from the late Arthur Hallam's solicitor, Duncan Meyer. It informed him that his inheritence had been released and, that day, his bank account swelled by more than seven and a half million pounds, a sizeable chunk of which had come from the sale of his father's share in Hallam Toys.

Harper & Vigo had been doing very nicely before Terence came aboard, but in the years since he had beaten Johnny Berman to the position of office junior, he had expanded the company's fortunes considerably, securing more new clients in one fiscal year than anyone preceding him in the job had managed in two.

In 1992 Terence was promoted to Chief Financial Officer.

His own expanding personal wealth was mirrored by his expanding waistline; this was in no small measure down to the fact that he regularly dined prospective clients at the swankiest restaurants, where he would indulge them in the richest foods and finest wines. With the onset of middle age, the once svelte, ten-stone young man ballooned to almost double that weight.

Turning away just as many clients as he signed, Terence gained a reputation as a tough man to deal with, yet even those of whom he fell foul had to admit they admired his accomplishments.

In 1999, Sherman Harper passed away. His son, also named Sherman, immediately stepped in as joint CEO alongside Sidney Vigo.

Sherman Harper Jr had a far more hands-on approach than his father. He was what Vigo once described to Terence as 'a spoiled, belligerent little arse-wipe', and it wasn't long before the two men were crossing swords. Fast approaching retirement anyway, Vigo sold his half of the company to Harper Jr and disappeared off into the sunset.

Vigo's departure hit Terence hard, and coming to blows with Harper Jr with increasing regularity forced him to decide it was time to move on, and he handed over his resignation. He departed with his secretary, Patricia Bianchi, in tow.

Fast approaching the age of fifty, he was so wealthy that he could have easily retired to a sunny isle and never worked another day in his life. But he had never been one to let the grass grow under his feet, and instead he immediately launched his own financial concern, Hallam Solutions, appropriating half of H&V's clientele into the bargain – much to the chagrin of Sherman Harper Jr.

H&V went under in 2004.

One of Terence's most influential clients, Aloysius Harlington-Forbes, was a respected Whitehall politician and a keen golfer; he seemed genuinely shocked when Terence one day remarked that he'd never played, nor had he ever seen the point of the game.

Harlington-Forbes invited him along to his club's annual charity dinner: 'Meet some of the chaps, see if we can't get you to change your infidel views on the gentleman's sport!' It was at that dinner in the autumn of 2010 that Terence first encountered the man's son-in-law, Crispin Partridge. They drank, smoked Habanas and talked, and Terence was delighted to discover that they were kindred spirits; Partridge had some agreeably radical opinions about the decline of society and how the government should be addressing it.

'You don't want to listen to that nonsense, old boy,' Harlington-Forbes said to Terence. 'He's had too much to drink. Bit of a fascist sympathist is our Cris. Always moaning at me about the great unwashed.' He chuckled. 'Here, have you asked Hallam about Cressida yet?'

'I was waiting for the right moment, sir.'

Terence looked at Partridge enquiringly.

'My little wifey to be…' he began.

'Who also happens to be *my* lovely daughter,' Harlington-Forbes interjected.

'Yes, Ally's daughter. She's in the market for some P.A. work. We were… well, that is to say, *I* was wanting to ask if by chance you might have any openings at Hallam Solutions?'

Terence couldn't help but wonder as to whether there had been an ulterior motive behind his invite to the dinner, this being it.

Regardless, by lucky coincidence, Patricia Bianchi had recently informed him that she was planning to emigrate to get married in November.

Terence smiled obligingly. 'I just might do at that. Have her come in for an informal chat.'

Unsurprisingly, Cressida Partridge was an inferior replacement for Patricia, but she was a pretty little thing, hard-working and eager to please, and Terence was happy enough to have her around.

At the company's office party just before Christmas in 2010, Cressida drunkenly came on to Terence and they ended up in bed together. He couldn't for the life of him figure out why she would cheat on Crispin; they had only been married for a month, and they enjoyed considerable social standing, an affluent lifestyle and were the owners of a sought-after property in Tunbridge Wells. Terence could only conclude that she must have a high sex drive which her husband wasn't able to fulfil and he didn't question the matter further. Why would he? Cressida had a desirable enough body, the sex was above average and in the weeks that followed he often took advantage of her eagerness to sleep with him for the price of a good dinner.

One evening, late in February 2011, Terence was driving his brand new Range Rover Vogue SE home from the office when his phone text alert sounded. He drew up at the kerb and, with the engine still turning, opened the phone. His sense of unease was founded; it was a message from Sid Vigo's wife, Coraline, informing him that her precious Sidney had died in hospital at four-fifteen that afternoon. The message went on to say that Sidney had always held Terence in the highest esteem and one of his requests had been that, when he passed, she let Terence know.

For the first time in years, Terence sat and sobbed. It seemed inconceivable that the man who had taken him in and turned his life around was gone. The tears swiftly turned to frustrated anger and a sense of regret that he hadn't taken the time to keep in touch with Vigo while he was alive. He banged his fist on the steering wheel.

Blowing his nose, he was about to get moving again when there was a tapping sound on the passenger side window. He looked up to see a young woman with a mass of tight blonde curls cascading around her shoulders peering at him through the glass.

He pressed a button on the dash and the window descended. 'Yes?'

'You alright there, babe?' The woman was chewing gum. 'You look a bit stressed.'

Terence frowned. 'I'm sorry, what exactly is it you want?'

'It's more a case of what *you* want.' The woman winked at him. 'I can help release some of that tension for you.'

'You're a prostitute,' Terence said sullenly.

'A sex worker.'

'Semantics. You can call yourself a teapot for all I care, but at the end of the day you're still a prostitute.'

'Well?'

'Well *what*?'

The woman leant into the open window. Terence could see her more clearly now; she wasn't quite as young as she had initially appeared. Her face was plastered with foundation make-up and she had the darkest red shade of lipstick on her mouth. 'Do you like what you see or not?' she asked, pulling aside her wrapover blue cotton top to reveal the swell of her left breast.

Terence stared at her blankly for a moment. Then he reached out and pushed a button on the dash. The door lock popped up.

The woman readjusted her top to cover herself and climbed into the passenger seat. She spat out a wodge of chewing gum onto the verge beside the car and slammed the door. 'It's sixty quid for a hand-job. A hundred gets you head. For one-fifty I'll take you to heaven and back.'

Without answering her, Terence pulled away and very soon the lights of the city streets gave way to countryside.

'I'm Lexi, by the way. We going to your place?'

Again, Terence didn't reply. It had started to rain and he turned on the windscreen wipers.

Lexi peered out into the darkness. 'Is it far? I hope it's not *too* far. I like to be home by eleven for my kids.'

They rounded a bend and Terence eased off on the accelerator and pulled in to a lay-by.

351

'You have *got* to be kidding me!' Lexi exclaimed. 'I haven't done it on the back seat of a car since I was a teenager!'

Terence switched off the engine. 'This isn't some spotty herbert's Escort. There's plenty of room back there. We can make ourselves nice and cosy.'

Lexi thought about it for a moment. She shivered. 'Alright, come on then, let's get on with it.'

She opened the car door and the rain gusted into her face. 'For fuck's sake! This is gonna cost you extra you know!'

Terence got out and quickly went round to join her at the rear passenger side door. He opened up and she climbed in, scooching across the suede seat to make room for him.

'This is alright actually, ain't it?' she observed, kicking off her stiletto heels. 'What's it to be then, babe?'

'Intercourse.'

'That's one-fifty then, yeah?'

Terence didn't answer her.

She held out her hand. 'Up front. It's my golden rule.'

'Afterwards.'

Lexi considered her options. If she played hard ball now, she might end up getting herself thrown out in the rain. She didn't trust him one bit, but what choice did she have?

Terence was already unzipping his fly. He moved a little closer and, putting his hand up Lexi's skirt, he roughly attempted to force her thighs apart.

'Oww! Easy there, babe. Cool your jets.' She playfully batted his hand away and reached up under her skirt. Pulling her panties down around her ankles, she removed her left foot, then flipped them with her right; they landed on the driver side headrest. She giggled and reached into her clutchbag for a condom. 'How do you prefer it? From the front or behind?'

Once again, Terence didn't answer. He accepted the condom and motioned for her to turn over.

Lexi grinned. 'Chatty bugger, ain't ya?'

'I'm not paying you for conversation,' Terence said curtly.

'Suit yerself.' Turning away from him, she muttered, 'You haven't actually paid me for nothing yet.' She got up onto the seat on her hands and knees, reached back and hitched her skirt up around her waist. 'My regulars reckon I've got a lovely arse.' She thrust her bottom towards him. 'They say it's my best feature.'

Positioning himself on the seat behind her, with his trousers and underwear pooled around his knees, Terence shuffled forwards and found her.

Lexi squealed. 'Easy, easy! Jeez! You really know how to turn a girl on, don't ya?' Glancing back over her shoulder, she shuffled her bottom against him – 'That's better.' – and manufactured a little moaning noise; it was common courtesy to let the paying customers believe they were turning her on. 'You never told me what your name is.'

'Stop talking.' Terence closed his eyes and, breathing heavily, he began to move his pelvis rhythmically back and forth.

'I reckon you look like a Clifford,' Lexi continued. 'Or maybe an Oliver. Yeah, definitely an Oliver.'

'I said stop talking.'

'Not that it matters to me one way or t'other. Most blokes prefer not to say. Or they make them up.' She idly scratched her nose 'Actually, I reckon I don't know the names of ninety-percent of the blokes I've been with.' She made another patently feigned moaning noise. 'There's this one fella though – he's one of my regulars, he's ever so sweet – we were going at it the other night and...'

Terence grabbed a fistful of her hair tightly and yanked her head back. 'Would you stop your infernal yapping, damn you!'

Letting out another cry, Lexi tried to squirm away, but he pulled even harder and she felt his large hand close around the back of her neck. 'Okay, that's *enough*! I'm not into the rough stuff.'

As Terence's thrusting increased in urgency, his fingernails sank into the soft flesh on her neck.

Lexi shrieked. 'Actually, you know what? Fuck this! We're done. Take me back to town right now!'

As the words left her mouth, Terence made a loud grunting sound. Then he shuddered and slumped forward across her back.

Grateful that the ordeal had come to an end so quickly, Lexi managed to scramble out from beneath him and sat up. She reached her underwear down from the headrest and slipped her feet into the holes. 'So that's one-fifty you owe me.'

Terence was already re-fastening his trousers. 'Get out.'

'Sorry, what?!'

'You heard me. Out.'

Lexi stared at him in disbelief. 'No, no, no! Just you wait a minute, mister. You've had the goods.' She held out her hand. 'One-fifty.'

'Get out of my car, you abominable harpy!'

Lexi shook her head. 'Not until I've had my money,' she said firmly. 'I let you put your nasty little Tic Tac dick inside me, so…'

355

Without warning, Terence's hand flew out and he slapped her hard across her mouth, splitting her lip. She could taste blood. 'Bastard!'

Throwing open the car door, Terence climbed out, reached back in and, taking hold of Lexi's legs, he started to pull her towards him. She managed to grab her bag and tried to kick him away, but he had a vice-like grip, and she was dragged swiftly across the seat and out of the door, cracking the back of her head on the sill.

Laying in the road, partially dazed, she stared up at Terence standing over her. As she blinked against the light rain, he tossed something and it struck her square in the face. It felt slimy and it dropped into her lap. She looked down to see the shrivelled condom. 'You cocksucker! 'Just you wait till my husband hears about this! There's nowhere he won't find you!'

Terence stamped down hard on her abdomen, knocking the wind out of her. As she squirmed on the tarmac, struggling to catch a breath, he reached into his trouser pocket and withdrew his wallet. 'I suggest you go and find a bus.' He threw a single note at her, then turned away and disappeared around to the other side of the car.

Lexi sat up and rubbed the back of her head. She could feel a lump where her head had hit the bodywork of the car and she suddenly wanted to be sick.

Retrieving the money Terence had thrown at her, she examined it; it was a crumpled five pound note.

'Cunt!' she screamed. 'You'll pay for this!' But her profanity was lost behind the roar of the Range Rover engine starting, and she watched in despair as the car pulled away.

She glanced down at her feet and realised that her shoes were still in the footwell of the back seat. 'Fucking cocksucking cunt!'

CHAPTER 28

Were it not for a report two weeks later on the nine o'clock morning news bulletin, Terence wouldn't have given Lexi another thought.

He would usually have been in the office well before then, but he had got caught in a traffic snarl up that left him staring at the back end of a bus and covering less than half a mile in forty minutes.

He had the radio playing on low and it was the name that caught his ear:

'...who was known professionally as Lexi was found dead in Sparkhill Park. Although ...'

Terence reached over and hastily turned up the volume on the radio.

'...police are currently saying her murder was drugs related, being as she was an active sex worker, they have reason to believe that she may have been with a client immediately prior to her death. Superintendent Brian Reed of West Midlands Police is leading the investigation.'

A sound bite of someone, presumably Reed, came on: *'Ms Bridges' body was found behind the public toilets. Most likely a coincidence, the park is situated adjacent to the school attended by her two small children. We are appealing to anyone with information that might assist in our inquiries to come forward, and that would naturally be treated in the strictest confidence. Whether you knew her under her professional name, Lexi, or her real name, Tia Bridges, we want to hear from you.'*

The clip ended and the newsreader came back on. *'Ms Bridges murder is the third in the area involving a sex worker in the past five weeks.'*

The newsreader cleared his throat and moved onto the next story. *'A teenager died yesterday evening when he lost control of the moped he was riding...'*

Terence switched off the radio. He was delighted to hear that somebody had taken steps towards doing something practical to decrease the numbers of slatterns on the streets; the police certainly weren't doing much about it. Prostitution was a dicey game and those playing it had only themselves to blame when the chips were down. Of course, the person responsible would inevitably be captured and subsequently locked up for the rest of their days, probably destined to become the subject of a book, or a documentary, or a feature film; everybody loves a good murder story.

But, in Terence's opinion, one man stalking the streets after dark wasn't even putting a scratch on the surface regarding the escalating problem with Britain's reprobate populace. Prostitutes were but one variety among the myriad of the maggot-ridden apples

359

beleaguering the barrel. There were too many Lexis; too many Lavises; too many like Chas, Danny and Rich. A lone vigilante was a starting point, but it would require a more ambitious strategem for England to stand a hope of ever resembling the green and pleasant land peddled in the aggravatingly patriotic song so often chanted at rugby matches.

The queue finally began to crawl forward again and a minute later the cause of the delay became apparent; the traffic lights had failed at a crossroads, and someone had taken a chance and pulled out, resulting in a nasty collision.

Once he got past the block, Terence had a clear run the rest of the way to the office.

He had just picked up the telephone to make a call, when there was a soft tap on the door. He returned the receiver to the cradle.

'Enter.'

Cressida Partridge's head appeared around the door. Her face was pale and drawn. 'Have you got a moment to talk, Terence?'

'Business?'

'No. It's personal.'

Terence glanced at his watch. 'That infernal traffic this morning has put me an hour behind and I've got a stack of calls to make. It'll have to wait until this evening.'

'It *can't* wait.'

Terence would have snapped at her to leave him be, but he'd detected a quiver in her voice. 'Very well. But make it quick.' Huffing, he got up from behind his desk and, taking his freshly lit cigar with him, crossed to the chaise longue in the corner of his office.

He sat down and patted the soft velvet cushion beside him. 'Come.'

Glancing furtively over her shoulder, Cressida stepped into the office and softly closed the door behind her. She winced as she recalled that the chaise longue was the first place they had made love. As she sat down, Terence placed a hand on her knee. 'What's the urgency?'

'There's no easy way to say this, so I'll just come out with it.'

Cressida paused as if she were waiting for a response, but she didn't get one. Terence was looking at her impatiently.

She took a deep breath. 'I'm pregnant.'

Terence didn't speak. But, almost imperceptibly, the corner of his mouth twitched and he removed his hand from Cressida's knee.

'Did you hear what I just said?'

'I trust that's a rhetorical question. Of course I heard what you said.'

'Well? Haven't you got anything to say?'

With a disinterested expression on his face, Terence took a puff on his cigar. 'Will congratulations suffice?'

Cressida stared at him, trying to determine whether or not he understood the inference of what she had just told him, let alone the ramifications.

'For Christ's sake, Terence, it's *yours*!'

'I assumed as much, or you wouldn't have come crawling in here with that frightened little mouse look on your face.'

'What are we going to do about it?'

'*We*?' Terence muttered, with a trace of amusement.

Cressida didn't appear to register his reply. 'Crispy is going to kill me. Or divorce me.' She put her face in her hands. 'Or both.'

Terence peered at her. 'Perhaps you should have thought about that before you flaunted yourself like a common Jezebel.'

Cressida lifted her head and stared at him angrily. 'As if you weren't like a hungry dog with two tails, happy to take advantage. God, you men are all the same!'

Terence gave her a thin smile. 'Interesting that you should bring God into it. I think you'll find that in the Book of Genesis, it was Eve who succumbed to the serpent's temptation. She ate first from the tree and it was *she* who led Adam astray.'

Cressida looked bemused. 'What the hell are you talking about? I'm pregnant!'

'Whoever sins sexually sins against their own body.'

'For fuck's sake, now you're quoting The Bible at me?'

'It feels pertinent.'

'And you *didn't* sin, I suppose?!'

'I'm not the one who only got married a few weeks ago.' Terence frowned. 'I have to ask: why exactly *were* you so eager to jump into my bed?'

Cressida started to colour up. 'That hardly matters now, does it?' She looked at him tearfully. 'So you're not going to support me?'

'Don't deflect the question. I asked you *why*. I want to know.'

'Because I found you attractive.'

'As I did you.' Terence returned his hand to Cressida's knee. 'But that's not all, is it? Why would anyone seek gratification outside of the marital bed when they had literally just wed?'

'He doesn't...' – Cressida faltered. 'I mean... Alright, look, I found out he gets off doing it with men too. Happy now?'

Terence frowned. 'Why on earth would you choose to marry a man like that?'

'Because by the time I found out, the wedding plans were too far advanced. Daddy would have thrown a blue fit! Besides, I love Crispy. Love isn't a switch you can just turn off, you know.' Cressida sighed. 'He wanted a trophy wife, and I can certainly be that for him. I just can't stand the thought of what he does with other men. So we hardly ever... you know, do it. And I have needs.'

Terence smiled. 'I thought it might be something along those lines, although, I must confess, impotence would have been my first guess.' Chuckling, he slipped his hand beneath the hemline of Cressida's skirt. 'It seems to me you're in a bit of a pickle, Mrs Partridge.' His fat fingers kneaded the soft flesh on her inner thigh through her tights.

Cressida clamped his hand in hers through the thin material of her skirt. 'Don't!' she exclaimed angrily. 'What the hell am I going to do?'

Terence withdrew his hand. 'It's obvious. You'll have to get rid of it.'

Cressida put a hand to her mouth. 'Get *rid* of it? How can you be so callous?'

'You say callous. I say practical.'

'I can't. I just *can't*!'

'It's either that or you'll have some explaining to do.' Terence's face darkened. 'I have no idea what you're going to tell him and, quite honestly, I don't care. But you'll keep my name out of it, is that clear?'

Cressida's tone became defensive. 'Wait just a minute. If you think for one moment…'

Terence's hand flew up and gripped Cressida's throat. 'I said you're to keep my name out of it,' he repeated angrily. 'Is that understood? Crispin and I have business together. I'm not going to let this silly nonsense interfere with that. Is that clear?'

Cressida tried to move, but Terence's weight was keeping her pinned against the backrest of the chaise longue. Her fingers clawed fruitlessly at his, but they were digging into her neck like iron rods and he merely tightened his grip.

'Well?'

'You're hurting me!' she gasped.

'Then answer the question.' Terence lifted the glowing end of his cigar up to within an inch of her eye. 'Is that *clear*?'

Cressida's eyes were filled with terror. She didn't reply.

'I'll ask you one last time. Is that…?'

'Yes,' Cressida managed to croak.

Terence squinted at her for a moment, trying to discern whether there was veracity in the frightened face. He decided that there was. 'I believe you do.' Putting the cigar between his moist lips, he took a puff and then lowered it towards her knee. He lightly touched its tip on her tights just above her knee; it burnt a small hole in the nylon and Cressida let out a squeal.

Terence released his grip and she leapt up off the couch.

'You're mad!'

'Well, you know what they say: madness maketh the man.' Terence chuckled at his little pun.

Cressida went to slap him, but Terence was too quick for her and caught her arm mid-sweep.

Getting to his feet, he towered over her. 'When the time comes to plead forgiveness – and, who knows, Partridge may decide to let you keep the little bastard – I do hope you'll not have a change of heart.' He let go of her arm. 'Just so that we're absolutely clear, should my name in any way be alluded to in connection with this unfortunate turn of events, as sure as I'm standing in front of you now, you *will* live to regret it.'

Cressida rubbed her sore neck. 'He'll never know who the father is. I swear he won't.'

Terence smiled and sat back down. 'I'm delighted to hear it. I've been musing on a possible new venture and your husband has, shall we say an *outlook* that I may wish to capitalise on.' His mouth curved into a smile. 'And, let's be honest, impregnating another man's wife isn't really conducive to a good business relationship, is it?' Stretching back on the seat, he chuckled.

'So that's it, is it?' There was hurt in Cressida's eyes. 'Fuck off and sort it out yourself, Cressida?!'

'Actually, there is one more thing. Under the circumstances, I'm afraid I shall have to let you go.'

Cressida wiped a tear from her eye. 'I don't understand.'

Terence sighed. 'Let me spell it out for you. I don't want you working here any longer. I have more than enough on my plate without having to look at you and your swollen belly, clomping about like some sort of obese elephant.'

'How am I supposed to explain *that* to Crispin?'

Terence drew on his cigar thoughtfully and exhaled the smoke. 'Maybe tell him the journeying back and forth between Tunbridge Wells and Birmingham – not to mention all the overnight stays – is getting too much? He might take pity on you and find you a cleaning job in his London office. As I said, my dear, it's not my concern. Go on with you now. Run along and clear out your desk.'

'*Now*?!'

'Well I don't see much point in you hanging around here.'

Cressida looked at Terence sadly. 'And to think, I actually fancied you. I must have been crazy. You're just another fucking bastard.'

'Not a bit of it. My Mother and Father were very happily married. Contemptible specimens both, mind you.' He winked at her. 'But you don't get to choose who your parents are, do you?'

CHAPTER 29

The Brighter Business Opportunities Expo, hosted at Brighton's Royal Albion Hotel, is an event at which affiliates of the financial sector converge annually.

When Crispin Partridge initially mentioned to Terence that the expo could prove the ideal venue to float ideas and gather support, Terence had been guarded, reminding him that the success of the proposal hinged on discretion and no small measure of anonymity.

Partridge, along with his partner, Tobias Swann, managed a private London-based concern offering financial advice, and he succeeded in talking Terence around: 'You're on Partridge and Swann's books as a client and as far as the world is concerned, that's the extent of it. There's no reason any of these guys need know you're the brains behind the whole thing. Not at this stage, anyway. Whether you choose to reveal that once you've got to know them is entirely up to you. I just feel that, for now, there's nowhere more inconspicuous for us to meet up with our new friends than a business conference where there will be thousands of people passing through over the duration. I assure you, we're talking about solid, like-minded people. And, as small a gesture as it may seem, a tête-à-tête and a physical handshake goes a long way to greasing the cogs. But hark at me, eh? You hardly need to be told that. You're a consummate professional, you could pull off this deal in your sleep. You already did a marvellous job getting the Professor guy and that boorish writer on board.'

Crispin's pitch had been convincing and now, here they were, preparing to go into a private meeting with three individuals of Partridge's acquaintance, the sole remit being to secure vital support for Terence's scheme.

Wednesday and Thursday had been the usual furore of seminars and frantic networking. By contrast, the third and final day of the event had proven to be a traditionally more relaxed affair, and those staying over for the weekend were looking forward to a couple of days unwinding and drinking with newly-made friends into the small hours.

Terence and Partridge had arrived late on the Thursday night and it had just turned four on Friday afternoon when they pressed the call button for the elevator.

'Solving tomorrow's problems today!' Partridge chuckled. 'You tell me that wouldn't make for a great slogan on a billboard!'

'I was mooting the concept as a vital public service, not a cheap promotional gimmick,' Terence said flatly, resting his briefcase at his feet. 'We're here to discuss a revolutionary initiative, not set up a toy shop.'

Partridge had sensed an odd tension building between them all afternoon, which he had pegged as pressure. He noticed that Terence wasn't smiling and rested a hand on his shoulder. 'Lighten up, my friend. It's going to be fine.' He saw Terence side-eye the hand and he quickly removed it. 'Sorry.'

Terence turned to face the younger man. Unlike himself – clad in an impeccable navy blue three-piece – Partridge had opted for a more casual look; light blue slacks and a white polo-neck sweater with a St Christopher medallion dangling from his neck. The result was manifestly tacky.

'It strikes me you're not treating our initiative with the gravity it commands. I've spent far too much time planning this to allow a cocky little bottom feeder to fuck it up at the final hurdle.'

Partridge's smile waned. 'Bottom feeder? That's a bit harsh, T. I'm putting a hefty wedge into this scheme too, you know. And just remember, we wouldn't even be here today if it wasn't for me. Besides which, I was joking. Sheesh!'

'We're not playing a parlour game here. There's no time for levity. When we step out of this meeting, I don't want anyone in that room left doubting our intent. We're talking about a multi-million pound investment program and we need them to be one hundred percent on board. So *you* keep quiet and let *me* do the talking.' His tone softened. 'All one has to do is dangle the right carrot. I appreciate you casting the line that brought these people here today, and for that I'm grateful. But I'll be the one to reel them in. Is that understood?'

Partridge nodded. 'Absolutely, Terence. Your powers of persuasion are exemplary. But, trust me, these three will be a doddle. They're under no illusions as to why they've been invited along and they're all ready to open their wallets.'

'Let's just wait and see what transpires, shall we?'

The elevator arrived and the doors slid silently open. As they descended to the lobby, Partridge said, 'By the way, I haven't thanked you for letting Cressida go. I know what an asset she was to Hallam Solutions and it must have come as a bit of a blow when she announced out of the blue that she intended to leave.'

Terence raised an eyebrow. 'Indeed.'

'She's in full-on mummy-mode already,' Partridge continued. 'The baby isn't due for another six months, but she's decorated the nursery and filled it with enough clutter to keep the kid happy until the day it flies the nest.' He chuckled.

The elevator reached the ground floor and they stepped out. Terence waited beside a potted yucca plant

372

while Partridge went over to the reception desk and spoke with the young man attending.

He returned with a smile on his face. 'They've arranged a private suite for us annexing the main conference room. Our friends are here already. This way.'

They walked through a set of double doors and along a corridor to a room at the far end.

It was small and the sparse furnishings comprised of a low table – it fell well below knee-height – about two metres long and ringed by half a dozen black leather chairs with high backs. Three of the chairs were occupied by Partridge's guests.

He introduced Terence to Toyah, Lee and Cole: 'As a precautionary measure, we'll refrain from mentioning surnames until we all get to know each other a little better.'

Terence shook each of their hands and he and Partridge sat down. On the table, there was a tray bearing a carafe of coffee, some empty mugs and a plate of plain biscuits.

Their guests already had drinks. Terence helped himself to a Rich Tea finger and poured a coffee. Partridge did the same.

They made smalltalk for a few minutes and Lee remarked upon his day walking around Brighton: 'This is a bloody strange place to hold a conference. Have you been out there? It's wall to wall nancy boys and rug munchers.'

'Really?' Toyah exclaimed. 'What century are you living in?

Lee looked at her scornfully. 'Yeah well, enough of that. With all due respect, I haven't come three hundred miles to make idle chitchat about gays and seagulls stealing your dinner.' He ran the back of his hand across his bearded chin. 'Let's cut to the chase, shall we? The thing bothering me the most is, does anyone here actually know who's behind this grand scheme? Has anyone actually met them? I'm sure I'm not the only one among us to have qualms about handing over millions of pounds to some shady character I've never even met.'

Partridge smiled. 'I'd find it out of character if you hadn't, Lee. But I assure you, the person you're referring to is no fly-by-night.'

Terence winced inwardly.

'His proposal...'

Terence interjected. 'It's *my* proposal. *I* am your shady character, Mr Galesko.'

Lee Galesko's face registered surprise.

'You know my name!'

Terence smiled thinly. 'I know all your names. You don't honestly think I'd come here today and reveal the months of intricate planning to people I knew nothing about.'

Galesko appeared to accept Terence's statement. 'Fair enough. So who the hell are you?'

'We shall get to that later. But let me tell you all a little story. There was an item on the news a couple of months ago. Prostitutes were being murdered around Birmingham. After the fifth body was discovered, the man slipped up and they caught him. He wasn't the sex-crazed psychotic the papers would have had the public believe. It turned out he was just an average Joe, married with a couple of kids.'

Galesko was frowning. 'Sorry, what exactly has a prossie killer got to do with us?'

Toyah spoke: 'Isn't it obvious?'

Cole was looking bemused too. 'Not to me, sweetheart.'

Toyah rolled her eyes. 'He'd had enough of the moral decline in society. Just as we all have.'

'Precisely that, Ms Leaky,' Terence said. 'Our murderer grew to abhor the dissolute activity of the proletariat in his neighbourhood. The police proved impotent – or unwilling – to act, so he decided to do something about it himself. He had the right idea, just not the wherewithall to tackle the situation single-handedly.'

'Keep talking,' Cole said.

375

'You all feel exactly the same about our country as that man did about his city. So do I. The difference is that, united, we *will* have the wherewithall to do something about it. There is a severe rot eating away at decency and sweeping through the cities like a contagion. The reprobates are taking over and before we know it we'll be knee-deep in them. Drunks, drug addicts, street whores, benefits scroungers and council hovel-dwelling cockroaches. They breed like rabbits, and every one of them is out to get something for nothing. They steal, damage public property, abuse animals, children, each other and...' – Terence banged his fist on the table – '...they're destroying our country, Goddammit! It's time for us decent people to seize control. You have already been invited to invest in this unique venture, and the fact you all showed up here today suggests you're also looking for something worthwhile to put your money to.'

Galesko laughed, but it was humourless. 'Don't count on that.'

Terence ignored him. 'But you're probably wondering what you get in return for your millions.'

'Too damned right,' Cole said. 'We're not talking bird feed here.'

'Indeed we aren't, Mr Smythe. Foremost you get the satisfaction of knowing your investment is facilitating a public service like no other. One that the country, indeed the world has never known before. But on a more cathartic level, the plan is that you will have the opportunity to witness the initiative in operation – in real time. We will discuss the finer points of that aspect later.' Terence lifted his briefcase onto the table and opened it. 'I have prepared for each of you a copy of my business proposition. You should find this dossier contains everything you need to know for now.' He distributed a folder to each of them. 'Myself and Mr Partridge will retire to the hotel bar for twenty minutes to give you time to assess it. I estimate it will take four or five years to have everything in place – at least to an operable level. But today will be our one and only face-to-face encounter, so when we return, I will be happy to answer any further questions you may have.' He looked at Partridge. 'Shall we?'

As soon as they stepped outside and closed the door, Partridge turned angrily to Terence. 'You knew who these people were before we arrived!'

Terence looked at him scornfully. 'Naturally. As soon as you floated their names last week, I had someone dig into their backgrounds. There's far too much at stake here to leave anything to chance.'

'I get that. But why didn't you tell me? You made me look like a fool in there.'

'You *are* a fool if you think I've invested months in the planning to waltz in and trust a bunch of complete strangers. And I'll tell you now, I have concerns about Galesko.'

'How do you mean?'

'Couldn't you read the room? Smythe and Leaky sat and listened. But every word that left Galesko's mouth was confrontational. I guarantee he won't be putting up any money. Unfortunately he already knows too much and that makes him a loose cannon.'

'I've known Lee for years. He's solid. If he pulls out, he won't talk.'

'That's not a chance I'm prepared to take.'

'What are we going to do?'

'Let me worry about that. Let's you and I go and have that drink and give them time to consider the proposal. When we return we'll see what the concensus is.'

Terence's assessment of Lee Galesko proved to be right be on the nose. The meeting had reconvened and, when it concluded forty-five minutes later, Leaky and Smythe had eagerly given Terence their verbal commitment. Galesko, on the other hand, had spent five minutes irately explaining the reasons why he wouldn't be investing in such a "harebrained project", and expounding upon how the whole thing was doomed to failure.

Terence and Partridge left the hotel just as it started to rain; they hadn't brought umbrellas and they had to make a quick dash back to the car. They had come down to Brighton in Terence's Range Rover.

They travelled the first five miles of the return journey without speaking. Partridge could still sense tension between them, but it was he who eventually broke the silence.

'I think that all went rather well.'

Terence kept his eyes on the road ahead. 'Do you now?'

'Sure. I mean, it's a shame about Lee, but two out of three ain't bad.'

'Three out of the three was the goal.'

'Oh, come on, T. Myself included, you have five people prepared to pour money into the pot. You can't possibly be dissatisfied with that.'

'Don't you dare lecture me on what I should or shouldn't be satisfied with,' Terence snapped.

'I apologise. But hopefully I've helped to secure a sizeable chunk of the funding you need.'

'This would have gone ahead with or without you. And your choices were questionable. You had no business inviting Lee Galesko there today.'

'I've said I'm sorry, okay? Honestly, T, as far as I was concerned, there was every chance he'd sign up.

Besides, you checked him out beforehand; surely you must have felt the same.'

Terence slammed on the brakes, causing the car behind them to swerve. It shot past them with it's horn blaring, and Partridge caught sight of a woman behind the wheel angrily mouthing something at them.

Terence shut off the engine and turned in his seat. He glared at Partridge. 'Firstly, let's be quite clear about this. I put my trust in *you* to select people who would be unwaveringly supportive of my cause. Not *possibles*. Not *maybes*. Cast iron guarantees! Galesko's failure to climb aboard has jeopardised my plans and now I'm stuck with an anomaly that needs to be dealt with. And a bigoted one at that. I've no time for anybody with attitudes like his.' He restarted the engine. 'And secondly, will you damned well refrain from addressing me as *T*. It's *fucking* disrespectful!'

Unsure how to respond, Partridge fell silent and they travelled on for another few minutes before he hesitatingly spoke again. 'So, er… about Lee…'

'What about him?'

'You said he's an anomaly and needs to be to be dealt with. That sort of implies…'

'Your rash decision to bring him in has left shit on the floor and it has to be cleared up. *How* is not your concern. You just need to be sure you don't let me down twice. This is the last time Mr Galesko's name is mentioned. Do I make myself clear?'

CHAPTER 30

It wasn't until Terence had dropped Partridge home in Tunbridge Wells that he started to feel hungry. He'd been running on adrenaline and realised he hadn't eaten anything since breakfast.

Shortly, as he approached the Dartford Crossing, his stomach started growling at him. His petrol gauge was tipping the red zone and he decided he would stop to refuel at Thurrock Services. There would inevitably be food outlets there too; it wouldn't exactly be fine dining, but needs must, he thought.

He circled the car park looking for a space, but when he found one there was a man and woman standing alongside the adjacent car, blocking him from getting in. They were arguing heatedly. Terence gave them short blast on his horn. The man shot him a filthy look and flicked up his middle finger, but they moved aside and continued their dispute. The sight of them screaming at each other reminded Terence that his reasons for avoiding such establishments weren't solely down to the dubious nature of the food they served. There was a time not so long ago when couples would take their disputes home with them; now it seemed to be par for the course to air one's dirty laundry in the street, without a care in the world for who it might offend.

He went into the diner and, while he waited to be served, studied his options on the wall behind the counter.

The young man serving him handled his order swiftly, but as Terence turned to leave, a little girl brandishing a tub of ice cream ran full pelt into him. The contents splashed down his trousers. Immediately she started to wail, and a woman who had been deep in conversation with her husband got up from a nearby table and came over.

'Did you drop your ice cream, chucky egg? Don't worry, Mummy will get you another one.' She took the child's hand to lead her back to the table.

'Is that it?' Terence exclaimed testily.

The woman turned back. 'Do what?'

He gestured to the white splatters running down his trousers. 'No apology? Your child has just ruined my suit.'

'It was an accident!'

'One that could have been avoided if you'd exercised some parental responsibility and kept her under control. This is a restaurant, not a playpen.'

The woman's face coloured up. 'Perhaps you should watch where *you're* going, mate. She's only a little girl.'

'All the more reason to keep her on a short leash.'

The woman scowled. 'Fuck you!'

'Ah, yes, there it is: the standard response of illiterate plebeians.'

'Double fuck you!'

The woman's husband was a wiry-looking individual wearing jeans and a scruffy T-shirt that looked as if it had never seen the inside of a washing machine. He had been holding back, but now he stood up and came over.

'What's going on?'

'You have a wayward child running loose in a busy restaurant, that's what's going on,' Terence said. 'You also have a benighted wife who, rather than scolding said child and making her apologise for slopping ice cream on me – a scolding which might help to ensure she grows up with a modicum of social awareness – she uses foul language and turns the situation around to make it appear as if *I'm* the one at fault. Exactly what sort of example does that set?'

The man was staring at Terence with his mouth hanging open. 'What did you just call my wife?'

Terence sighed. 'Benighted. Go and Google it. But don't procrastinate. Your time is finite.'

The man frowned. '*What*?'

The woman pulled the little girl back to the table. 'Ignore him, Shane. Toffee-nosed cunt.'

Terence returned to his car. Not wanting to let the pungent smell of his food take up residence inside, he spotted a bench near the fence and went and sat down. First using his handkerchief to wipe the ice cream off his trousers, he unwrapped his food and dejectedly examined the flaccid triple-stack cheeseburger he'd been given; it bore no resemblance whatsoever to the tasty-looking offering pictured on the menu.

Gingerly, he took a bite. Not that he would ever have admitted it, but it actually tasted better than it looked and he greedily consumed it in six large mouthfuls, washing it down with a beaker of cola that seemed to have more ice in it than liquid.

He had just finished, when he heard the click of heels on tarmac and a woman's voice spoke.

'Hello there, baby.'

Terence looked up to see a young black woman smiling at him. She had a pretty face that Terence suspected might be even prettier without make-up, and her hair was braided in cornrows. He looked her up and down. She was wearing a red leather jacket over a cropped white T-shirt that ended just above her navel, revealing an expanse of smooth skin. A short black leather skirt fell short of the tops of black fishnet stockings, revealing the tops of her thighs. On her feet were black shoes with three-inch heels.

Terence estimated she was probably about twenty years-old; no more than twenty-two. He returned her smile. 'Good evening, my dear.'

'I was going to ask you if you fancied having good time.' She giggled. 'But it looks like you're already having one.'

Before Terence could ask what she meant, she reached down and wiped a blob of tomato sauce from his chin. She slipped her finger into her mouth and sucked it clean. 'Mmmm. That's *soooo* good.'

Terence felt a warm sensation pulse through his loins.

The girl touched her finger to his nose. 'So?'

'So *what*?'

'*Are* you looking for a good time?'

'I think not.'

'Awww. That's real a shame, baby.' The girl turned around and casually raised the hem of her skirt to reveal the flawless twin curves of her buttocks, divided by an insubstantial strip of red lacy material. 'Are you *sure*?'

Terence glanced around the car park. There was nobody around. Reaching out, he pressed a chubby finger into the soft flesh.

'Oi! Naughty!' The girl stepped away and spun round, readjusting her skirt. 'You don't get to touch the goods until I've seen the colour of your money.'

Terence smiled. 'You're a very forthright young woman, aren't you? How old are you?'

'Nineteen.'

'It's a dangerous way to earn a living, hanging around places like this, propositioning strange men.'

The girl shrugged. 'Doesn't bother me.'

Terence stood up, fished in his pocket for his wallet and withdrew a twenty pound note. He handed it over. 'On account. You'll get the rest afterwards. What do you say we take a little drive?'

The girl took the money and stashed it in her jacket pocket. 'It'll be another hundred.'

'That's fine.'

She grinned, showing perfect white teeth. 'Okay, baby. Where are we going?'

'Somewhere where we can get to know each other.'

He escorted her over to the passenger side door of the Land Rover. 'What's your name?'

'Jo.'

Terence's heart skipped a beat. '*Jo*?'

'Yeah. It's Josie really, but I prefer Jo.'

Terence held open the door while she swung her slender legs inside. 'Well then, Jo. Let's see where the road takes us, shall we?'

As soon as he got into the office on Monday morning, Terence lit a cigar and reached for the phone.

The man on the end of the line answered after just two rings.

'I have a problem that needs cleaning up as a matter of urgency,' Terence said.

'Name.'

'Lee Galesko. I'll send over the details on an encrypted email as usual. I need you to pay him a visit.'

'Understood.'

'I don't expect to hear from him again. You get double your usual fee for swift results.'

Terence could almost hear the man smiling.

'Consider it done.'

There was a click and the line went dead.

Terence took a draw on his cigar. 'And *that*,' he said aloud, 'is the last we'll hear of Mr Galesko.'

The intercom on his desk buzzed. Terence reached over and pressed a button. 'Yes, Hilary?'

'There's someone here to see you Mr Hallam.'

'Who is it?'

'A lady. She says you're expecting her?'

Terence glanced at his watch. 'Oh my word, yes, of course. Send her in.'

He rested his cigar in the astray and stood up. As he adjusted his tie, there was a knock on the door.

'Come.'

The door opened and a young woman dressed in a beige trouser suit and carrying a small briefcase stepped into the room.

'Mr Hallam?' The woman extended her hand. 'The agency sent me. I'm Caroline Smart. Your new P.A.'

THANK YOU FOR READING

MADNESS MAKETH THE MAN

If you enjoyed it – or any of our books – please consider visiting Amazon or Goodreads and leaving us a short review (both would be great!). It only takes a moment and means so much.

Acknowledgements:
The authors would like to thank Sandra Watson and Sara Greaves.

We would also like to thank Sally Swift for being our "voice", and wish her a very Happy Birthday on the very day this book is released.

Cover design by TimBex.

Also from Rebecca Xibalba and Tim Greaves:
Misdial (2020)
The Break (2021)
The Well (2021)
Reset (2022)
3.2.1 (2022)
Hazelwood (2023)
Available from Amazon, for kindle and in paperback

From Rebecca Xibalba:
Shootin' Starz: 20 Years Behind the Lens
Available in hardback from Amazon

The following titles are available in Audiobook format
from Audible and itunes:
Misdial (read by Paul Kendrick)
The Break (read by Sally Swift)
The Well (read by Sally Swift)
Reset (read by Keith Cruden)
3.2.1 (read by Sally Swift)

Printed in Great Britain
by Amazon

29020485R00223